STILL THE ONE

AIMEE BROWN

Boldwood

First published in Great Britain in 2024 by Boldwood Books Ltd.

Copyright © Aimee Brown, 2024

Cover Design by Alice Moore Design

Cover Images: iStock and Shutterstock

The moral right of Aimee Brown to be identified as the author of this work has been asserted in accordance with the Copyright, Designs and Patents Act 1988.

All rights reserved. No part of this book may be reproduced in any form or by any electronic or mechanical means, including information storage and retrieval systems, without written permission from the author, except for the use of brief quotations in a book review. This book is a work of fiction and, except in the case of historical fact, any resemblance to actual persons, living or dead, is purely coincidental.

Every effort has been made to obtain the necessary permissions with reference to copyright material, both illustrative and quoted. We apologise for any omissions in this respect and will be pleased to make the appropriate acknowledgements in any future edition.

A CIP catalogue record for this book is available from the British Library.

Paperback ISBN 978-1-80426-842-1

Large Print ISBN 978-1-80426-841-4

Hardback ISBN 978-1-80426-843-8

Ebook ISBN 978-1-80426-840-7

Kindle ISBN 978-1-80426-839-1

Audio CD ISBN 978-1-80426-848-3

MP3 CD ISBN 978-1-80426-847-6

Digital audio download ISBN 978-1-80426-844-5

This book is printed on certified sustainable paper. Boldwood Books is dedicated to putting sustainability at the heart of our business. For more information please visit https://www.boldwoodbooks.com/about-us/sustainability/

Boldwood Books Ltd, 23 Bowerdean Street, London, SW6 3TN

www.boldwoodbooks.com

Congratulations to my husband for surviving his dirt bike attempting to kill him.
Those were a few close calls too many, dear.
Also, well done me, for writing through the above nightmare – you did it.

1

EVE CASSIDY

'Morning, Eve.' One of the emergency surgeons I see regularly greets me with a lift of his coffee cup as we pass each other in one of the endless employee-only hallways.

The walls of the hospital are crisp, sterile white, with shiny black marble-looking floors, and local photography, or healthcare signage, hanging every ten to twenty-five feet. I've worked here long enough that I've got the photos memorized but I still glance at each one to verify I haven't forgotten a single one.

'Good morning, Doctor Sully,' I say. 'I hope I don't see you today,' I tease, glancing back at him as I pass.

'Amen to that,' he chuckles.

I wouldn't want to put money on whether or not we'll meet, but I would love for today to be as low-key as possible because it's my Friday, and it's easier to roll into a weekend without the unsettling feeling of turmoil lingering from the day before.

As usual, the morning shift-change employees crowd the in-hospital Starbucks with a line to the doors of the tiny coffee shop. I claim my spot behind a face I don't recognize, which means small talk is unnecessary, and pull my phone from my scrub pocket – might as well catch up on social media while I wait.

I scroll through Instagram first – nothing new since I left for work. So I flip to Facebook. Immediately I double-tap my sister Jess's most recent story (she gets auto likes): a rambling about home remedies rumored to help evict a stubborn fetus. At thirty-six weeks pregnant and confined to her bed via doctor's orders (but hesitant to do so since this baby looks to weigh in the double digits, judging from the size of her), she's giving all the labor-inducing wives' tales a try. Her latest attempt: consuming castor oil from a spoon. Ick. I shiver at her near-gag on screen. Why didn't she have a trigger warning, jeesh? Note to self: never get pregnant.

'Well, well, well, isn't it my lucky day,' the barista chirps as I approach the counter. 'What can I get the girl who completes my story?'

I cock my head, rolling my eyes. 'Every day, Adam?'

He grabs a clear Venti cup, scribbling my name on the side, complete with a heart. 'God would be disappointed if I didn't at least acknowledge fate,' he says with a sly smile.

Adam has asked me out at least once a month for the last few years he's worked here. He claims it's fate that we end up together. But I'm pretty sure he's only in it for the puns. My answer is always no because after a couple of dud exes, I no longer date, and I definitely don't date the under-twenty-five crowd.

As Adam swirls my usual iced latte to perfection, I lean against the counter, watching him work his magic. He slides the cup toward me with a wink. 'On the house today, Eve. Consider it a bribe for future consideration.' He chuckles, his eyes playful.

I shake my head. 'Have I ever told you that I don't believe in fate?'

He gives me a mock pout before moving on to the next customer. I take my drink and head toward the exit, my mind drifting back to my sister's impending motherhood. Jess has always been the brave one, ready to leap into any adventure without hesitation. I mean, do you know what castor oil is for? Constipation. She's trying to shoot that baby out of her vajayjay explosive-diarrhea style. Ouch. She's been talking for months about doing this life-changing event medication-free. Double ouch.

Not once, in any relationship, have I ever considered procreating. I made that decision when I unexpectedly delivered a baby at the front entrance of the ER a couple of years ago. The expectant mother and I just happened to be walking in at the same time (for once I'd gotten a good parking spot!) when I realized what was happening in front of me as she dropped to the filthy ground. I knew it was either medically trained me or the wide-eyed, horrified-looking security officer standing in the breezeway to my left. I stepped up. Not one ounce of that disgusting mess was beautiful, as soon-to-be parents claim. I wish my eyes could unsee it because my brain has it filed in the '3 a.m. file' and nothing in that sleepless mess is a good time.

The bravest thing I've ever done is mistakenly get married on a whim.

I swipe my badge over the magic lock that keeps society out, and employees safe. The doors swing open, revealing people scattered here and there, meandering between ER departments.

Time for my morning pep talk. 'Please God, since I'm your OG human, give me an easy day today, would ya?'

'Morning!' Catalina calls while in motion.

I lift my coffee, acknowledging I've heard her.

'Hello, Miss Cassidy.' Dale, today's charge nurse, greets me with a sleepy smile – even though I know darn well he's probably on cup of coffee number three. He gets here an hour before the rest of the morning shift so he can give room assignments and catch up on who's still lingering from the overnight shift.

'You're in Trauma 2 today,' he says, glancing at the giant whiteboard on the wall behind his counter.

'My favorite room,' I say, lifting my cup. Cheers to that.

'It's weird you have a favorite trauma room.' Genevieve, my work bestie, appears at my side from a hallway to my right.

'It's weird you wait to get out of bed until fifteen minutes before your shift with your hair looking like that,' I tease.

'What's wrong with it?' she asks, patting the oversized messy bun perched on top of her head – her favorite pen, the one she takes to and from work with her, pokes out of her hair.

As usual, she's wearing a set of scrubs from the in-house scrub shop's 'that's so eighties neon line' (named by *moi*). She can pull off highlighter pink. I cannot. I went a little lighter with my already light blonde hair this month, and even though it's nearly fall, I still don't have that summer glow that I usually do, so I feel like neon scrubs are only going to attract attention to that. I'd look like a glow stick. I'm perfectly OK sticking with my boring 'cool' colors scrub wardrobe, mixing and matching – mostly because I don't turn on my closet light on my way to the shower – and hope the pairing isn't too wild. I got lucky today with navy pants and a pastel purple top.

'Your hair looks fantastic, I'm just teasing you. Also, there is nothing weird about preferring the single bay over the multi-patient. Less chaos,' I say, my reasoning sound.

'You know what else prevents chaos?' Genevieve asks.

'Huh?' I reply, sitting my coffee on the desk in front of me as I read through the electronic room board, familiarizing myself with my patients.

'Not working eighty hours a week,' Gen says, giving me a knowing look.

'It wasn't eighty last week,' I confess.

'What was it then?'

'Um.' I sit at my computer, typing in my unique login. 'Seventy-six.'

Genevieve chuckles, shaking her head in disbelief. 'You seriously need a vacation.'

'And saving for that is exactly what I'm doing with all this overtime.'

'Who's going on vacation?' Dr Bradly, our assigned physician, asks. A very full backpack hangs off one shoulder and a dark green Stanley cup, the biggest size they offer, is in one hand, filled with black coffee to keep himself focused. He's wearing his usual dark blue scrubs and by the look of his tousled hair, I'd say he just woke and ran. 'And did I approve it?'

'HR approves vacations, not doctors,' I remind him.

'Thank God,' Gen mumbles behind me.

She's right. Most doctors I know are also workaholics, partly because the healthcare industry is severely understaffed right now. So putting the fate of our vacation days in their hands would be a terrible idea.

'But nobody is going on vacation,' I reassure him. 'Gen is just dreaming again. I mean, look at her monitor background.'

Troy (aka Dr Bradly) glances at Gen's workstation. 'Bahamas?'

'Fiji,' Gen says with a happy sigh. 'Honeymoon shot.'

Troy chuckles, shaking his head. 'You're not even dating anyone, Genevieve.'

She shrugs playfully. 'A girl can dream, can't she?'

I finish scanning through the patient charts for Trauma 2, mentally preparing myself for whatever may come through those doors today. As we settle in for our shift, the ER starts bustling with activity. The chaos – also known as controlled pandemonium – is oddly comforting to me. Saving lives is a dance I know well, the steps familiar even when the music changes.

A couple of fender-bender patients – one with a broken nose from hitting his steering wheel, and another with 'claimed' whiplash – fill my morning, and after lunch seems to be the calm before the storm. After checking in on a couple of patients still awaiting a hospital room, I pull up my email to make sure I haven't missed anything. And by anything, I mean extra shifts I could take via the internal employee-only hospital site. Nothing.

I grab my phone, sipping my coffee as I scroll through socials again. My mom's 'book post' on Facebook stops me as I read her thoughts on the most boring book alive – *Moby Dick* – her favorite. She's always described the novel as the perfect example of the monster your mind can create if you let it. 'An idle mind is the devil's playground,' she used to say. A lesson she learned after being married to my father for ten years too long (her words).

I scroll again. Kait got her Botox redone and is announcing it to the world, which is weird. Then I stop... a Facebook memory. Crap. I hate these. I scroll to the post, sucking in a breath at the sight of it. I glance at the date on the top of our patient board – September 27. Christ on a motorbike. Suddenly, I remember why I prefer Instagram to Facebook. The latter enjoys taunting me with the anniversary of past nostalgic happenings that I've tried really hard to forget – along with all the feelings that come with them. They've been sufficiently buried under my heart for five years now.

I bite my bottom lip as I tap the photo. Wow. Not gonna lie, twenty-two-year-old me looks so incredibly innocent. This version of me still believed in love. I'll never be able to get that back, and the reminder feels like someone twisting the knife.

With a deep sigh, I scroll through the comments on the photo. I do this every year and each time, my heart beats a little faster as I read each one. They're all from the same person, and all the exact same comment: 'xx, Fost'. Once each year this memory probably pops up on his Facebook as well.

'Fost', also known as Foster, is the guy who broke my heart into a million pieces and left me questioning everything I thought I knew about love and trust. Five years have passed since we last spoke and even though I'm the one who decided to walk away without a second glance, my mind sometimes wanders to what would have happened if I'd stayed.

The memories that have always slightly lingered flood back as I stare at the photo, the pain still raw beneath the surface. I quickly scroll to see if he's added this year's comment yet but don't see it, so I close the app with a shaky hand. Gen shoots me a concerned look from across the nurses' station, but I only offer her a weak smile in response.

'Everything OK?' she asks, leaning over the counter that separates us.

'Yeah, just a little unwanted social media trip down memory lane,' I reply, trying to sound nonchalant.

Gen's expression softens with understanding as she glances at the date board. 'Happy anniversary?'

I nod slightly, my attention now on my badges attached to my scrub top pocket. I straighten them, then grab my stethoscope from the desk, draping it around my neck and overly adjusting it to my liking.

'Thanks,' I say, only slightly bitterly. 'It's such a happy day,' I joke.

She frowns. 'You know you don't have to torture yourself like this. Just delete the original post.'

'I can't,' I admit, a hint of regret in my voice. 'I hate it, but I also don't know if I'm ready to forget it.'

'You're—' With her mouth open, the sound of commotion near the ambulance entrance catches our attention. We both turn to see what the fuss is about.

'Trauma 1 crew to the bay,' I hear Dale's voice echoing from the ER overhead speakers through the halls.

'Sucks to be them,' Gen says, leaning back in her chair and tossing a piece of SkinnyPop into the air, catching it in her mouth as we watch multiple patients being pushed past us toward Bay 1.

'Don't curse us,' I warn, grabbing my now buzzing phone from my scrub pants pocket.

I glance at the screen, blinking rapidly as if there's something wrong with my vision. No. He. Didn't. But I see it with my own eyes. He did. Again.

xx, Fost

Comment made, one minute ago.

I scrunch my face. Why, Foster? Why every year? I inhale deeply, exhaling slowly. Do I respond to this? No. It'd be weird (like having this exact conversation with myself every year is normal). I reach across the screen and tap the thumbs up with my index finger. It's what *I* do every year in response to his comment. Passive-aggressive is our new vibe as we play a silent game of 'You still alive?', 'Yep, I acknowledge you'. I just wish I knew what it meant.

2

GUY 'FOSTER'

'Feeling good?' Matty asks. He's my trainer – a guy with graying hair, a solid flavor savor of a mustache, and a slightly growing retirement gut proving his wife really is the cook she claims to be. (She is, I eat there all the time. We live like five minutes away from each other.) He pats me on the back.

It's been a long time since I've been in Oregon – five years to be exact. A refreshing crisp breeze has the recently dropped leaves dancing around the track and swirling through our tent as I sit on a stool inside with the rest of my team. Honestly, it feels exactly like what I remember a late West Coast summer day feels like. The September heat and humidity of Florida isn't something I miss right now, that's for sure.

'Are you kidding?' Travis, one of our mechanics, asks. 'I've never seen Foster anything other than calm, cool, and collected. He makes this sport look like a party game.'

I chuckle. 'I don't know about that,' I say, appreciating the compliment.

Years of hard work is how that happened. I've been a motocross and Freestyle Motocross Rider (also known as FMX) since I was a kid. I won my first trophy at the age of four, and my first big title at fifteen. After that, I'd caught the bug for extreme sports. Backflips off a ramp on a motorcycle, love it. That time I skydived, I'll never forget it. Extreme sports and me, we jibe. I'm addicted to the adrenaline. To me, cutting through the air on my motorcycle, hitting the power band at just the right moment toward a ramp that will launch me forty to fifty feet in the air so I can do some insane flip, is what life is about. I love the smell of gasoline and engine oil. And the ringing in my ears at the decibel of some of these supped-up engines excites me to my core.

'Dude...' Matty, an ex-motocross and FMX superstar, says, 'I'm telling you, Jeff's trying it. He's been landing it and if he does, you've got to up your game.'

My riding rival, yet frenemy, Jeff Hunt, is currently making his way up the track to the start. This is his final chance of the day to outdo me, and I can feel the tension building. We've taken the top two spots according to the announcers and now it's up to us who will take first and second places.

'Nah,' I say, not even looking up while the announcers ramble off Jeff's stats as he rides the track, working the crowd up with wheelies and ground tricks we could all do in our sleep. 'He ain't trying it. At the last minute he'll do a California Roll, guarantee it. Jeff will come in second just like he always does.'

'You cocky son of a bitch,' Matty toys.

'Yeah, yeah... I learned from the best,' I say, shooting him a finger gun.

Matty rolls his eyes, turning to face the track once again.

I'm not entirely paying attention to Jeff's run because honestly, I can't. That kind of pressure has been known to stress me out; instead, I'm scrolling social media, trying to focus on myself when Facebook reminds me of a memory.

Holy shit. September 27. I tap over to my main screen to verify the date, then back into Facebook. I almost forgot this year. I can see this photo with my eyes closed (and often do). The woman to my right has never truly left my mind – or my heart. My favorite daydreams are being transported back to when we were young and in love. In the picture, she's wearing a white veil draped over her light blonde wavy bob, and I am wearing a black T-shirt with a tuxedo print. Classy, I know. Even so, we look ridiculously happy, and if my memory is correct, we truly were in that moment.

Despite her still owning a part of my heart, things didn't work out. I messed up – I'm not afraid to admit it. But she didn't exactly do the right thing either. Without notice, I came home from a gig one day and she was just gone. It destroyed me, if I'm honest. Our break-up was the one time I was heartbroken and lost, but I bottled it all up inside because that's what I do. Is it healthy? Not even a little bit. But I'm not from one of those 'talk out your feelings' families so I'm honestly not sure how to get over it. I truly don't think I ever could. But that's only because if I could go back and change it, I'd still choose to follow my heart and marry Eve. After all, that's who I am – I take extreme risks. Marrying a woman thirty days after you meet is extreme. But God, was it worth it when it was good.

How can it already have been five years? I rub my hand across my chest, my heart beating a tad erratically right now – like I'm in the middle of a trick or back in that moment of our wedding day. Those two events felt the same.

I'm not even in her presence, so how on earth can a photo of her gorgeous face have my heart topsy-twirly? Eve and I haven't spoken in years, yet I could never bear deleting her from my phone altogether. And this anniversary post always gets me. I glance at the comments, which are all written by me, and tap the reply button. I've done this yearly, and with each comment, I pray she says something in return. *Please, God – any words this time. Hello. Go away. Not if you were the last man on earth. Fuck all the way off. Anything.* But so far, it's never happened, and her reply is only ever a 'like', moments after my comment has been posted. A simple thumbs up, acknowledging that she is still alive.

I wonder if her heart flutters in the same way mine does when she's notified of this memory. I hope I'm not the only one feeling that. Well, why let this year be any different than the four before? Here goes nothing. Maybe this will be the time she finally responds. Fingers crossed.

I type out my comment, then hit send before glancing up at Matty who's now getting loud.

'No hands!' he yells from the edge of the tent. 'I told you!' He points my way. 'I fucking told you!' Both of his hands are now clasped on the top of his head as he rocks back and forth on the balls of his feet, his eyes on the track.

I follow Matty's gaze and see Jeff performing an impressive trick called the Bundy, which involves executing a backflip above the front of the bike while holding onto a handlebar with one hand, usually. But Jeffy boy has let go completely and the crowd is ecstatic about it. Cheering and roaring with excitement as he maneuvers through the air like it's easy. Even I stand from the stool I'm on, watching as he repositions his hands on the bike to maintain balance before landing it without even a wobble.

'Ho-ly shit!' I yell to Matty, patting his back this time. 'Clinton Moore himself would be impressed!' The trick was made famous by Clint, a legendary rider, and it's widely regarded as one of the most technical tricks in FMX history.

'I can't believe he landed it. Yes!' Matty cheers, throwing a fist into the air proudly.

'Wooo!' I holler with him. The moment's thrill is palpable, and the excitement from the crowd is infectious. Jeff and I may be rivals on the track, but I know a well-done stunt when I see one. He killed it.

Matty glances at me, his gaze meandering to the phone in my hand. 'Get off your phone and get ready,' he yells. Comp days tend to stress him out. He wants all the guys he works with to win – but not all of us can, so he will settle for two out of the three 'places' given at each event, and usually that pans out.

'Relax,' I say to Matty, as if saying that ever helped anyone. 'You know I got this.'

I hand him my phone, then the single earbud from my ear, taking my helmet from him and hanging it off one handlebar so I can do my entry ride, working up the crowd because the more adrenaline involved, the better I ride.

'Volt?'

'Probably,' I say somewhat confidently. But not for my first run. For that I'll go with the Double Superman Seat Grab, during a backflip. Backflips are my 'thang'. Basically, I'll let go of the handlebars mid-air, holding on only to the back fender Superman-in-flight style, then remount the bike and land solidly.

Double Superman for my first run. Volt for my second. Pep talk time: *You got this, Fost! Beat Jeff. Kill it! Also: Stop. Thinking. About. Eve.*

I ride the track, rocking my head back and forth, trying to shake her memory out so I can think clearly. I was still deciding if I'd do this stunt today, but with the success of Jeff's last run, I've probably got to pull out the big guns of FMX trickery to beat him. I've done Volts in our foam practice pit over the years, but I've only landed my twist on it about fifteen times on solid ground (out of hundreds). Now it's time to do exactly that for the first time in a competition in front of a crowd.

The Volt is a 360-degree turn next to my mid-air bike – no hands. As I spin back around, I'll catch the bike and mount it from the side before landing. Only in my usual style, I'm doing it in the middle of a backflip.

'You got this, Foster. Take the energy from the crowd and nail it.' Matty talks me up, patting me on the back hard and then clapping his hands loudly. 'Famous 15! Get it!'

Matty and my crew watch as I ride toward the track, impressing the crowd with little stunts – no hands, wheelies, the Captain Morgan – shit I taught myself as a kid when I was still considered an amateur – while riding the track slowly. At one point, I stop altogether. The fans yell louder as I get off my bike and do my 'Famous 15 backflip'. I don't remember exactly when my gymnast floor routine started, but I get the best reaction, proving my thirty-five-year-old ass can still do a backflip from the ground without my bike and not kill myself. Thank you ten years of gymnastics my uncle insisted I did as a kid to help with my balance.

The announcers ramble off my stats over the loudspeakers. 'Number fifteen, Guy Foster, thirty-five years old, has decades in the business and is an X-Games superstar...' Yada yada yada.

I lift a fist into the air, allowing the track's energy to sink into my soul. I scan the stadium seating before putting on my helmet as I ride to the start. It's always fun to see if someone stands out. Maybe an old friend showed up? You never know unless you look.

Stopping at the flag guy, I let go of the handlebars, balancing my bike with my feet on the ground. I shake off the nerves that are always a part of this at first; that never goes away. I'm well aware this gig is dangerous, I just try not to think about the risks.

Just like Matty said, *You got this, Foster. You'll be popping that champagne cork after accepting first place*, and then – my gaze stops on a woman who looks vaguely familiar as I give myself my usual internal *Win this!* speech. I squint, trying to see her better. My eyes – and possibly my heart – have got to be playing tricks on me though, because there's no fucking way she's keeping up with the sport her ex dominates. When she said she never wanted to speak to me again, she meant it. That much I'm sure of.

'Yo!' the starter yells, earning my attention, waving the signal to go again. 'Go, man!'

Fuck. I hardly have the time to daydream when seconds are eating away at my possible score. I don't even have my helmet on yet. I slide it on, patting it hard on the top to wake my ass up, then with a twist of the throttle, my head returns to my job and now it's time to give my fans what they came here for and win this event. I'll figure out the Eve thing after.

3

EVE CASSIDY

'Trauma 2 crew to bay.' I hear Dale's voice requesting Gen, Troy and I go to our room assignment and like always, a buzz goes through my chest with anticipation.

'Here we go,' Gen says, pulling a yellow paper gown over her scrubs exactly like I am. 'Any guesses?'

Guessing how bad something coming into our trauma room is, is a thing we do to occupy our minds, to prevent 'stage fright'. On a scale of 1 to 10, the 'what are we walking into' game.

'Five or less, I hope,' I say as we walk in, flashing my crossed fingers at her.

'Male, mid-thirties, unresponsive after a motorcycle accident. Required intubation on scene due to severe respiratory distress,' one of the medics relays breathlessly as they maneuver the gurney into position. Sweat glistens on their foreheads, a testament to the high-stakes race against time they've just endured.

The room buzzes with a symphony of sounds – the beeping monitors, the soft murmur of the ventilator, the urgent rustle of gowns and gloves.

'Freeway? Off-road? Type of accident?' Genevieve asks.

'FMX rider. We were on-scene medics; he seemed distracted before his second run and he didn't land it, a forty- to fifty-foot fall, easily. The bike landed on top of him.'

With those words, my heart starts to slow, and panic builds in me at the sight of our patient's dark hair and green riding gear. I'm positioned near his feet, but as I begin cutting up the leg of his pants, my gaze hesitantly moves across to his one tattooed arm, black and gray ink from elbow to wrist – and to the one in color. A hot pink tiny heart just under his right thumb. I have the exact same one; we did it when I went to Florida to stay with him. My fingers have traced the outlines of those tattoos many times. Almost shyly I force my eyes to his face and recognize him immediately – yep – Foster. Crap. Crap. Crap. This is bad. He's hardly aged at all, and is just as handsome as I remember, only now he's pale and lifeless, framed by an endotracheal tube and an oxygen mask.

Time seems to slow down as a wave of emotions crashes over me – shock, fear, and an overwhelming sense of helplessness. Luckily, my training kicks in, forcing me to focus on the immediate tasks but beneath the professional facade, my mind is racing, my heart is pounding. I used to love this man.

'Vitals are unstable – BP 90/60 and dropping, pulse erratic between 100 and 150. Board and collar in case of C-spine injury, suspected internal bleeding,' another medic continues, their voice tight with urgency.

Every detail feels like a knife twisting deeper, yet I have to listen to every word because that may help us save him, but all I can think about is how I once knew the warmth of this man's smile and the comfort of his presence.

Dr Bradly is issuing orders, but his voice sounds muffled like I'm underwater. 'Get him on the monitor, full vitals. I need an ABG stat. Let's prep for central line.'

With his clothes now cut off to his boxers, I move mechanically, helping to transfer him to the trauma bed, attaching leads and checking the ventilator. My hands are steady, but inside I'm trembling. I'm torn between the need to be professional and the overwhelming urge to break down, to hold his hand, to tell him to fight, to stay with me. But there's no time for personal grief. My colleagues are relying on me – and most importantly, Foster is relying on me.

'Who is he?' Troy asks, moving like he's doing a ballet. He's got every motion memorized and it comes to him like second nature.

My lips press together in a determined line, my eyebrows furrowed in concentration as I try to force the words out. 'His name is Guy Foster, thirty-five years old, date of birth is…' I give the information I know which the doctor and the terrified-looking registrar hanging at the door are looking for – without even looking at the medic's paperwork that I've yet to lay eyes on.

Genevieve side-eyes me. She knows his name, his face, and all the details of our past relationship but she's never met him in person. I'm thankful she's keeping her cool right now as the realization hits us both simultaneously.

'Mr Foster!' Troy says loudly, shining his pen light into each eye. 'Welcome to OHSU Emergency Department. I'm sorry to meet you in this condition, but we're doing everything we can to get you home and healthy.' Dr Bradly has always been the most empathetic doctor here and despite the situation, is very aware that even the unconscious can likely hear what's going on, so he attempts to keep everyone calm, including the patient.

Monitors beep incessantly, their digital read-outs displaying a cascade of vital signs – each beep a marker of Foster's precarious state. My heart can barely take it.

'Please – stay, Fost,' I say in what I thought was a whisper, my hands moving automatically as muscle memory guides me through procedures and my mind stays acutely aware of every change in his condition.

'Fost?' Dr Bradly asks, his gaze jetting to me only for a second. 'Do you know him?'

I nod, glancing at Gen who doesn't say a word, just continues with her duties. 'He's my ex-husband.'

'Shit!' Troy says.

Shit feels like an understatement.

I think back to just an hour ago, getting the notification that he'd commented on our anniversary reminder post, and what that did to me compared to what's going on inside me right now. Chaos. Pandemonium. I feel like I'm in a trauma room full of people while our relationship plays for all to watch on a screen big enough to block out practically all else. What the hell happened?

Dr Sully enters the room and I realize my comment during my coffee run may have jinxed us earlier – like a bad curse laid on us by someone practicing voodoo. Our eyes meet and he lifts his chin as a hello.

'Sorry to ruin your day, Nurse Eve.'

Usually, I'd chirp back a response casually, lifting the mood slightly – at least for us employees. But seeing him means this is as bad as I'd worried it was.

'Truthfully,' I say, 'I've never been happier to see you.'

'He's the husband,' Troy announces, stepping away from the bed Foster is on as transport take over and wheel him away.

'Whose husband?'

'Eve's,' Troy answers.

'You're married?'

I shake my head, following Foster out and into the hall and avoiding the question Dr Sully just asked. 'My God, Fost, this was always my fear,' I say, holding his uninjured hand and speed walking with his bed. 'You'll be OK, though,' I add. 'This is a great hospital. And uh... I'll be waiting for you when you go to a room. Alright?' The two young men wheeling the cart toward surgery stop as they wait for the secured door to open. I can't walk with them any more but I stay for what feels like hours watching them disappear into the halls of the surgical unit until the doors click closed, separating us.

'Oh, my God,' I breathe out in a shaky sigh. It's finally over. At least my part is. I was beginning to think the moment would never end. I know he's in good hands but I'm not sure I can handle this. I've never worked on someone I know intimately.

I march down the hall, tearing off my gown and peeling off my gloves, tossing them into a garbage can and beelining to Dale's desk. 'I need to take a break,' I inform him, giving him zero other explanation. 'And no is not an option.'

His gaze meets mine, then the clock. 'Little late for a break, but since I can't say no, I guess go ahead?'

I'm glad he picked up that I was going whether he said yes or not. With his permission, I practically run through the halls toward the staff room. The door closing behind me feels like relief as I separate myself from what just happened.

Foster. He's the best of FMX. How could this have happened? First the anniversary reminder, and now this. It sort of feels like the fate I no longer believe in is playing a cruel joke on me.

Seeing him like that – my God. Tears spill down my cheeks as I pace the small lunchroom. Foster has always been a whirlwind of excitement and charm, with his short dark curly hair and that mischievous twinkle in his eye. In the past, I could never resist his flirtatious banter or his contagious laughter. God, he has to be OK.

'He'll be alright,' I say to no one in particular, sinking into a chair, my hands trembling. The room is quiet, a stark contrast to the storm still actively swirling through my mind. *How is this happening*? I say to myself, rocking with anxiety as exhaustion, relief, and profound sadness overtake me like a tidal wave. My mind replays every moment of the past thirty minutes, the clinical tasks interwoven with flashes of Foster's and my very short life together – arguments, laughter, the mundane and the meaningful. Our story wasn't simple, and neither are the feelings that linger.

The sound of the break-room door opening causes me to try and pull myself together and I'm thankful when I hear Genevieve's voice.

'I've been looking all over for you.'

'I'd like to change my guess from five to 500,' I say, wiping unexpected tears from my face with a sniffle.

I underestimated that one for sure. The adrenaline of the trauma room that had kept me focused is fading, leaving a raw, aching void in its place, knowing I've done all I can and maybe it won't be enough? *Please, let it be enough.*

'How ya doin'?' she asks gently, sitting down next to me.

I shake my head. 'Not great. Not great at all. Everything I never wanted to remember I am, and nothing feels OK right now.' I glance up at her. 'Nothing. What do I do?'

Right then, my phone vibrates in my pocket, and without really thinking about it, I answer the call.

'Is this Eve Cassidy?' the caller asks.

'This is she,' I say, curious about who would be so formal when calling me.

'My name is Sarah. I work with Oregon Health and Science University. I'm calling about your husband, Guy Foster. He's had an accident and—'

Her words nearly stop my heart and I suddenly realize what this phone call is. *I'm* still Foster's emergency contact. I remember him adding my name to his FMX paperwork that Matty keeps on file for emergencies, all those years ago, and hoping I'd never get that call. This call. Yet here it is. After I participated in stabilizing him. My phone slips from my hand, landing on the floor with a thud.

Genevieve grabs it.

'Hello?' she says, noticing that I'm frozen in place. She listens for a moment, her gaze on me. 'Where should she wait for him? OK. Yes. Thank you.' Gen hangs up with the caller then wraps an arm around me, pulling me close. 'Go,' she says. 'Wait for him in the ICU family room. She said it may be a few hours. I'll smooth everything over with Dale.'

4

EVE CASSIDY

After many cups of stale hospital coffee and attempting to preoccupy myself with whatever HGTV show is playing on the remoteless TV in the ICU family waiting room, I decide to badge myself into the unit and see if Foster's out of surgery and in his room yet. Yes, this is frowned upon. No, at this moment, I don't care. It's been hours; surely they're done in the OR by now. I approach the front desk, stopping anxiously in front of a woman I don't know.

'Who are you looking for?' she asks, not even looking away from her computer.

'Foster—er, *Guy* Foster?'

He hates his first name – always has. It's why I'm stumped every time I hear it. I've never known him as Guy. In his words, every dude on the planet gets called 'guy', so how is he to differentiate the people actually speaking to *him* from one of the other billions of 'guys' on the earth?

The receptionist scans her screen, and a click or two of her mouse fills the silence between us.

'Guy Foster.' She nods like his name rings a bell. 'And you are here because...?' Her gaze drops to my hospital badge, still attached to the breast pocket of my scrubs, her eyebrows furrowing. 'You're from the ER? Didn't he come in via ER?'

'Oh, um, yes. Sorry, I'm not here on the clock, I'm off-duty.' I cover my badge with my hand.

The receptionist looks confused but taps on her keyboard again like she's writing a novel. 'Are you family?'

'Yes?'

She narrows her eyes.

'I'm his... uh—wife.' I blurt out only the tiniest of white lies. The sentence is really only missing one word. *Just please don't ask me for a marriage certificate, because I burned that years ago.*

Miss Receptionist scans the screen, clicking in and out of the system. 'Eve?' she asks.

I nod.

Her pursed-lip smile says anything but 'it'll all be OK'. 'It looks like he's just arrived in the recovery room so it's going to be another hour or so.'

'But he made it through the surgery?'

She glances at the screen again then nods.

Oh, sweet relief, he's alive. Thank God. My heart stabilizes from its erratic run since seeing his face and for the first time in hours, I feel like I'm back on planet Earth and not just hovering above it watching chaos unfold.

'Can you make a note to have someone come get me when he's brought to a room? I'm in the family waiting area.'

'Will do,' she says, right as my phone vibrates in my pocket.

I pull it out as I walk back to the waiting room and see Kait's name flashing across the screen.

'Hey,' she says when I answer. 'What's going on?'

Really, I'd rather not give anyone a play-by-play of my day right now, but I know she's not hanging up the phone until I do. Prying is what best friends do best. Plus, I've known her too long to lie.

'Foster is in ICU – here.'

The other end of the line is momentarily silent.

'Here?' she asks. 'As in at *our* hospital?'

I like how she calls it ours as if we own it, not simply work for it. Kait is technically my sister's best friend – originally. But the three of us are only a couple of years apart so we've become a BFF trio. Jess is home and has no idea what's going on right now – thank God – because if she did, she'd be blowing up my phone with opinions I'd rather not hear. But Kait is here and works on floor six of the OHSU Doernbecher Children's Hospital in labor and delivery, and I'm sure she was filled in on what's happening by Genevieve, who has befriended us both.

'As in, I had to leave my shift early because I was in the trauma room when he got here.'

'Holy be-Jesus, Evie. Are you alright?'

I sit back on the couch in the family waiting area and rub a hand over my face. Emotions surface just from considering if I'm alright. 'I don't know.'

'Is he...?' she asks very hesitantly.

'He lived through surgery, but I have no idea what his injuries are and I haven't seen him since they took him to the OR.'

'Did you really get the call?'

I wipe my eyes, hoping to stop the tears before they flow far too easily. 'I did and I don't know why, considering we've been apart for five years. He should have changed it a long time ago. How am I supposed to help with this? I don't even know how to contact his family.'

'What about Matty?'

'Don't know how to get ahold of him either.'

'Shouldn't he be here if he was hurt during a ride?'

'He could be, for all I know, I just haven't seen him.'

Her silence says so much. She's choosing her words wisely here as after I left Florida (and Foster), I was a total mess. I thought three months after marriage I'd be floating on cloud nine still, but instead I found myself alone, far away from home, and wishing I'd made other choices while he toured without me. I didn't get married and change my entire life only to be alone 92 per cent of the time.

'Are you sure you don't want to be happy with how much you've already helped, and let someone else figure this next part out?' Kait asks.

'You think I should leave him when he's in this condition? Alone? We both know patients who are on their own heal slower than those with support. I once loved this man. No way can I just leave.'

'I know, but this is a slippery slope, Eve – you have no idea who's in his life now and things may get super awkward for you before they get better if you stay.'

'What do you mean?'

'Love-*dddd*. Past tense, darling. Really, harsh as this may sound, he's not your problem any more. He didn't even show up at your wedding reception.'

'That is a technicality. He tried to make it, his face via iPad made it, but his flight got changed last minute.'

'OK, fine. What if he has a girlfriend now? Or a wife? Or children? What will you do if they walk in and see you there?'

'Children? God, are you trying to kill me?' I ask, planting a hand on my thumping heart. 'You're worrying about nonsense. I already know he's single as a pringle. I googled him as I sat here in the ICU waiting for him to get out of surgery. Only one other woman besides myself was listed as one of his partners and they broke up publicly a year ago. Her name is Gia.'

'He's got a thing for girls with three letter names, eh?' she asks with a slight chuckle. 'Well, I'm sorry for being a worry wort. I forgot he was famous and Google knows all. What about his family? Shouldn't they also get "the call"?'

'If they were in his paperwork. But considering he's a grown man who probably no longer has his parents listed anywhere for anything, I'm not holding my breath.'

'Hi.' A brunette woman dressed in navy scrubs, with a stethoscope around her neck and a badge with her photo, and the name 'Chelsea – RN' attached at the breast pocket, steps into the doorway of the waiting room. 'You're here for Guy?'

'I gotta go,' I say to Kait, hanging up before she can even say goodbye. Slippery slope or not, I'm going in. My heart won't say no.

'Foster,' I correct Chelsea. 'He never goes by Guy.'

'Oh! Good to know! And you're his wife?'

'Yes.' I don't even feel guilty saying it at this point.

She looks at my scrubs, lifting a single eyebrow. 'I recognize you. Don't you work here?'

It's a big hospital but if we work the same hours, it's possible to meet in the halls or cafeteria. I don't know this nurse, but that's not to say I've never spoken to her on the phone or run into her at some point.

'I do,' I say with a nod. 'Trauma ER.' I pull my badge from my pocket to prove it.

'Oh, you poor thing – you were there when he came in?'

'I was.'

Her bubbly persona fades and she frowns. 'Well, come with me. He's just been wheeled in from recovery. You must be worried sick,' she says, touching my shoulder with concern.

'You have no idea,' I mumble, glancing at each room we pass, fear building in me.

What am I about to walk into? It can't possibly be as bad as it was earlier but that doesn't mean he's not still struggling. I have no idea what's really wrong with him at this point, other than what I heard in the ER, and none of that sounded promising.

Chelsea stops outside a room, sanitizing her hands and pointing to the wall where the dispenser is for me to do the same. As I lather my hands until they're dry, I glance at the wall of glass separating us. The curtain within the room is pulled, so I can't see him just yet, but I hear the medical machinery beeping steadily enough that I know he's stable.

'I know you see a lot of horrifying things, but brace yourself, it's always different when it's someone you love,' she warns, slowly pulling back the curtain, stopping me in my tracks. My steps falter, and I have to steady myself against the doorframe, my breath catching in my throat. Despite our painful separation, my now stunned heart is telling me the connection is still there, like an unbroken thread binding us together.

'Freaking. Hell.' The words tumble out of my mouth without trying.

I approach his bed slowly, my heart galloping through my chest. His hand lies limply at his side, and I hesitate before gently placing my own over it. The contact is electric, a stark reminder of the bond we once shared. His skin is cool, and I squeeze his hand lightly, willing him to feel my presence, to know he isn't alone.

'Foster,' I whisper, leaning into him and speaking in his ear, my voice trembling. 'It's Eve, again. Surgery's over. You're doing great,' I say, glancing at the numbers on the monitors. All of those words feel inadequate, but they're all I have.

I scan the room, taking in the array of medical equipment – the IV drips, the infusion pumps, the tangle of wires and tubes – all working to keep him alive. I struggle to maintain my composure, my professional mask slipping in the face of personal crisis. Chelsea was right, the years of training and experience as a nurse couldn't shield me from the raw, aching vulnerability of seeing someone I once loved in such a critical state.

Tears well up, but I blink them back, knowing I need to be strong – for him. For the person I once promised to love and protect. I speak again, my voice steadier this time. 'You got this, Fost.' No response as I plant my lips on the side of his forehead.

Standing, I glance at Chelsea and another nurse I don't know who's also in the room, documenting something on the computer near him.

'What, uh—' My mind is not moving the way it usually does considering it's now clouded with every moment I've ever spent with this man. '—What injuries did he end up having?'

'Might be easier to talk about the injuries he doesn't have,' the nurse at the computer says with half a grin.

Chelsea is checking his monitors but glances at me. 'Well, let's see.' She props a hand on her hip. 'He has a deranged left shoulder, his left wrist is fractured, and he's got many broken ribs on both sides. He also has a collapsed lung, ruptured spleen, a bruised liver, and multiple internal injuries that surgery just repaired. No brain bleeds, luckily – thank God for helmets. And his cervical spine looks good – but bruised. As you probably know, the next forty-eight hours will be his biggest challenge, but we're keeping him as comfortable as possible. If he stays stable for the next few days, the doctor will extubate before he has another surgery on that shoulder and wrist.'

Jeesh. He needs more OR time? Oh, God this is bad. So, so bad.

My gaze meanders to the many wires and tubes that are everywhere. It's terrifying from this side of it. He's shirtless – which I've always enjoyed – but his left arm is strapped to his side, probably to stabilize both his shoulder and wrist until they do the surgeries she mentioned. Machines on either side of him beep with different patterns. His dark loose curls are a mess, and he's dirty, as is usual with his career choice, but his face is perfect – besides the tube taped between his lips. To quote Chelsea, thank God for helmets.

'Wow. OK. Typically, he's a way better rider than this. I can't believe this has happened.'

For years, he's tempted fate with every ride he takes. It only ever gave me a mini heart attack watching him mid-air doing a death-defying stunt with a two-hundred-pound bike hovering nearby. Which is why, since we broke up, I haven't really kept up with him because who does that after someone breaks your heart? No one willingly stresses themselves out. I made a clean break.

'Keep talking to him,' Chelsea says. 'He can hear you.'

That's sort of what I'm afraid of. Sure, it was a clean break, for me. However, when we parted, I didn't exactly leave things on a good note. In fact, I *only* left a note. He didn't question it. And until today, besides his yearly FB comment, we've never spoken again. So... I have absolutely no idea how this is going to go down. Will the sound of my voice flatline the poor guy? It hasn't so far.

'We'll be back to check on him in a few, or when something starts beeping,' Chelsea says, motioning between her and the nurse now logging out of the computer. 'If you need me, press his call button,' she says while washing her hands. Then they exit the room, closing the curtain and door behind them, leaving just him and me in the scariest place I've ever been.

I spend a moment looking him over – something I didn't allow myself to do earlier. Five o'clock shadow, present. That's his 'look'. God – and his home gym – blessed this man with strong shoulders, muscley (but not 'overdone') arms, and an oh sweet six-pack. Maybe I can't see that part now, with his arm stabilized across his mid-section – but a girl never forgets a body like his. He has a single scar through one of his dark eyebrows that looks intentional, but it's from the first fall he ever took on a bike when he was four. And though I can't see them now, his eyes are such a light blue they look like sea glass – it's the first thing you notice about him. The man is devastatingly handsome. Seeing him like this, even though I see this kind of thing daily, is terrifying.

'Didn't quite land this one, eh?' I ask, holding his hand gently in mine.

No answer. Not even a grin. I heave a sigh. 'I don't even know what to say, Fost.' My voice cracks, which surprises me as I'm pretty emotionless these days. 'And no, I'm not crying. I just—God, you're so broken that I'm scared. I'm also certain I'm not the girl you want to wake up to, so give me a hint somehow. Is there someone I can call for you? Your parents? Matty? A girlfriend Google doesn't know about? Blink once for yes.' I sniffle, wiping away tears with my free hand.

His eyes stay closed, not even a flinch. He's still as a corpse, with a mechanical lung keeping him this side of the earth. What do I do? I glance around the room again, spotting a bag with the words PERSONAL BELONGINGS on a nearby chair. Surely, his phone is in there, and I can call his family; it's the least I can do.

I dig through the bag. In it is his riding gear that I cut into shreds so I could get it off him – we won't tell him I did that personally because that's going to piss him off. He's very protective of his gear. I push aside his boots. Gloves. Socks. Underwear... and at the bottom of the bag are his wallet and cell phone.

I grab the phone and tap the screen on. It's locked with a passcode. Great. I haven't talked to this man in years. How am I going to figure this out? I flash the phone in front of his face, but nothing happens. Either the intubation tube is confusing it, or he doesn't use Face ID. What about his thumb? Gently, I lay his right thumb over the reader. Still locked.

Think, Eve, think. What are some of the most important things to this man?

Motorcycles. Possibly not after this, though?

Doughnuts. Should I look up Voodoo Doughnut's phone number? I don't think so...

His birthday? Maybe. I tap it in, but his phone buzzes no.

My birthday? I should be concerned if this one works, but enter it anyway. Buzz. No go.

Wait, what year was he fifteen? He's thirty-five now... so twenty years ago would be 2004. I tap in the numbers, and his phone magically unlocks. He won his first title that year. Fifteen is his rider number. He considers it lucky – I'm not so sure at this moment.

I tap on his list of contacts, scrolling for some cutesy candy nickname he's given a new girl, or for his parents. I come across his mother first – Donna Foster. I stop at her name, hesitantly hovering my index finger over her listing. We've only briefly met and I didn't feel like she loved me. She was not happy to hear we'd eloped after thirty days either. Nope, can't call her. I scroll again, landing on Matty's number.

'Foster?' he says, confusion in his voice.

'No,' I say. 'It's Eve.'

'Eve?'

The glass door slides open and Matty walks in, phone still to his ear. Our eyes meet. A look of puzzlement is plastered on the older man's face. 'Eve?' He drops his device after spotting me. 'Why, uh—why are you here?' he asks.

I lift my shoulders. 'I didn't plan to be, but I work here,' I tell him. 'I was in the ER when he came in. I'm also shockingly still his emergency contact.'

'Really?' he asks, frowning at the sight of Foster. 'I didn't know you two were involved again. He hasn't mentioned it.'

'He wouldn't, because we're not.'

He lifts a curious eyebrow. 'Keep talking,' he says, now across the bed from me, inspecting the parts of Foster that are injured.

'I didn't even know he was in the city. We don't talk any more.'

Matty's eyes are on me and he looks... interested, to say the least. 'When's the last time you two actually spoke?'

'When I left Florida,' I admit, sheepishly. 'Actually, not even then, really, so I guess just before I left?'

'You haven't talked to him in five years?'

I shake my head, glancing down at Foster, my heart stuttering painfully. Tangled, messy emotions swirl through my head, confusing me almost to tears. I sniffle hard, looking up at the ceiling to will them away as I plant a hand over my mouth to stop it from quivering because that's when I'll lose it.

'How bad is it?' he asks, nervousness in his voice.

'He's critical. They've got him sedated into what we call an induced coma until he's been stable for a minimum of forty-eight hours. Mostly internal damage, except his left arm. No brain bleeds. No serious spinal injuries.'

He shakes his head, closing his eyes painfully. 'Damn it,' he mumbles, now looking at Foster with worry.

'Was it as bad at the track as it was here?' I ask after pulling myself together.

Matty nods, frowning at the same time. 'Worst crash I've seen in a while. I don't know what happened, but I've got my suspicions.'

Really? I want to ask what those are, but he continues speaking.

'But Foster's tough as nails. We both know that. He's healed broken bones so many times he's pro. Even survived a broken heart once.' His gaze meets mine and I feel instantly guilty. 'He'll pull through – eventually.'

Message received. 'Should I go?'

Matty is like a second father, a trainer, a coach, and a best friend all wound into one for Foster. He's who should be here – especially after his broken heart jab and his protective fatherly persona. I get it. I hurt this man. But I didn't leave with a whole heart either. The breaking was mutual.

A soft smile creeps up on Matty's face. 'Nah, I think you should stay.'

'*Why?*'

That I did not expect. Truthfully, I figured whoever might show up for him would hate me with the fire of a thousand suns, just like Foster probably does.

Matty shrugs. 'He was distracted at the track today and considering the date, I have a feeling that distraction may have been you.'

'*Me?*' My head almost can't comprehend this news. I never even had the chance to know if he saw my thumbs up on his message. My memory distracted him?

'You know our boy believes in signs – what do they call it? Fate? And considering his distraction and the fact that he ended up here with you as his nurse, that seems fateful. I think he may have something to say about that when he wakes up.'

I feel a slight squeeze on my hand, and I nearly jump out of my skin as I jerk mine from his. I'd forgotten I was even holding his hand.

'Swedish meatballs!'

'What?' Matty asks.

'He squeezed my hand!' I say, repeatedly tapping the red call button. 'He squeezed my hand,' I say again, softer, feeling instantly like a weight is lifting slightly from my soul. He's in there. And he can hear me.

5
GUY 'FOSTER'

Chelsea, my nurse, who announces herself by name each time she walks in – which is helpful given my condition – was right: I can hear what's happening around me. Thankfully, I can't feel much, and I'm not really sure how I got here. What I do know is that since the moment I arrived, the woman I was briefly married to has been at my bedside, and the sound of her voice hurts something inside me that I'm pretty sure is more emotional than physical.

'I think you should stay,' Matty says softly.

Yes, Eve. If this isn't some kind of nightmare and you're really here, please, please stay. I don't know what happened, but I need you.

'*Why?*' She sounds stunned. Which, seeing our history, I shouldn't be surprised at.

'He was distracted at the track today and considering the date, I have a feeling that distraction may have been you.'

'*Me?*'

I don't know if it's the tone of her voice, or the fact that I'm following a conversation between the two of them while my head feels like it's off-duty at best, but something about this conversation seems real. Like I'm not dreaming it. I didn't know I was distracted earlier but it sort of makes sense that if I was, she'd be behind it. It's pretty much been that way since I lost her.

'You know our boy believes in signs – what do they call it? Fate? And considering his distraction and the fact that he ended up with you as his nurse, that seems fateful. I think he may have something to say about that when he wakes up.'

I do. I have shit to say! I can't die right now – I've got regrets. Unfinished business on all fronts and the last thing I need to do is try to make this up to her when I'm a ghost, lingering around the hospital attempting to get her attention. Nobody's got time for death at the height of their career! *Come on, Foster, acknowledge her before she's gone again.*

It takes everything in me to attempt to squeeze her hand. A tiny 'he's right' gesture that she'd not understand, but I know, and if I ever get this tube out of my throat and don't feel like I'm floating on the edge of the matrix, I plan to tell her exactly that if she'll hear me out.

'Swedish meatballs!' There's panic in her voice, along with what sounds like relief.

'What?' Matty asks.

'He squeezed my hand!' She holds my hand tightly, grasping it with her other after a few seconds. 'He squeezed my hand,' she says in a near whisper, but I can hear the hope intertwined with the fear she's probably feeling.

Seconds later, water flows from the sink as Eve chatters about what just occurred with whoever just entered my room. She's worried about me waking up too early and risking my stability. I just want to know what the hell happened to put me in this position.

'Hi, Foster, it's your nurse, Chelsea. How are you feeling?' she asks as if I can answer as she touches the side of my face. 'I brought Dr Sully this time. Can you open your eyes, sweetheart?'

I am trying, lady – with everything in me, I'm trying. Ahhh! No. Not the bright light. *Stay back, Foster. Don't let this death shit tempt you.* When the blinding light flashes into my other eye, I'm confused.

'Might have just been a reflex,' a male voice says.

'No.' Eve insists. 'He responded to a statement.'

Yes, girl. Read my mind. I know you have the ability. That was part of what scared me about you the most.

'Matty said something and Foster squeezed my hand as a response. I know it. Watch...'

A hand grabs mine again, and I know it's Eve's. She's one of those women with dainty hands. We compared hands once. She's got long, slender fingers, brightly painted nails at all times, thin gold bands on the forefinger of her right hand and thumb of her left, and skin as soft as silk. She always has a bottle of lotion in her purse because she can't stand sandpaper hands – which I sometimes have.

'Do you have something to say to me, Foster?' she asks, her voice tinged with worry.

So many things, Evie. Some that might piss you off. But a guy's got to start somewhere now that he's got the chance, right? *Squeeze her hand, Foster. Could you help me out here, brain? I know you work – nine times out of ten.*

With everything in me, I focus on one thing. The signal from my brain moves through me like molasses. It's not the speed at which my mind usually works. But finally, what feels like hours later, she squeals when my hand clutches hers.

'Huh,' the doctor says. 'He may be coming to, but we've got him pretty sedated and would like to keep it that way for now, considering his condition. Chelsea, you want to up the meds a tad?'

Up the meds? No. But it's too late, whatever meds they're talking about she must have administered immediately because I feel as if I'm floating.

'I know you're worried, Eve, but for his safety, we need to keep him sedated,' the man continues. 'My main focus is getting him through the next couple of days. After that, we'll re-evaluate and, if possible, ease up on it. Obviously, he can hear you, so talk to him?' he suggests. 'I usually advise light conversations, listening to music, reading, or reminiscing about happier times.'

Happier times. Reminder: you married this guy.

The room falls silent for a moment and all I hear is shuffling.

'Hey—oh, sorry—didn't realize it'd be a full house. Should I come back?' the voice asks.

'No, she works here,' Eve says to someone.

'I took lunch and wanted to come check on you.' The woman, whose voice I don't quite recognize, is speaking to someone in the room. Maybe me, but I'm not sure.

'Who's this?' Matty asks.

'This is Kait, my best friend,' Eve tells him. 'Kait, this is Matty, Foster's trainer.'

'Trainer. Friend. And stand-in father figure,' Matty explains.

I've heard of Kait, but only met her a handful of times.

'Gawd,' Kait says, dragging out the word. 'He looks awful. Will he make it?'

How awful? Am I grossly deformed? Get hit by a semi? Eaten by an alligator? Wait, aren't I in Oregon? There are no alligators there to my knowledge. What happened to make me look awful?

'I hope so,' Eve and Matty say in unison, both of them stopping after their words.

'Crazy,' Kait says softly. 'Anyway, I remembered something about him after we hung up and since someone brought these into the unit this morning, I thought we'd give it a shot and see if he's still in there. You know what they say, do anything you can to remind them of who they are, to keep them fighting.'

'Good idea,' Matty says.

I hear a shuffling then it hits me – a whiff of something sweet and delicious. Doughnuts. A surge of hunger and anger rises in me. How dare this stranger bring in my favorite food when I'm unable to chew or even acknowledge their presence? I'm tired of this 'induced coma' they're calling it. *My mind works, y'all!*

'He's gonna hate you for that,' Eve says, inhaling deeply. 'I've never met a box of doughnuts he didn't devour on his own.'

'I know – you mentioned that years ago. Maybe they'll work like smelling salts?' Kait says, clearly hopeful.

'No smelling salts, ladies,' the doctor says as he sanitizes his hands, ready to leave the room. 'We want him sedated, until I say otherwise.'

If only I could communicate and tell them what's happening in my head because my body feels like it's rolling across ocean waves, bobbing through the water hoping for a rescue boat. In reality, I've got an itch on the back of my left knee worthy of amputation at this point, and the smell of my favorite food is luring me into a medically induced daydream while the veil between life and coma is thin.

* * *

Five Years Ago

I'm meeting Eve at Voodoo Doughnut, my favorite spot in Portland. There's one in Orlando, but the original is always better. This place is like a portal to a world where all your wildest doughnut dreams come true. With its playful pink exterior and whimsical signage, Voodoo stands out among the surrounding buildings.

Inside, the atmosphere is lively and bustling. Every inch of wall space is covered in funky art and voodoo-themed decorations, giving off a vibe that's equal parts carnival funhouse and rock concert venue. The scent of freshly baked doughnuts fills the air, mingling with the sound of cheerful chatter and upbeat rock music.

The display cases are packed with a variety of sweets, ranging from classic options like glazed and chocolate to more unconventional choices like the iconic Voodoo Doll doughnut, shaped like a gingerbread man and filled with raspberry jelly, complete with a pretzel stake through its heart. Other eye-catching options include the Bacon Maple Bar topped with crispy bacon strips and the Grape Ape boasting vibrant purple frosting dusted with grape flavoring. I love every single one.

As I enter the bustling shop, a staff member greets me with a cheerful, 'Good morning!' Their colorful attire and sleeves of tattoos add to the unique atmosphere of the place. 'Need a recommendation? I'm considered a doughnut connoisseur.'

I order an assortment and snag a rare free table in the usually crowded indoor seating area. As I wait for Eve to arrive, my nerves start to get the best of me. It's silly, really. How could I already be falling for this woman? We've only met once and have been chatting through text for a couple of weeks. But I feel something with each buzz of my phone. They say the heart never lies, and mine is beating faster than ever before – especially when I see her walking in.

Jay-sus. She's even more stunning than I remembered. Her hair is hanging freely at about shoulder blade level, with a hint of a wave that could be natural or could be manufactured by a curling iron. She's wearing a shiny black bomber jacket over a sheer white V-neck T-shirt, with an eggplant-colored bralette peeking out from underneath. Her torn jeans fit her perfectly, and her white Converse sneakers complete the effortless yet sexy look. I can't take my eyes off her.

Her dark blue eyes sparkle with gold glitter on her eyelids, and she's wearing bright red lipstick again. A pair of bangle-sized gold hoops dangle from her ears, and a delicate gold necklace with a cursive 'e' charm hangs at the base of her neck. She has multiple bracelets on one wrist, including a black rubber one with a single green stripe engraved with my riding number. Instantly, I recognize it as something she got at the event where we first met. She's wearing my merch on our first official meeting – adorable.

As she approaches my table, she smiles. 'Doughnut fan, are ya?'

I can't help but grin back at her. I've set up a spread of Voodoo's finest pastries and can't wait to see which is her favorite.

I shrug nonchalantly. 'There are two things I can never say no to: adrenaline rushes and doughnuts,' I say with a mischievous grin.

She tilts her head, studying me with a confused expression on her face, but also showing genuine interest in what I have to say.

'A doughnut-loving adrenaline junkie; who knew you were so complex?' she remarks with a nervous grin. Her eyes linger on the sugary treats before me. 'This place is like the extreme doughnut shop, isn't it? So, tell me,' she asks, 'which one is your absolute favorite?'

I scan over the options, considering her question. 'It depends on my mood,' I reply. 'Sometimes I crave the classic Voodoo Doll, while other times I can't resist the allure of the Old Dirty Bastard.'

She laughs to herself. 'Chocolate frosting, crumbled Oreos, and peanut butter... it's enough to make anyone's heart skip a beat.'

I laugh as well, leaning back in my seat and nervously running a hand through my hair. Curiosity gets the best of me. 'Do we have the same favorite, Evie?'

Without hesitation, she reaches for the Old Dirty Bastard. 'Perhaps,' she says, not waiting a second to take a bite. 'So, as someone from out of town, do you come here often?' she asks, mouth full of doughnut.

I chuckle. 'Only when I want to impress someone special,' I respond with a sly wink.

'Well then, color me impressed,' she says, lifting her doughnut in a mock toast.

I raise my doughnut in response.

The playful banter between us is easy, a natural flow that makes me feel like I've known Eve for much longer than just these few interactions. As we both take a bite of our chosen pastries, a comfortable silence settles between us.

The atmosphere around us buzzes with energy, the mix of excited chatter and the sweet aroma of doughnuts creating the perfect backdrop for our growing connection. I find myself stealing glances at her, admiring the way her eyes light up with each enthusiastic topic we touch upon.

'So, Miss Cassidy, what other hidden gems of Portland should I know about?' I inquire, genuinely interested in her perspective on this city that she calls home.

Eve's eyes narrow playfully as she leans back in her seat. 'Ah, so you're looking for insider tips now? Well, buckle up, because Portland has a lot more to offer than weird doughnut shops.'

She starts rattling off a list of quirky places and hidden gems around the city. From a tiny bookstore with a resident cat named Whiskers to a cozy speakeasy hidden behind an unassuming door in an alley, her excitement is infectious. I listen intently, hanging on her every word as she paints vivid pictures of each location with her animated descriptions. As she speaks, I can't help but marvel at how effortlessly charming she is. Her passion for her city shines through in every recommendation, and I find myself falling even more under her spell.

'Wow, I never knew Portland had so much to offer,' I say, genuinely impressed by Eve's knowledge of her city.

She chuckles, her eyes crinkling at the corners with amusement. 'Oh, this is just the beginning. Portland is full of surprises if you know where to look.'

I lean in closer, intrigued by the idea of discovering more of this city with her by my side. 'Then I'm counting on you to show me all the hidden gems only a true Portlander would know.'

A playful glint sparkles in her eyes as she nods, and her smirk widens into a grin. 'How long are you here for?'

I playfully drum my fingers on the table, pretending to contemplate. 'Hmm, let's see... I could probably stick around long enough to explore a few of these "weird" places you speak of,' I say.

Eve leans back in her seat again, crossing one leg over the other. 'Well then, it's settled. Consider me your official Portland guide until further notice,' she declares with a mock air of authority, her tone light and playful.

A warm feeling spreads through me at the thought of spending more time with her. 'I've never looked forward to anything more – besides, of course, this date.'

'Date?' she asks with a surprised smile. 'Is that what this is?'

I shrug. 'Did you try on more than one outfit?'

She drops her head, pink filling her cheeks. 'Maybe...'

'Me too, Evie. Me too.'

Relief fills her face and her shock at me titling this a date fades away as we both fall into an easy silence, savoring the last bits of our doughnuts as the noise of the shop surrounds us. It's in these quiet moments that I find myself watching her closely, noticing the way her laughter lines crinkle when she smiles and how her eyes light up with every story she tells – and I realize I might be in Portland for years with this woman if I'm not careful.

6

EVE CASSIDY

'You took time off?' Kait asks, surprise in her voice as we stand in line at the hospital Starbucks. She's in her usual pastel-colored scrubs and I'm in black leggings, an oversized Timber hoodie, black Converse, with a bag stuffed full of things to entertain Foster hanging off one shoulder.

'I only have a million vacation days stacked up, and HR wasn't pleased with me calling in sick for three days in a row, so yeah. Gen thought this would be smarter because Dale is irritated with having to replace me last minute every morning.'

'I get that, but you're spending your vacation days at work, in the ICU, with your comatose ex-husband. That's not healthy.'

'Currently I'm concerned more about his health than mine. He's alone, Kait. I can't leave him until I know he'll pull out of this. He's got no one else. If it were you, Gen or Jess, I'd do the same,' I offer, hoping she'll understand.

'That's because you love us. We hate Foster, remember?'

Hate is a strong word. But one that I truly believed I felt except for one day a year until he showed up in my trauma room a few days ago. Now my insides are muddy and I can't figure out what I feel, but I know I can't let him do this alone.

'Of course I remember.' A break-up like that isn't something you forget.

'But honestly, how bad could things get with him? He can't talk or work, and those are pretty much his biggest flaws, right?'

'What are you going to do today if he can't talk? Admire his pretty face?'

'Noooo,' I say. 'I did that yesterday.' And the day before, and the one before that too – not that I'm reminding her of that. 'Today, I chose a variety of things. Cards, my iPad so I can annoy him with shows he hates, and a book; I may even clean out my purse while I'm here.'

'Wow. Reading, binge-watching, solitaire, and purse cleaning; sounds like a full day. What it doesn't sound like is a vacation. You do realize this could be the worst idea ever.'

'Bad ideas are my secret talent, so I'm not sure why you're so surprised. Anyway, I gotta go...' I say, taking my latte from a barista that is not Adam.

'Update me?' Kait requests as I leave the shop.

'Will do,' I say over my shoulder as I head toward ICU.

Every day since they found out, she and Jess try to talk me out of stopping by to see Foster; what they don't realize is I'm not just spending an hour a day with the man. I've been here from sunup to sundown, just watching him. Counting the beeps of the monitors for hours on end and memorizing all the parts of him I thought I'd forgotten. I had a dream about him last night and that hasn't happened since I met him.

'Eve!' Chelsea greets me with a smile as I approach her. 'How are you holding up?'

'I'm good. How is he today?' I ask, my voice laced with the concern that continues to linger, as I draw near the room where Foster is being treated.

'There's been some improvement,' Chelsea replies, and for a moment, I feel relieved. But then a wave of nervousness washes over me.

'Improvement?'

She nods. 'He was wiggling his toes last night – on command,' Chelsea says.

'Really?'

Chelsea's friendly smile grows even wider. 'I think he may pull out of this sooner rather than later. Come on, I'm sure he'll be glad to hear your voice again.'

I'm not so sure about that, but I follow her into his room anyway.

'Oh, he's got more color,' I say. Those words leaving my lips surprise me as they're what my mother always said to my sister and me after we'd been sick. It was like a reflex that I haven't had in years.

I drop my bag onto the guest chair and approach his bed, brushing his hair from his forehead. His cheeks are pink, and his freckles are prominent this morning. To my surprise, his eyelids flutter at my touch.

'See,' Chelsea says, across his bed from me. 'He even squeezed my hand this morning when I got here. His vitals are good, lab work is improving, and he's starting to look less corpsey and more human, so I wouldn't be surprised if his progress is enough to make the doctor ease up on the sedation soon.'

'How long will it take him to wake up once they start that?'

'Usually, it's relatively quick,' she replies with a smile. 'He'll be back to his old self in no time.'

'Define quick?' I ask. 'Five minutes? Five hours? Five days? I'm not usually on this end of these situations.'

Chelsea laughs. 'Excited to gaze into your husband's eyes again, are you?'

The thought of this makes me giddy, which turns my stomach a little, making me wonder if this truly is the worst idea ever. I can't imagine what he will say when he finally wakes up and finds me standing at his bedside.

'You guessed it,' I say.

'How cute are you two?' she gushes. 'Every patient is different, so I can't give you an exact time frame. But, if you're not here when it happens, then I'll call you so you can come in.'

'Great,' I say, worried. Note to self: block Chelsea's number. I'm kidding – mostly.

'Got plans for entertaining him today?' Chelsea asks.

'Yes,' I say, walking to my bag and pulling out my 'plans'. 'I'm going to read to him from Matthew Perry's autobiography and then catch up on *Bachelor in Paradise*. And I brought cards so I can kick his butt at poker.'

'So sad about Matthew, isn't it? Gone far too soon. Otherwise, sounds fun! I'll leave you guys alone and I'll be back later.' Chelsea exits the room, leaving just the two of us for the fourth day in a row.

'Hey, Fost,' I say, sitting at the chair near his bedside. 'It's me again, your "wife" – sorry for lying about that by the way. I just couldn't let you do this alone, if you're wondering why I didn't include the "ex" part of that title.

Anyway, today we're reading about Matthew Perry. I don't know if you follow anything other than adrenaline-filled sports, but he died recently, and I'm not ashamed to tell you – mostly because you can't laugh in response – I shed a tear. Truthfully, I turned on *Friends* that night and full-out sobbed for the first few episodes, but then I realized Chandler Bing would live forever with only a click of my remote. Not that you care. If I remember correctly, you aren't a sitcom watcher. But it's OK because I know you like music, and if you're not into this story, next up is the Britney Spears autobiography, and that one will be a wild ride, I bet.'

'Mr Foster.' Dr Sully walks in – mid-chapter – greeting Foster cordially. 'Mrs Foster,' he says, giving me a knowing look.

'Ha ha,' I mouth.

'I'm hearing good things about your progress.' Jeremy (aka Dr Sully) looks at Foster's monitors, does a small exam, listening to his heart and lungs, and then turns to me. 'How do you feel he's doing, Nurse Eve?'

'Well, I'm less anxious he's going to die. And he looks better. I feel like he's much more stable than he was.'

'You are correct, Miss Cassidy. I think today may be "wake up Foster day".'

'Really?' I ask.

'I'm going to run it by another physician and be in with our decision this afternoon. Sound good?'

'I'll be here,' I say.

My heart races in my chest knowing they're considering 'mission unsedate Foster'. It's one thing to be here when he can't talk to me, call me stupid nicknames he knows I'll hate, or look into my soul with his intoxicating crystal blue eyes, but knowing that soon he may *know* I'm here makes me nervous. What will he say? *Get out? What the hell are you doing here? Hello there, Jellybean?* (That stupid nickname). I'm not excited to find out.

I read for a while longer, occasionally glancing over at him. He looks so peaceful, as if he's sleeping. I wonder what he's dreaming about. As for me, my mind is wandering. I've read the same page twice, retaining exactly nothing as I remember the last time I saw him and all the stupid things we fought over. Please don't let him be dreaming about all that.

My phone buzzes on the table beside me, my sister's name flashing across the screen.

'Did you finally pop?' I joke.

'Why are you there again?' she asks, her tone demanding an answer.

Damn it, Kait.

'Have you forgotten the disaster that break-up was?'

'No,' I moan. 'But you and Kait are great reminders.'

'Well, the memories of him that you shared with me are intruding my thoughts. You can't go back to a guy who never cared you left, Eve.'

'I'm not here to take him back,' I say, defending myself. 'Which is why the second he opens his eyes, I may run out of this hospital like an Olympic athlete. But for now, even he deserves to have someone here for him, doesn't he?'

Jess lets out a heavy sigh, her frustration palpable. 'Evie, listen, I know he's pretty, but there are countless pretty men who don't let the supposed love of their life walk away without following them or even asking why. Fall in love with any of them instead?'

I scoff. 'As if it were that easy. I tried that, remember? That one was an even bigger disaster than this one.'

For a second she's silent because she knows I'm right. 'You're acting insane.'

'And you're being overbearing. I'm completely sane, I'm just acting like someone who gives a crap about a guy she once loved. In sickness and in health, remember?'

'You can't break out the vows when they work for you,' she moans.

'I can't let Foster suffer through this alone. No one deserves that.'

'I'm sure they'd send in a priest so he wouldn't be completely alone.'

I gasp. 'Rude. Clearly, you're the sister without the soul.'

She laughs into the phone like she's proud of it. 'That's right. If need be, I'll drive my enormous ass down there and drag you out.'

'Do not, Jess. Also, I'd really appreciate it if you and Kait would stop discussing me and the situation behind my back. I know what I'm doing. I'm a full-grown adult. He's nice to look at, and I haven't had a vacation from work in years. Let me enjoy this.'

'Holy shiitake mushrooms, Eve. You're considering *this* your vacation? Vacations include tropical drinks and reading by a pool.'

'I'm reading; and as for the tropical drinks, I momentarily considered sneaking in a hard lemonade, but I don't need that reputation – though it would make these conversations easier. Also, I have a pool, in the basement. I'll be there three times a week, just as I always am, with my elderly aerobics class and baby swim class. Maybe tomorrow I'll lay out a towel and bask, just to appease you, since I won't have to jet to work immediately afterward.'

'Yes, please, I'll take that photo proof of you basking at the edge of an indoor basement pool.' She says the words sarcastically, but I know she's being serious. She doesn't want every minute of my day to be Foster, but whether I'm in his room or not, he's on my mind.

'I'm warning you now; this could all go completely tits up, and when it does...'

'As usual, you'll be the first to say "I told you so." I know, Jess. It's not going to happen, though. Foster probably hates me as much as I hate him – hence him not coming after me all those years ago. He'll likely demand I leave. And I will, happily.' Just saying the words makes my heart feel anything but happy.

'Why don't I believe you?'

'Because I'm your little sister and you never do. Listen, I appreciate your concern, Jess, I do. I'm just hoping to get some good karma on my side when it comes to love – if it even exists. Maybe I'll use this as a reminder of what to avoid in the future. This time I'll take notes.'

'Eve,' she says sympathetically. 'I know you've been hurt and I feel for you, I really do. But I have a sinking feeling this will all go terribly wrong, and you'll end up hurt again. I'd rather not see you go through that.'

'Lessons learned is all heartbreak is. You'd know that if you hadn't married the first boy you met,' I tease. 'I'll live through this. I promise, Jess, I'm being careful. And if anything does go wrong, I'm a survivor. A cynical, cold-hearted survivor.'

Amid a deep sigh, Jess reluctantly utters, 'Fine. You're an adult, and you can make your own decisions. I just have opinions and your best interests in mind. He doesn't.'

'Not sure he's currently got anything on his mind, but I get it.' How will we really know if she's right about that until he comes to?

7

GUY 'FOSTER'

Even though I'm starving, in pain, itchy, and hazy at best, hearing Eve speak is comforting – even if it is about the life story of Matthew Perry. The only time I've heard her voice until recently was in my dreams, and I find myself wanting to keep her talking just to remember her. I can't get enough and didn't realize how much I'd missed it – her – until now.

'Pretend you didn't hear any of that phone call,' Eve says, touching my hand gently. 'Jess is overly protective of me because I have horrible taste in men, as you know.'

Offensive.

'Not that you're horrible – an unreliable dumbass at times, yes – but I think you being in the condition you're in sort of confirms that. Anyway, despite us being way in the past, I'm reliving every part, and now Jess has me anxious as all get out.' She sighs heavily. 'I also remember why I deleted all your photos from my phone. You're too easy to look at, even with a tube between your lips. But, in case you *can* hear me, know we're staying divorced – I think fate lied to us. I'm just here to make sure you don't suffer through this on your own with a strange priest offering you up to a God I'm sure you don't believe in.'

She has no idea how much I appreciate that. A few more chapters of Matthew Perry's life entertain me, but then the book slams closed.

'I can't focus,' she says. 'Want to play a game?'

A game I will obviously lose? *Sure, Jellybean. If it keeps you here, yes, I do.*

She shuffles around, and I wonder what she's up to.

'I brought playing cards. Wanna deal?' she asks with a laugh. 'I'm kidding. I've watched you attempt to shuffle cards, and you're bad at it when you're conscious. I'll deal. Three-card draw. Good luck.' She deals the cards and then giggles to herself. 'Ooh, tough hand, mister, I win without even trying. Man, you suck at this game, awake *and* asleep.'

Shit-talking, is she? It's hard to listen and not be able to respond. The sounds of her re-dealing bring back so many memories of when we did this together.

'Oh hey!' she says excitedly. 'You won! Three kings and I've got zero. Congratulations! Too bad you're not conscious to see it.' She laughs. 'I'll photo document it,' she says. After a few silent seconds, she speaks. 'Perfect! This one's going on the fridge. Maybe I'll bring you a prize tomorrow since we didn't bet anything.'

Please don't let it be the Britney Spears book. I have nothing against her personally, but now I'm invested in Matthew Perry's life outside of *Friends*, and I'm not sure my brain can handle jumping around different stories. I can barely stay in the moment for longer than ten minutes when Eve's here because the past continues to take over, and I'm starting to like it.

'How's he doin'?' Chelsea's voice enters the room.

'Well, he's not as terrible at poker when he's asleep, but no conversation or anything.'

'Bad at motorcycles *and* poker?' Chelsea jokes.

How dare she! The poker thing I'll accept, but I am not bad at motorcycles. I can ride them, build them, flip them (and stay alive), and they pay for anything I want. Plus, it's fucking fun! *Do not criticize my riding ability, woman.* To my surprise, I attempt to respond to defend my talent, and a grunt leaves my lips. Machines start beeping like mad.

'Holy crap!' Eve exclaims. 'Did he just try to talk?'

'Maybe? It almost sounded like I offended him,' Chelsea says.

*I am man*fended*, Chelsea. My masculinity is on the line here. Is that stupid? Yes, the fuck it is. But I am who I am – best in my industry.*

'Foster?' Eve says my name, gently touching my cheek. It's the weirdest sensation I've ever felt – like the fuzz of an old TV screen, but just under my skin. A tingling that lasts for longer than the actual touch. A sensation only created by my gorgeous Eve. Well, maybe not 'my' Eve. I screwed that up, yet here she is in the worst possible moment of my life. Worried.

'Foster, honey.' Chelsea pats my cheek. Her touch doesn't do the same thing Eve's does. Interesting.

Focus, Fost.

'Foster! Are you in there?' Eve hollers, grabbing my hand.

I immediately clutch hers back. *I'm here.*

'Hand squeeze,' Eve says.

'Good!' Chelsea praises.

'You know what it probably was?' Eve asks. 'You said he was bad at motorcycles. That's forbidden in Foster's world. He's the best in the sport, and he knows it. He'd be so mad if I were to say something like "Foster, you suck at riding. I'd bet that was probably your last event. You almost killed yourself! Looks like Jeff will finally be the top dog".'

Jeff?! This girl. I want to laugh and cry all at once. I grunt again, suddenly very aware of the tube down my throat. I jerk Eve's hand toward it. I'll pull this damn thing out myself if I have to.

'Oh! He's trying to reach the tube,' Eve says, yanking my hand back and holding it steadily against her chest.

I have to do *something* so they know I'm here.

Come on, Fost. Eyes. Open. Open your eyes, dude! Defend. Your. Honor. Your. Title.

'Can you relax, Foster?' Chelsea asks calmly.

I feel Eve lean into me, her face brushing against mine as she speaks softly. 'Dream of winning hands at poker until we can figure this part out, Fost. Maybe I'll see you soon?' she says, her voice almost hopeful, which tempts my mind to wander off without her again. It doesn't take much, that's for sure.

* * *

Five Years Ago

'You ever played?' Matty asks as he walks into my place.

Us boys get together for a monthly poker night. Even when we're on the road, we do this. It's a nice break from the one thing that connects us all – motocross. Not to mention, no one leaves injured or bleeding. Pissed sometimes, yes. But we get over it.

'Didn't Foster tell you? I'm a pro,' Eve says. 'I don't tell a lot of people because how else would I dupe stupid boys who think women are inferior at everything?' She is sitting to my right, a beer in front of her and my usual poker night buddies are around the table. We all stare her way, our faces blank with her words. My God, I think I just fell in love with her more as she shit-talked my buddies.

Matty glares my way.

'She's kidding,' I assure him.

'He's right,' she says. 'I've never played, but Foster did explain it to me on our way here.'

Laughter erupts around the table. 'Well, he sucks, so don't get hopeful that you're going home with the jackpot, sweetheart.' Jeff looks proud of himself for slamming me in front of my girlfriend. I'm not *that* bad. Just a little unlucky.

'I hope y'all went to the ATM,' Charlie, a motocross God, teases. 'My upcoming honeymoon won't pay for itself, and Fiona wants to go to Fiji.'

'Fiji, that'll be cheap,' I joke. 'It's surprising someone would marry you at all.'

Charlie flips me off. 'You're the only old maid at this table.'

'Hey, I brought a date, and I'm younger than you, Grandpa.'

He rolls his eyes, sipping his beer, turning his attention to Jeff and Matty who are explaining the rules to Eve as he deals. She's cute the way she hides her cards, holding them close to her chest to ensure no one else gets a peek. One by one, we each toss our bets and draw cards face down onto the table and she follows suit, raising the bet by ten bucks.

'Upping the bar already, eh? Pretty ballsy for a newbie,' Matty says, dealing draw cards.

Charlie folds.

'You in or you out, girl?' Jeff asks.

'Um...' She glances at her cards, then her chips, and throws a fifty into the pot.

'What?' Jeff groans. 'Seriously? Your first game ever, and you want to go home broke?' He matches her bet. 'I'm not a complainer; might as well hand over your wallet now.'

Eve glances at me. 'You in or out, princess?'

I laugh. 'Princess?'

She nods.

'He's in,' Matty says, tossing in a chip. 'As am I. Read 'em and weep boys – and girl.' He lays out a straight.

Jeff lays his hand of cards across the table. 'Fucker. I've got three queens.'

'Loser,' Matty says with glee.

All eyes are now on Eve and me.

'Who will it be?' Jeff asks. 'Is Foster finally going to win a hand or what?' He and the guys laugh as they pick on me.

'Do you really lose every time?' Eve asks.

'Not every time.'

'Once,' Matty snaps out the truth, 'he won fifty bucks; one time in years.'

Eve grimaces. 'That is bad.'

'Motorcycles are my game, not cards.'

'This is going to be fun,' she says.

'You think you can beat me, don't you?' I ask.

She shrugs.

'Fine, I'll go first.' I lay my cards on the table proudly. 'Full house. Beat that, Jellybean.'

She lays her cards on the table with a playful roll of her eyes. 'Good thing you're good at something because you're right, poker ain't it, Pumpkin – royal flush, boys.'

Matty stands from the table, nearly knocking all of our beers over, pissed off and running a hand through his hair. 'Are you fucking kidding me?'

Jeff's jaw drops. 'Oh, yeah, "I've never played before",' he mimics her earlier words in a high voice. 'You little liar!' he laughs, staring at the hand that beats us all.

I glance at her, confused, raising an eyebrow.

'Truthfully,' she admits, 'poker was my family's holiday game. I've been playing since I was about five. My dad's dream was to go pro, but Mom didn't love the idea of him being in Vegas that often because alcohol always trumped gambling, and mix those two addictions and you can imagine the fallout. However, I do know a rule that you guys forgot.'

'What's that?' Matty asks, still mad.

'The first rule of a good poker player is to be good at bluffing.' She doesn't hesitate to pull the pile of chips her way, obviously eager for the next round. 'You dummies believed every word I said.'

'My God, I underestimated you…' I laugh.

'She's scary,' Matty says, re-dealing the cards.

'Three hundred dollars,' Charlie moans an hour later. 'Fiona is going to *kill* me.'

'Well,' Matty says, pulling on his coat. 'That was the fastest I've ever lost five hundred bucks.'

'Like you guys wouldn't be dancing around the damn room if you'd just walked away with thirteen hundred dollars,' I say, defending the queen of poker.

Eve laughs as she rolls a wad of cash up and stashes it in her purse. 'You guys act like I robbed you blind. I didn't plan it.'

Jeff glares her way. 'I hope you call your dad tonight and tell him *you're* the one who should go pro. Girl don't even need dark glasses to lie. You better watch out,' he warns me, poking his finger into my chest. 'She's dangerous.'

'Am I invited to the next game night?' she asks jokingly.

'No!' Jeff, Matty, and Charlie all say in unison.

8

GUY 'FOSTER'

As soon as I hear the words 'extubation is a go', I pull my hand from Eve, but another hand stops me. One stronger than Eve's.

'This is normal. Patients waking from a coma while intubated can be confused and combative. Why don't you wait in the hall while we get this out and examine him,' a male voice says.

I grab Eve's hand to keep her close. No way am I doing this without her. *Stay, Evie.* I try to open my eyes to see her. Ouch! Bad idea. Retreat. Light hurts. Wait, no, I have to do this. I squint. Blinking a few times, attempting to get Eve's attention.

'His eyes are open!' Eve says. 'He also won't let go of my hand, so I can't go out in the hall.'

Success! (Eye-burning blindness aside.)

'Mr Foster.' A man comes into my blurry gaze, the light I once thought was the white light of death flashing before each eye again. 'I need you to stay calm while we remove this tube. It'll be just a few minutes. Breathe through your nose and try to relax.'

I nod as much as I can, my gaze moving to where Eve's voice has been coming from. I can't see her clearly, but I know it's her. She's got both hands around mine, holding it to her chest, and I can feel her shaking.

Before, when I'd answer 'would you rather die by drowning or shooting',

I'd choose drowning – seems like a peaceful way to go. But I'd like to change my answer. *Please, just shoot me. This is torture.* After a few terrifying minutes where I thought I'd die, the death hose has been extracted from my trachea, and I pull in a deep breath. I can't get enough. Each time, I cough uncontrollably.

'Let's slow down the breathing, Mr Foster. Try not to panic.' The voice of the doctor is calming, and that helps me follow orders. A nurse slips a face mask with air blowing over my face. 'Breathe in through your nose and out through your mouth. Chelsea will give you something to help you relax a little.'

I do the breathing technique they're giving me but can't relax at all because my gaze is locked onto Eve's. She's actually here. My wife. Er – ex-wife, but it still counts, considering I was beginning to wonder if her voice was just a hallucination to help me get through this. Now that my eyes are open and I can almost see her clearly, I know every word was real and that she has been here, every single day I have.

'E...' I try to say her name when I feel like I've caught my breath, but a gravely sounding E is all that leaves my lips.

'No talking, Mr Foster. Right now, we breathe. Later, we chat,' the doctor coaches.

'Focus, Foster. Breathe like this.' Eve holds my hand tightly to her chest, inhaling deeply, encouraging me to follow along. So I do. I'd probably do anything she asked after dreaming about her for what feels like months.

She's nice to look at, even prettier than the photo that haunts me. The woman I assume is Chelsea is now injecting something into my IV line and it takes a matter of seconds for the so-called 'relaxation medication' to kick in and my mind starts feeling as malleable as putty on a scorching summer sidewalk. It's like an out-of-body experience, with me hovering over my damaged shell, floating high in the sky. *Earth to Foster – don't fade out yet.* I attempt to pull myself back to real life, gripping Eve's hand, but it's not happening. How much relaxation do I need? I don't even know if it's day or night.

As I lie here, my chest heaving, I feel every second ticking by like hours. Nurses and doctors hurry in and out of the room, their footsteps echoing through the sterile space. But amidst all the chaos, Eve stays, her eyes fixed on me. I can't help but stare back, completely captivated by her. Every fiber of my being aches, a constant reminder of how fragile life can be. Yet all I can think about is her. She's different, yet somehow more beautiful than ever.

Despite the temporary pandemonium of the room, it's as if nothing else exists except the two of us. The rest of the world fades away, and all that's left is her and me. I want to ask her all the questions that are swirling around in my head. But as I open my mouth to speak, all that comes out is a ragged gasp.

'Eve, why don't you talk to him?' Chelsea suggests.

After a moment of hesitation, she finally speaks up with a timid voice. 'Oh... um, OK. Hey?' she says meekly. 'How's your day?' Her adorable, crooked smile hints that she's teasing me. 'Honestly, that was terrifying to watch. I thought I was going to witness you taking your last breath more times than once.' She pauses, swallowing hard. 'For the record, I'm glad you didn't.'

Considering her last spoken words to me were, 'You'll probably kill yourself on that thing, and I won't miss you at all,' it's a bit bewildering to hear her say that last part.

'Keep talking, Eve. His vitals are settling. You're soothing him.'

'That's probably just the medication,' she says, flashing a smart-ass smile. 'So, did you at least place?'

I lift my good shoulder and nod, implying that of course I did. But honestly, that's doubtful.

She rolls her eyes playfully.

'He lived,' the man wearing the white coat says. 'Seems like first place to me.'

And I woke up just in time to not listen to the Britney Spears book next. If only I could say that out loud.

'No Britney.' I croak the words out, a hair above a whisper, but Eve somehow hears them.

Her lips part, and her jaw drops open, revealing a smile. 'She's going to be so offended by that when I tell her.'

Despite my attempt to let out a chuckle, the persistent coughing takes over. The tickle in my throat is relentless, and no matter how hard I try to suppress it, the coughing persists, sending waves of discomfort throughout my body. Once I get the coughing under control, I attempt to speak again.

'Also, Chandler Bing lives forever.'

Eve's eyes grow wide, as she probably realizes that I could indeed hear her, just like the nurses warned. Even so, she laughs at my croaking voice. 'Sshhhhh,' she says. 'Doctor's orders.'

'How about a Popsicle?' Chelsea asks enthusiastically.

I nod. It's no doughnut, but considering I haven't eaten or had anything to drink in years (or so it feels), it's a yes from me.

'You've got a lot of injuries,' the doctor says after thoroughly inspecting me.

'But I woke up,' I say with a gravelly voice.

'You did wake up,' he agrees with a slight smile. 'Do you remember how you got here?'

I think back but my mind is like quicksand – thoughts popping into my head and sinking away before the words reach my lips. I had a competition. It feels like ages ago, but that's the last memory that comes to mind.

I shake my head. Slowly I move my eyes downwards to see what exactly I'm looking at here. My left arm is immobile and strapped to my chest, probably to avoid any further injury based on how it feels. At first glance, nothing appears to be a severe injury, but as I shift my weight slightly, a sharp, piercing pain shoots through the back of my neck, sending shivers down my spine and causing me to groan involuntarily. The discomfort is so intense that I can't help but clench my teeth and close my eyes tightly, hoping that the pain will subside soon.

'You bruised your cervical spine pretty badly, so move slowly,' the doctor says, gently pushing my head back on the pillow. 'Last thing you remember, Mr Foster?' the doctor asks.

'I had a competition.'

He nods. Must've gotten that answer right. 'How'd that go?' he asks.

'I dunno,' I answer honestly.

'Hmmm, tell me about one of your FMX titles.' The doctor changes tactics.

Despite my voice cracking in and out like I'm going through puberty, this is a topic I could talk about for days. 'Moto X Big Air. Best Trick at the X

Games in Philly. Gold at Red Bull X-Fighters Grand Slam tours in Madrid. Three golds at the FMX Nitro World Games. A few silvers at the Summer X Games...'

Eve and the doctor lock eyes, their expressions revealing much about their thoughts. The doctor appears impressed.

'I said one, but wow. Congratulations.'

Meanwhile, Eve's face wears a familiar expression – a mix of skepticism and mild amusement, as if she's thinking, 'Yep, he really is this cocky.'

'Your long-term memory seems fine. But you've got no memory of your recent race that put you here?'

I shut my eyes tightly, trying to remember. As far as I know, we had arrived at our destination on a Thursday. But after that, everything is blank. I shake my head again.

The sound of shoes sliding on a slick floor suddenly interrupts us. All eyes turn toward the door as Matty, with his disheveled, dark, graying hair and prominent crow's feet, rushes into the room. His face is creased with worry as he slides to a stop upon catching sight of us.

'You're awake?' He sounds relieved. 'They called me yesterday to tell me this would be happening soon, but I hoped to make it beforehand. How do you feel?'

'Shitty,' I say.

The doctor leans into Matty and says, 'Mr Foster's having a hard time remembering what brought him here.'

Matty lets out a hearty laugh. 'You didn't quite stick the landing, my friend,' he says with a grin. 'I'm not exactly sure where your head was at' – he shoots a look at Eve – 'but it was pretty clear to everyone watching that your timing was off midway through your second run.'

I furrow my brows. I didn't land a jump? How don't I remember this? I look over at Eve, whose eyebrows are raised with concern as if she knows something I don't. The memory feels so close, yet so far, like it's just on the tip of my tongue, tantalizingly out of reach.

'I'm going to order an MRI and have another look at his head, and consult with Dr Greene in Neurology. Him not remembering could be nothing, just part of coming to after this critical of injuries. No one worry yet. Just as a heads-up, Mr Foster, you'll be headed in for another surgery on your shoulder and wrist in the coming days, so save your energy for now, and do not even attempt to leave this bed.'

'Yes, sir,' I say, knowing when to follow orders.

'How long will he be here?' Matty asks.

'Oh, probably another week or so,' Dr Sully says. 'For now, you'll head down for an MRI and a CT within the hour. Maybe tonight you could have some dinner?'

Oh, finally, food. I feel like I've been on a hunger strike – dreaming of doughnuts and no way to eat. Now, I can. I hope this place has an all-you-can-eat buffet.

'Do you have lobster?' I ask, mostly kidding.

'You can have the lobster bisque,' the nurse suggests with a light smile. 'For hospital food, it's pretty good really. We'll have to start slow on the solids since you haven't eaten in a few days. Soup. Crackers. Jell-O. Popsicles.'

She hands me the red Popsicle now unwrapped, causing Eve to release my hand. I've got no qualms about a Popsicle. Food is food. I glance at Eve. 'Stay for dinner with me?'

'Aww,' Chelsea says with a gushing smile.

Matty groans. 'Slow down, Casanova, it's been five minutes and you're already asking her out on a date?'

'I think it's cute,' Nurse Chelsea says. My eyes have finally focused on the badge on her chest and I'm putting together her face and voice. 'They're in love.'

Both Matty and I raise an eyebrow. 'Love, huh?' He says it first, and by the look on Eve's face, she's unsure.

She nods slightly, ignoring the statement altogether. 'Sure, the least I can do is stay for dinner,' she says. 'How about you, Matty? You staying?'

Three's a crowd, girl – has no one ever told you that? I know everything there is to know about Matty. It's her I want to catch up with. But like I can say no to having my best friend here with us. Maybe he will help with the awkward vibe now pulsating through the room. I'm not sure what it is, but I'm sure I'll find out shortly.

9
EVE CASSIDY

'You're having dinner with him? At his request? What, like a date?' Gen asks when I stop by the ER to talk to our boss. Or rather, kiss her ass so I don't get fired for taking all fourteen of my vacation days at once, unexpectedly. Sure, she approved it, going off my description of my current hell, but it never hurts to make sure things are A-OK, so I'm not assigned Trauma Room 1 for the rest of my life. I've brought a gift basket, full of every snack item I know Teri (the head of our department) loves. If this doesn't win her over, nothing will.

'No, not like a date,' I reassure Genevieve. 'Like a dinner. In his hospital room. There's nothing weird about that. Everyone eats dinner.'

'Not with their ex-husband...' she reminds me.

'Sure,' I say, sitting the huge basket that takes two hands to carry on the counter, separating me from her. 'Technically, that's true. But, if I ran out now, I'd look like a real asshole. I've already done that once with him. Now I need to see him through getting released from the hospital to clear my conscience, and that's exactly what I'm going to do.'

No need to tell her that every time he and I touch, or our eyes meet, my heart melts for him like he's got a freaking flamethrower to it. But it'll never work between us, because we've got very different lives. *Be strong, Evie girl.*

'What are you going to talk about?' Gen asks.

I shrug. 'Don't know. Maybe the weather. His career. Food, if I know him. You know, casualties.'

'And if he asks about you leaving a note...?'

'I will promptly change the subject,' I finish.

She grins. 'To doughnuts?'

'Perhaps.'

'Which will then loop you right back to your first official date and then the next thing you know your relationship is the topic. Are you ready for that?'

I inhale sharply. Why must she be a truth teller when I need anything but the reminder right now. No. I'm not even a little bit ready for that. I'm about to say those words when we're interrupted with a hand on my back.

'Eve, I thought you'd be happily floating across the ocean waves in the Pacific by now.' Teri, a slight woman in her fifties who's got decades of nursing experience, eyes a can of Pringles in the basket in front of us.

'Or entertaining past mistakes in room 117,' Genevieve mumbles.

I shoot her a glare, then turn my attention to my boss. 'I got you something,' I say, sliding the basket of goodies her way. 'As a thank you.'

'For me?!' Teri exclaims with surprise.

'Kiss ass,' Dale says through a cough from his desk behind us, and with a sly move, I throw a single finger his way behind my back, hearing him scoff, and feeling pleased with myself.

'It's just a token of my appreciation for allowing me time off on short notice.'

Teri nods, but her eyes are on the basket of treats. 'It's not every day your most dedicated employee asks for time off.'

Just about everyone sitting in the nurses' station lets out a groan. Great. Now they all hate me for being titled 'most dedicated'.

'Thanks, Eve,' Genevieve says sarcastically, sipping from her coffee mug.

I roll my eyes and turn back to Teri. 'There may not be ocean or giant flamingo-shaped floaties in my future but perhaps when this nightmare is over, I'll make a weekend trip to the coast before I come back.'

Teri nods in approval, then digs into the basket, pulling out her favorite brand of chocolate bars. 'As long as you return ready to work, which I have no doubt you will.'

'Absolutely,' I reply, feeling a weight lift off my shoulders. The tension eases as I see Teri enjoying the snacks, and I know my job is safe.

'I'll walk you out,' Gen says. 'Goin' on break, Dale!'

She steers me out of the ER through a side door only employees use to get some fresh air. 'You sure you're OK with this dinner?' she asks, concern evident in her voice.

I nod, adjusting the strap of the bag on my shoulder. It's packed full of things I thought Foster might enjoy in his state. Extreme sports magazines. My iPad so he can watch whatever he wants. Cards, in case he wants to practice his skills. And a couple of books that are not about celebrities.

'Yeah, it's just dinner,' I say. 'Plus, Matty will be there.'

'Ah,' she says with a sly smile. 'Invited a third wheel to make it less weird. Smart.'

'It just worked out that way.'

'Well, when shit hits the fan, you know where to find me. I'll bring the floaties and margaritas and we'll bob around that hospital pool you so love and cry it out.'

I laugh, but truthfully, that might be as much of a vacation as I get this year – or any year since I've worked here. Me, Gen, and probably my favorite over-sixty-five folks, all getting lit on hospital facilities while floating in the Olympic-size pool on water floats shaped like summery shapes – it's not exactly my dream vacay.

'Here's to a dinner of all the best hospital cuisines. Wish me luck,' I say, backing away from Genevieve so I'm not late.

'Don't eat the fries!' she reminds me. Our hospital can't seem to work a fryer for the life of them. They're either so crispy they taste like rocks or so mushy they'd stand in as mashed potatoes. I let Foster order for me, so we'll see how well he still knows me.

'Knock, knock?' I call, lightly tapping on Foster's ICU door as I slide it open, peeking in.

He smiles, his eyes crinkling at the corners. He looks genuinely happy to see me.

'Evie,' he says with relief in his voice. 'I'd have dressed up, but this is all I've got.' He glances down at the hospital-issue blue scrub pants he's now wearing. Otherwise, he's still shirtless and it's showing off his hard shoulder (singular, since I can only see one) in a way that's bringing back memories I'd rather not relive.

I glance down at my outfit: black skinny jeans, a white ribbed button-down tank, a wheat-colored bomber-style sweater, and white Birkenstocks. The top part of my hair is braided and pinned behind one ear, just to keep it out of my face, and I didn't exactly throw on a face full of make-up. Instead, I went for my 'easy' routine: quick foundation, under-eye brightener, a dab of blush, mascara, and nude lipstick.

He's sitting up in his bed, still attached to wires, IVs, and a nasal cannula of air to help his oxygen levels. Machines beep regularly next to him. His dark hair is tousled and he looks comfortably glazed over on pain meds so I'm not sure how much of any conversation he'll retain. But besides all that, he looks good. Almost exactly like the Foster that easily wooed my heart in our past.

'Wow!' he says, his eyes on me. He blinks a few times, looking me over like it's been a while. Which it has. 'I sort of wondered if you were just one of the many dreams I was having. But I'm glad you're not. Also, you never change, Jellybean,' he says in a soft voice, still shaky from the intubation ordeal. 'Actually, you do, I'm pretty sure you're even more gorgeous than I remember.'

Heat rushes to my cheeks and I'm sure it's visible. He's been awake one day and already he's got me blushing. I want to tell him I'm not any more gorgeous than I was, but come on, what girl doesn't want to hear that from a man?

'I go by Eve now,' I joke at the sweet but a tad too much nickname he gave me a long time ago. 'But thank you. You look... a lot better than I expected.'

He laughs, coughing when he does so. 'I feel 50 per cent alive.'

'That's something,' I encourage, glancing around the small room. 'So, where's Matty?'

'He's on his way. Refused to eat hospital food so he's stopping by the In-N-Out for the good stuff.'

'Ah,' I say with a nod. 'Smart man. On that note, I brought you some stuff too.' I make my way to the empty chair near his bed and set my bag down, unloading things one by one and setting them on the tray in front of him.

Once the items are fully displayed, he looks to me with a hint of worry. 'Does this mean I'm on my own for entertainment now?' He frowns.

'Why do you look disappointed about that?'

He shrugs his one good shoulder. 'I was sort of looking forward to hearing the rest of Matthew Perry's story. I'm intrigued by MattMan.'

My jaw drops. I had mentioned Matthew's last social media post only one time, in the middle of two paragraphs in his book. I can't believe he remembered that. 'You really were listening?'

He nods. 'A guy's not got a lot to do while in a coma, except listen.'

'Do you remember anything else?' I ask, sort of nervous to hear his reply but ready for it.

'A lot of things. Just not what brought me here.'

'I've got the remedy for that.' Matty's voice startles us as he makes his way into the room, In-N-Out bag in one hand, his phone in the other. 'Red Bull sent me the video – and this.' He sets a Red Bull bag with handles on the end of Foster's bed. I peek in, seeing a couple of cases of Red Bull and enough merch to decorate this whole room.

'The video?' I ask, confused.

'Of his wreck.'

I suck in a breath. Of course, I should have expected it to be on film. Most of these events are televised. 'Should he watch that, considering his condition?'

Matty looks him over, then looks at me. 'He's alive, and a grown man, why shouldn't he watch it? We already know how it ends.'

How can I argue that logic? 'Yeah, but what if it horrifies him?'

'What if it helps him regain his memory,' he counters.

I clench my teeth together, nervous for Foster. 'What if it makes him never want to ride again?'

Matty waves a hand at me, implying I'm being ridiculous. 'We could "what if" all day. Question is, do you want to see it?' he asks Foster, now leaning over his bed, his phone planted in front of his face.

Foster grimaces, obviously not completely sure of his answer. 'For now, I'm going to pass. Let's get beyond the hospital, then maybe I'll take a look.'

Wow. He's matured. Usually, he'd be all over watching himself on film. But he's choosing his peace of not remembering over his ego.

'Alright,' Matty says, shoving his phone into his pocket.

'Plus, look at her.' Foster nods my way. 'She's terrified and she's standing on solid ground. I can't make her worry about me more than she already is.'

'That's right,' Matty says. 'How could I forget that you always hated his job.'

'Not hate. I worried. About exactly this scenario,' I say, motioning toward the injured Foster.

'Hey,' Foster says, reaching out and touching my hand. 'I lived, and according to Nurse Chelsea, I'll even get to walk out of this place. You don't need to worry any more.'

'Easier said than done,' I mumble, staring down at his hand wrapped around mine; and for a second, I undeniably feel that spark that I always did with Foster. The longer we're in contact, the stronger it is. 'I was there in the immediate aftermath and I'm still trying to forget that part.'

He says nothing, but his eyes say thank you. I only nod.

Despite the rumors about the bisque, Foster downs it like he's been on a forty-day fast. I opt for one of the burgers Matty brought – because Foster sweetly also ordered me the bisque, and having made that mistake before, it was a real quick 'no thanks' from me. But the blueberry crumble dessert he also requested is to die for. I won't lie when I say I begged Miguel, the house chef, to sneak me the recipe that he claims was his great-grandmother's favorite finger food for guests, and I now make it at home and sometimes eat it as a meal in itself.

'Aww,' Chelsea says when she walks in for her next round of vitals. 'I'm so glad to see you two reunited. You're just adorable together. This must have been so hard to see, Eve.'

'Yeah,' I respond, hoping she doesn't say anything further.

'So, how many years have you cuties been married?'

Matty's attention is on me like a beacon. It was going too smoothly. I should have known I'd not get away with this.

'Years?' he says with a laugh. 'More like months.'

I shush him under my breath.

'Months?' Chelsea asks with surprise in her tone.

'Yeah, you're backward. They were married for only months, and ended things years ago,' Matty continues, not reading the cues on my face for him to shut up.

Chelsea stops what she's doing, placing a single hand on her hip and staring me down like I've done something wrong. 'I thought you said you were his wife?'

I nod, shoving the rest of the blueberry bliss into my gullet so maybe she'll mishear my words. 'I *was* his wife,' I say, my mouth full.

My gaze meets Foster's and he gives me this look – one that I know well. It's of admiration and forgiveness. How on earth can we still have silent conversations when we haven't laid eyes on each other since I left?

'Now she's his ex-wife, sort of,' Matty says, earning a glare from Foster that I'd know anywhere. That's his *shut the fuck up* glare. I feel like there's more going on here than just my original lie to get in to see him.

'You know what?' Chelsea says after jotting down his vitals. 'I'm going to just let you three be, and we'll talk later.' Her eyes are glued to me, and even though I don't know her well, those are the accusatory eyes of someone who's just realized I lied. Oops. Does it help that it was for a good reason? I sure hope so.

10

GUY 'FOSTER'

I don't know what the uncomfortable silence radiating through my hospital room is exactly. But I wish Matty would read me and shut the fuck up before he says too much and sends Eve sprinting away from me already. Sure, I've daydreamed about this moment for the last five years, but honestly, I never expected to see her again, and certainly not in this way. But she's in my hospital room and has been for days on end. I feel like that's a big enough sign that I need to spend some time with her until I can figure out when the right moment to say what I've meant to say and have never had the balls to say is. All I know is that the time is not now.

'You told her you two were still married, didn't you?' Matty accuses Eve.

Her eyes widen. 'I had to, because to get into ICU you must be close or family.' She glances up at Matty, then at me and guilt flashes across her face. 'My heart couldn't let him be alone, so I left out one word and nobody asked questions. Anyone could have walked in here and done it, had they known Foster's full name.'

Her heart couldn't let me be alone. The beeping to my left speeds and Eve's gaze moves to the monitor.

'You alright?' she asks, standing with worry.

'Fine,' I lie, rubbing my chest. *Slow down, heart. She's gonna know what you're up to and that'll make her run.*

'Wow,' Matty says with a laugh. 'If it's that easy, you could have ended up with way worse than your ex-wife here. Gia could be sitting in that exact chair right now complaining about that soup. How she hates plastic cutlery. Bitchin' about the AC blowing down on her and drying out her hair. And I don't doubt sterile environments make her feel just as icky as hot days on the track do.'

Matty and I share a full-body shiver, only I groan through mine as it sends pain through my body.

'Who's Gia?' Eve asks, suddenly interested.

'Asks the girl who knows Google me better than I do,' I tease, drinking the last of the lobster bisque that I don't remember ordering. It's alright – sort of bland, but I'm pretty sure I'm on the bland food diet right now. I've got apple juice, a now-empty soup bowl, and green Jell-O sitting in front of me. I wonder if Chelsea specifically requested the green because of my bike color? Not that she's a fan, but by now I'm sure Eve's convinced her to do a little digging – it was one of Eve's favorite things to do, Google Foster – then quiz me on the information to see how much of it was true. I didn't hate the game because it gave me a chance to clear some shit up.

Based on the shy smile creeping up on her face, I'd say she doesn't want to admit the Google thing, or she's not done it this time. But I know this woman – or at least I did – and I'd say she's for sure googled me recently. And she knows exactly who Gia is.

When neither Matty nor I answer her question, she continues. 'Did you really refuse to marry her?'

I chuckle, coughing as I've still got a tickle in my throat that's driving me up a wall. 'Yes. I refused to marry Gia.'

'Why?' she asks, seemingly perplexed. 'She's like – perfect.'

'She *did* Google you,' Matty says, midway through a third burger.

Eve looks at me, her interest clearly piqued.

I grab my juice cup, peeling off the metallic seal. 'Gia wasn't my girl.'

Matty is nodding his head repeatedly. 'He found that out when he called her by the wrong name when she popped the question.'

Eve's eyes widen and her brows furrow in curiosity. She tilts her head slightly to the side, her gaze fixed on the object in front of her – me.

'Whose name?' she finally asks.

Matty laughs, not holding back even a little, shaking his head and taking another bite of his burger. *Thanks for the help, man.*

'Uh—yours,' I admit.

Yep. It happened. After casually dating Gia for about a year, she one day dropped down onto one knee at the side of the track after a comp and actually said the words: 'Will you marry me?' I swear, my heart actually stopped. And in that second, the name of the one person who could make it start again left my lips. A name that got me punched – the video's online – by Gia, right in the fucking nose. It wasn't my finest moment, that's for sure. The only thing that still stands out about Gia for me is her smile – she had a great smile. Too bad it was a facade for the entitled thirty-year-old beneath. I'd never missed Eve so much as I did while I was dating Gia.

'Google "Famous 15 gets punched",' Matty tells her.

'Don't,' I advise. 'How about we change the subject? I dreamed of you.' I say the words I wasn't planning on saying, catching Matty off guard as he glances my way curiously. I look at Eve instead. 'While I was sleeping, after the accident, I dreamed of our first date. And that poker night where you whooped everyone's ass.'

She smiles, her cheeks growing pink again. I don't remember her blushing this much before, but my mind is foggy.

'By the way, tell your friend Kait she owes me a Voodoo box before I leave this place, as payback for tormenting me with the smell as I lay in confusion a few days ago.'

She grins. 'OK...'

'They didn't feel like dreams,' I continue. 'It was more like... I was there. In the moment. Then something would snap me back to reality and I'd know I'd been awake the whole time, but it's like my soul went to revisit the past.' I run my hand over my head, shaking out my hair that hasn't been washed since I got here and is probably filled with dust from the track. 'Does that even make sense?'

'I get it,' Eve says. 'Like an out-of-body experience. But instead of seeing the present, you relived the past.'

'Yes,' I say with as much enthusiasm as I've had since I got here. 'The only thing missing was the ghost of Foster's past.'

She laughs.

'Pain meds can be a real roller coaster of an experience according to patients I've worked with. When I had my wisdom teeth pulled out a few years ago, I got an unexpected package days later.' She shakes her head. 'Do not shop while medicated, is my only advice. I now own what Amazon calls a naughty boy lamp, which is a lamp shaped like a boy wearing a black lampshade, and the off and on toggle switch is located where his wiener would be.' She presses her lips into a flat line, clearly regretful of this purchase.

I let out a laugh that sends me into another coughing fit. I hold my injured arm closer to my side, attempting to reassure my broken ribs that they will survive this.

'I named him Willy,' she continues, this time making Matty nearly spit his black coffee at her. 'I smile every time I turn him on and off.'

This is the Eve I remember. She's funny. Witty. Laughing at her own joke. Note to self: look this lamp up to get a full visual later.

'Don't trust your judgment right now, is all I'm saying.'

Touché. This girl just changed the subject without me even noticing. Distracting me from telling stories of daydreaming of her. Do I make her nervous? We're quiet for too many seconds and Matty can't take it; I see him fidgeting.

'So, Eve, you work here? What do you do?' he asks.

She works here. That's right. My mind is loopy at best and that day in the ER feels like forever ago. I do remember her saying my name. The rest of her words were a jumble because I thought my heart was going to stop right then and there with her familiar voice. Never had I let myself forget this woman. I'd memorized everything, and I think of her often. I just always hoped she'd reach out to me so I wouldn't look desperate. She left me. I wasn't going to chase down a woman who only left a note – a note I've had memorized for five years.

'I'm a trauma nurse in the emergency room.'

'Oh,' he says, stunned. 'You were there when Foster came in? Like *in* the trauma room?'

Her eyes meet mine as she nods her head softly. 'I was.'

'How was that?' Matt asks.

'Um...' She takes a breath. 'Terrifying.' Her gaze doesn't leave mine and I see fear in her eyes.

She was terrified, yet she's here now. Not Gia. Maybe there is a God.

'I didn't realize you'd become a nurse,' Matty says. 'But I didn't know you long either, did I?'

'My early twenties were kind of messy,' she says, scrunching her face. 'Got my nursing license when I came back to Oregon and I've worked here ever since. Lots of hours – so I don't have a lot of time for myself. But, on Saturdays, my best friend and I go to the farmer's market, that's always fun.'

'Huh,' Matty says. 'Well good for you. You still single?'

My heart nearly flatlines. Why is he asking that?

'I got engaged—'

'You're engaged?' The words just tumble out of my mouth, surrounded by disbelief and jealousy.

'Two years ago,' she finishes her sentence. 'It didn't work out.' She frowns, clasping her hands between her knees and fidgeting with a ring on her middle finger.

Matty and my eyes meet. I don't know what he's trying to say to me but I feel like it's 'Do not do this again, dumbass.' Or maybe I'm seeing, 'Shoot your shot, bud.' Either way, he should know by now that I never listen. I'm alive and that feels lucky. I don't want to press that.

'I'm sorry,' I say to her, sincerely being sorry that she was so obviously hurt, but not denying that knowing she's single sparks something up in my chest. Something I don't have the brain capacity to think through right now.

11

EVE CASSIDY

I don't know how to describe that first conversation we had after Foster woke recently. I've been thinking about it ever since. He seemed stunned when he found out I was engaged, and then relieved when I admitted I wasn't still. What was that about? If he had something to say, I'd have hoped he would have done it back when I needed to hear it. But he didn't. He just disappeared. No phone calls. No texts. Not even a freaking note. Just the once-a-year comment that he does still exist via FB anniversary reminders, each one spearing through my heart like an hors d'oeuvre skewed by many toothpicks.

Wake up, Eve. You're attempting your routine again, remember? This morning is elderly water aerobics day.

I snap to, forcing Foster out of my mind. Pop music of the sixties blasts through the room's speakers.

'Paul, you've got no rhythm,' I kid, counting along to the beat of the song. 'One, two, three, four, five,' I count with him, a hand on his shoulder, leading him along, but I don't think Paul's seventy-something body will allow it.

I'm back on my schedule again. Sort of. I'll spend the hours I'd usually work with Foster until he's released from the hospital. Otherwise, I've got to get back on track before I lose my mind. Work would help take my mind off things, but when you love someone the way I loved Foster – blindly and with my entire soul – turning your back on them for a second time isn't an option. I have regrets and I have a feeling he does too. No, I don't believe in fate, but something is telling me to follow this through.

'I got it!' Paul waves me away like I'm an annoying fly.

What kind of nonsense will leave these folks' lips today? I glance around at my three attendees. Usually there are six, but we lost Freddie a few months ago – he passed peacefully in his sleep while his wife slumbered next to him. Wanda, Freddie's wife, moved into a home recently. I was sad to lose them because even though I no longer believe in love, those two kept a piece of my heart filled with hope. But back to my morning crew here. Jeraldine called in 'tired' last night after going through a bout of insomnia that had her 'homicidal'. Pretty sure she was kidding when she said that, but I advised her to stay home and sleep in for my own safety.

My other attendees today are eighty-four-year-old Dolly and her little sister, Margaret – a young seventy-nine and one year. Her words. Paul is seventy-seven and has on a leopard print speedo and definitely can't hide his wandering eye. Honestly, he's really doing great in this class after his stroke.

'That's it, Dolly, let's march it out for ten more seconds,' I say, modeling the correct way to water march – knees high – hitting my palms that are sitting just on top of the water. Though they're trying, no one's knees are reaching the waterline in this group.

My group are sporting brightly colored swim caps and goggles, floaties and life jackets. They mimic my moves, swaying and stretching in almost unison.

'Good.' I come to a standstill, feet planted on the bottom of the pool in the shallow end. 'Let's go for a stroll,' I say, now jogging in place – still with the Strangeloves playing in the background.

The three of them each attempt to not let the 'elderly float' – as I call it – overtake them, forcing their feet to the bottom with enough force that the water sloshes around us.

'You ladies know how to skip any more?' Paul breaks the silence a minute into the jog, his voice loud enough it's startling when it reverberates back to us in the otherwise empty pool area of the hospital gym. 'It's harder than you think,' he continues. 'My great-granddaughter challenged me on the TikTok.'

'Lord, Mags, he's got a TikTok,' Dolly says, the two women laughing.

'My failure to skip got thirty-seven thousand likes, girls.'

'Impressive,' I say to Paul, causing him to scrunch his face like my voice makes his skin crawl.

He's not looking for my approval; it's the women next to him he's trying to impress – with skipping, at that. Unusual card to play but now when I leave here, I'm going to need to make sure I still know how to skip so I can pass this challenge when it's my turn. I don't think I've done it since I was in grade school.

The heavy door into the pool area opens, earning our attention, and I glance to see who's invited themselves in.

'Oh, my,' Dolly says. 'Who is this stud?'

'Me?' Paul says, pointing to himself. 'My name is Paul Westwood.'

'Not you,' Margaret says, now pointing toward the edge of the pool where my eyes are also on the three men walking our way. 'Him, in the middle.'

My eyes are already on him, Mags. 'Hi,' I say when he stops poolside. 'What are you doing here?' I ask, glancing at Matty on one side of him and his physical therapist on the other.

Despite the IVs hanging from a pole that Matty is pushing, and Foster's hand secured onto the hospital-issue cane, he looks better than I've seen him all week.

'I asked him where he wanted to walk and he asked to come here,' his physical therapist says.

'Really?'

'I thought you had to be sixty-five to take this class?' Paul hollers over the music, obviously miffed over the potential newbie the ladies both have their eyes on.

'I may look thirty-five, but I assure you, I'm a spry sixty-five,' Foster says with a smirk, earning a chuckle from Dolly and Margaret. Paul's eyebrows shoot up in surprise.

'Not sure "spry" is the word,' Matty says. 'It took us thirty minutes to get here from his room.'

Matty has been in and out of Portland since Foster's accident. This time he can only stay twenty-four hours, but I've noticed how Foster seems happier when he gets calls from buddies back home and especially when Matty shows up. He's his stand-in father after Foster's real dad proved a long time ago that he wasn't reliable – with anything. We understood each other in that way. Each of us had an absent father (mine not until I was a teenager), so I guess that would mean that we share some of the same issues – daddy ones.

'I was almost dead last week,' Foster reminds him. 'I feel like a thirty-minute mile should be celebrated at this point in my recovery.'

'I agree,' his physical therapist says, thrusting a fist in the air.

'You seem pretty lively today for someone who was on death's door last week,' I say.

'Lively, *and* sexy,' Dolly murmurs behind me.

Foster chuckles, his cheeks growing pink at the attention of the two women not trying to hide their approval of his exterior.

'Well, you know me, always making a grand entrance.' Foster winks, his crystal blue eyes twinkling mischievously.

I can't help but smile at his jest, the dimples in his cheeks deepening. Despite the circumstances that brought him here, his charm and humor are as present as ever. It's refreshing to see him in such good spirits.

'Well, you're just in time for our grand finale,' I say.

'Welcome to the water ballet,' Paul takes over, motioning to him and the two ladies. He then touches his fingers above his head and turns in the water, his yellow float tube acting as his tutu as his spin turns sideways and he ends up in an uncontrolled wobbly float.

'You've probably got to have life insurance for this class, huh?' Foster kids.

I laugh. 'I haven't drowned anyone yet,' I say, grabbing onto Paul and steadying him once again.

Despite the playful banter around us, there's an unspoken understanding between Foster and me that goes beyond words. It's been happening all week. We haven't really had any conversations about us or the last time we were an 'us', besides briefly alluding to the topics and realizing they were still too hot to touch. We've just existed and focused on him recovering. His eyes hold a hint of gratitude and warmth that makes my heart skip a beat. It's moments like these where I wonder if we'll ever have those conversations we probably both need to get closure from this mess. Do I want to relive that fresh hell? For closure? Maybe.

'Take a bow, ladies, you're the stars of the show,' Paul says when his feet are once again solidly on the bottom of the pool.

'You guys can go ahead and free-swim,' I tell the group, swimming to the side and hopping up, grabbing my towel and wrapping it around my shoulders.

'Floating it is,' Dolly says, shoving off of the shallow end and bobbing into the deep end. Paul and Margaret follow suit.

'Is there a reason for this visit?' I ask Foster.

'The guy torturing me wants me moving and I needed a change of scenery.' He shrugs his one shoulder, grimacing when the other one moves too.

'A change of scenery to Paul?' I point at my elderly swimmer. 'Who, under that water, is wearing a very tight leopard print speedo?'

Foster's eyes jet to Paul, who gives him an obnoxious thumbs up. He looks back at me with a shake of his head, a grimace on his face. 'I'm more here for the pretty blonde instructor.'

I swish my feet in the water below me, unsure what to say about him calling me 'pretty' again. The basement is filled with the thick scent of chlorine, humidity and steam as warm water meets the coolness of the walls.

'Thank you,' I say.

Trust me, Fost. I've already noticed your half-bare chest.

'Is this your longest walk?' I ask.

'Yep,' he says, a proud look on his face. 'The doctor mentioned going home tomorrow.'

'Tomorrow?'

That's quick. I mean, it's not really but it feels quick.

'The details haven't been ironed out.'

'Well, that's – amazing.'

'Yeah?' he asks, his tone unsure.

'Very. When you were first brought in, I was worried we wouldn't be having this conversation at all.'

'You worried?' he asks as if he's not sure he believes me. 'For real?'

I nod. 'Since the moment you were wheeled into my trauma room, Fost.'

He cracks half a smile, looking suddenly shy but also relieved to hear it.

'Ready to head back?' his physical therapist butts in, motioning in the direction they came from.

'Yep,' Foster says, nodding. 'I think I've pushed my luck far enough for today.'

Matty gives him an appreciative yet gentle pat on the back. 'You did great, buddy.'

'I'll see you later?' Foster asks, shooting me a charming grin before turning to follow his physical therapist.

'Yep, I've got a bag full of bedside activities in my locker. Just got to get through my baby swim class next and after the toddlers, I'll probably make it up to your room for lunch?'

'Perfect,' he says, flashing me the smile that has always been hard to say no to.

'See ya then,' I say, watching them walk away, his IV pole clinking softly with each step. As they disappear through the heavy door back into the hospital corridor, I smile. Am I excited to see him for lunch or at the news that he's being discharged soon? I'm not sure.

Dolly elbows me in the calf playfully. 'Hot lunch date, huh?'

I roll my eyes, trying to hide the smile that threatens to break through. 'It's nothing.'

'Nothing but longing gazes and unresolved tension?' Margaret chimes in with a smirk.

I give them both a look. 'You got that from the last two minutes?'

'A girl never forgets those looks and at our age, seeing it is a rarity. Who is he?'

'His name is Foster, and we were once married,' I say, tossing my towel aside and hopping back into the pool with them.

'Marr*ied*?' they say in unison, bobbing on floaties in front of me. 'Why the past tense, darling?'

I've never actually tried to explain this part. 'We got married impulsively in a five-minute ceremony after only a month of knowing each other. We threw our cares to the wind, and we jumped all the way in. Which was so, so good as it was happening, but in the end, love wasn't enough. He had his life and I had mine. It was destined to fail.'

'A serendipitous moment that wasn't meant to be?' Paul asks like he's experienced it before.

'Exactly,' I say, realizing he's described it perfectly.

I'd never want to have not experienced it, because it was great in the moment. But reality had different ideas and considering that's where we live most often, I had to listen because I deserved to be happy too. And I wasn't.

12

GUY 'FOSTER'

'Hello,' Eve says as she enters my room. 'I brought food from the outside world.'

She's got a pink bakery box in her hands with a brown paper bag balancing on top, grease already staining through, and a plastic grocery bag hanging off one wrist. On her shoulder is her stuffed bag she brings daily, filled with all the necessities a woman on the go may need.

If only I could hide the smile that automatically fills my face each time I see this woman.

'You didn't have to do all this,' I say. 'Though I'm not going to say I hate that you did.'

'I figured. Now what do you want to start with, doughnuts or burgers?'

I think about it for half a second. 'Burgers.' I can't resist, after smelling Matty's the other day.

'Excellent idea,' she says, dumping four burgers wrapped in red and white paper on the tray near my bed. She takes one herself, along with a container of fries, and sits in the chair facing my bed.

I unwrap one and take a bite, leaning my head back against the pillow and closing my eyes to savor every morsel. 'Mmmmmmm!' I moan, making Eve laugh. 'This is so much better than hospital-issued lobster bisque.'

'Only the brave order it,' she says. 'Someone once suggested we use it as colonoscopy prep.'

I laugh. 'I'm glad it didn't have that effect on me.'

She obviously made herself up after her elderly swim class this morning – though she didn't need to because even make-up-less and soaking wet, she's easily the most gorgeous girl I've ever laid eyes on.

'Did you know there's a doughnut burger?' I ask, just making conversation.

'Ew. Where?'

I shrug my one good shoulder. 'A food truck in Orlando. It's called the Luther Burger. Krispy Creme glazed doughnuts, with a bacon cheeseburger inside.'

Her scrunched disgusted face is adorable. 'Sounds like the recipe for acute coronary syndrome.'

A single eyebrow jets up my forehead as I question her silently.

'Heart attack,' she clarifies. 'Have you eaten this Luther Burger?'

I nod. 'A few times.'

Eve's bright eyes widen in mock horror. 'And you're still alive to tell the tale?' she teases, a playful grin tugging at the corners of her lips.

'I'm invincible,' I say with faux bravado, winking at her. 'Obviously.'

She shakes her head, but there's a lightness in her expression that says she's enjoying our banter.

'Obviously...' she repeats.

We finish our burgers silently and I go in for another while she eats fries one by one, without ketchup.

'There's still a rumor of me going home tomorrow,' I say, causing her to pause with a French fry midway to her mouth.

The thought of leaving this hospital room where she's been my daily visitor is bittersweet. Sweet because it means progress and recovery, but bitter because it also means I'll be headed home, thousands of miles from Eve once again.

She smiles, but I swear I see a hint of sadness in her eyes. 'That's great news, Foster. I'm sure your buddies and bike miss you immensely.'

'I miss them too,' I admit, feeling a pang of disappointment that surprises me with its intensity.

For a moment she's in heavy thought over something but when she finishes her fries, she stands, grabs the pink bakery box, and opens it to reveal an array of colorful doughnuts.

'Well, we'll have to make the most of the time we have left then. Doughnut?' she offers, holding out the box to me.

I grin and select the Old Dirty Bastard, our favorite.

She settles back into her chair, her eyes lingering on mine as I take a bite of the treat. The taste explodes in my mouth, and I can't help but let out another appreciative moan.

'Oh, my God. How is this better than I remember?'

Eve quirks an eyebrow at me, a mischievous glint in her eyes.

I swallow, trying to keep my heart rate steady under her gaze. 'I swear on every insane stunt I've ever done, this is the best doughnut I've ever had.'

She laughs, a sound that feels like music to my ears.

As we sit there in comfortable silence, the sound of our munching filling the room, I catch her stealing glances at me when she thinks I'm not looking. It warms my heart to know that she still cares at least a little bit, even after all these years.

Eve breaks the quiet. 'Can I ask you something?'

'Anything,' I reply.

'Why am I still your emergency contact when I'm not even your last girlfriend?'

Honestly, I don't know because I think as a stunt rider, you try not to think about what could go wrong and instead pretend you're invincible, so the reality doesn't set in and kill your courage. Though, there is another reason.

'It's because…' I trail off, searching for the right words. 'Well—' I start again, my voice softer than before, more serious, '—this feels weird to say out loud because my actions haven't proven this, and even though you might not know it, you've always been my constant. No matter what happened between us, you never left my mind. I knew if something were to happen, I could always count on you.'

Eve's expression softens at my words, a hint of confusion crossing her face.

'Hello!' Matty's voice interrupts us as he pulls back the curtain and stops in his tracks.

He's got the worst timing but the best taste, as he too is carrying a pink bakery box and a grocery bag full of stuff.

'Damn,' he says. 'She beat me to it.' He sets the box of doughnuts on top of the one already sitting on the tray in front of me and grabs one of the leftover burgers. 'My favorite. Doctor been in yet?'

'Not yet,' I say.

'By the way,' Matty says, still chewing. 'I checked on your bag and Jeff said it's back at the shop.'

'Damn,' I moan, glancing at the scrub pants a nurse brought in to me since I've got no clothing with me. 'Not sure how I'll get home without a shirt or shoes.'

'I brought you both to tide you over,' Matt says, nodding toward the plastic shopping bag he's set at the end of my bed between my feet. 'Also, I can't get you on my flight home, but I did manage to book one for the day after tomorrow.'

Eve watches the interaction between Matty and me, her expression unreadable. I can see a flicker of something pass through her eyes, but it's gone before I can decipher it fully.

'Thanks, Matty,' I say.

He waves me off with a greasy hand, busy wolfing down his burger.

The sliding door to my room opens and in walks Dr Sully, wearing a pair of the exact same scrubs I am but with his white coat, proving he's the doctor here.

'Mr Foster,' he says as he sanitizes his hands. 'You're looking good. Is this your going-away party?'

Eve interjects before I can respond. 'It's his first day of outside food since his accident. I went all out.'

Dr Sully chuckles. 'She always does,' he says to me. 'Eve's the best nurse I've ever worked with.'

I glance her way, watching her smile with a confidence that's new to me.

'But back to you, Foster. You're doing exceptionally well. I think we are shooting for discharge tomorrow. What do you think?'

'I'm beyond ready to sleep in my own bed again,' I admit.

'Good, because bed is where you'll spend a lot of time in the coming days.'

'But not too much time if you want to get back to work,' Matty follows up.

'No rest for the wicked,' I say, mentally groaning at the idea of things like physical therapy and home workouts that will feel like torture for a while. I look to Matty. 'You better make that plane ticket first class.'

'Plane ticket?' the doctor asks, shaking his head. 'No. You're in no condition to fly.'

Eve's eyes go wide. 'But he lives in Florida,' she informs him.

'That's too far for you to be traveling with your injuries,' the doctor reasons, peering down at me with a stern expression.

Eve's fingers drum on the arm of her chair, a worried expression flickering across her face. 'What do you suggest then?'

Dr Sully ponders for a moment, adjusting his glasses before speaking. 'He needs someone to monitor his recovery closely. So, I'd recommend staying with a friend.' His gaze jets to Matty.

He's hardly even listening – because cheeseburger – but he shakes his head. 'Can't,' he finally says through a mouthful. 'I also live in Florida.'

'In that case, perhaps you've got a medically trained wife who could help you out until you're cleared for more extensive travel.'

Everyone in the room, myself included, directs their attention at Eve, who's never looked more uncomfortable in her life. She uncrosses her legs and then recrosses them, her fingers fidgeting with one of her rings.

She looks conflicted, her jaw agape and her eyes darting between me, Matty and the doctor. 'Ex-wife.' The word leaves her lips softly, barely audible, yet we all pick it up.

13

EVE CASSIDY

'I get the feeling that you're implying I should bring him home with me?' I ask the doctor I know all too well before glancing at Foster, who can't keep his eyes off me.

Sure, I've been here every day since his accident. But this isn't going the way I expected. My original plan was to quietly tiptoe out, escaping undetected before he stirred from his sleep. Now I'm unexpectedly being volunteered to nurse the man back to health.

'He's going to need round-the-clock care as his mobility needs supervision. He's still got a great deal of internal injuries healing. His cervical spine is bruised, and he'll probably be wobbly on his feet for a bit. You're literally the best person for the job.'

My heart speeds as I try to maintain my calm exterior. 'OK,' I say, my mind racing with fear and uncertainty.

'As I'm sure you're aware, Mrs Foster, every injury is unique and requires a customized approach. He's lucky to have you in his life right now.'

My mouth involuntarily falls open in surprise and I shoot Jeremy, my co-worker, a glare – he knows damn well my last name isn't Foster.

'Cassidy,' I correct him. 'It's been Cassidy since the day we met.'

Dr Sully smirks. 'My apologies,' he says under his breath with a chuckle.

'I don't know if I can take that much time off work,' I say.

'You can with a doctor's note,' Doctor Sully reminds me, a sly smile on his face.

Matty nods like he knew that all along.

'Can I, uh... talk to you?' I ask Matty, refusing to see how Foster is reacting to my hesitation. 'In the hall?'

He raises his eyebrows in confusion. 'Sure? Just let me grab a doughnut first.'

As he stands, I make my way outside Foster's room. Matty walks out a moment later with a famous Voodoo Doll doughnut whose head he's currently biting off.

'Shall I quit my job too?' I ask, lowering my voice so we're not overheard.

'What else is he supposed to do? He can't road-trip *or* fly, you heard the doctor – you're the best fit for this job.'

I sigh heavily. 'I know, but besides the last couple of weeks, I haven't seen Foster in years. We're divorced! I can't bring him home with me.'

'Yet you were good with pretending to be his wife since he got here.'

I moan. 'Only because I have a heart. But moving him into my place? My tiny, one-bedroom apartment? That is hugely different to visiting him in the hospital.'

'Can't be that bad. I'd bet it's probably got all the same things he's got here. Why can't you play home nurse? Clearly you like to help people. Maybe it'll be fun? You two used to have so much fun together that you decided to get married after a month. Why not explore that a bit longer?'

'Because exploring that will probably include wiping his ass – those are wife duties.'

Matty grimaces. 'Maybe buy a bidet?'

I drop my head back, frustrated but also wondering why I don't already have a bidet. I'll look into that.

'Despite the fact that I once loved him, and those feelings are slightly stirred within, I'm pretty sure I no longer do. So, I don't think him moving in with me will be all sunshine and rainbows. Do you realize the responsibilities that come with taking care of someone injured the way he is? I'll have to help him get dressed, prepare his meals, assist him to and from the bathroom, shower, make sure he's moving enough and doesn't overdose on his pills or get addicted, and drive him to his doctor's appointments – all on top of possibly going back to work because my vacation days are going to end very soon.'

'Or you could pretend you once loved the guy and make sure he gets the best care possible.'

I cross my arms over my chest.

'I bet he'd pay you,' he says, taking another bite of his doughnut as if this conversation is as casual as it gets.

I glare. 'Matty, I don't have the room or the time.'

'The fact that you're standing here says you've got the time. Plus, how much room could he take? Just make sure he doesn't die. Easy-peasy.'

'Easy-peasy? Ha! What if I miss giving him his meds on time? And shall I give him my bed too?'

'That's up to you. I'd suggest the couch but you're the professional, if you think he needs to be in your bed I don't think he'd shy away.'

I glare. Hard. But it's almost like it spurs him on. 'You're delusional.'

'You haven't said no, so – sounds like we've got a deal?' Matty says before heading back into Foster's room. As I follow, he whispers into my ear. 'Why are you *really* here? For a man you pretend you can't stand. Maybe think about that.'

I groan to myself, following him into Foster's room. I shift my gaze toward Foster, captivated by his piercing blue eyes which seem to reflect the depth of his soul. His unwavering stare makes me feel vulnerable, almost as if he can see right through me – like he knows what I'm about to say. A strange sensation takes hold of me, but I can't quite discern whether it's the flutter of butterflies or the sting of bees.

'It's complicated,' I say, attempting to soften the blow of me saying 'no' to this.

Foster nods. 'Eve,' he says, glancing at my hands.

I look down, my fingers intertwined as I spin my ring around my finger. 'This is a fidget ring. I'm using it exactly as it was intended.'

'I don't expect you to take care of me. I'm a grown man. I'll check into a hotel. Maybe I can sweet-talk a maid into helping me out here and there. Uber Eats can feed me, and I'm sure it'll be fine.'

My heart slows. I don't doubt he could sweet-talk a maid into doing whatever he wants, but he sounds so disappointed by the idea of it. His tone doesn't match the mask of the casual smile he's wearing either. How would he get the food Uber leaves outside his door? A hotel room is *smaller* than my apartment. What if he doesn't take his meds right and gets worse? What if he bleeds out and dies in his sleep – alone?

'No,' I say, surprising even myself. 'You're not going to a hotel.' I sigh heavily, sitting in the chair near Foster's bed and resting my head against the back. 'My apartment isn't far from here. I'm sure we can make it work.'

The smile on Foster's face makes the swarm of fluttering in my chest feel less lethal than it did earlier. Maybe this will be fun? I mean we did used to have fun together. Matty's not wrong about that.

I block out the chatter between the three of them now and worry about what my friends will think of me having just volunteered to nurse Foster back to health, in my apartment.

14

EVE CASSIDY

I've spent the last morning picking up items from the shopping list Nurse Chelsea gave me. Shower seat, a cane, and my own addition at Matty's suggestion – a bidet.

Yes, he could have gone to a hotel but my stupid heart spoke for me. Honestly, I'm a little worried about how this is going to go down. Recently it's been easy to leave the hospital when visiting hours are over and detach myself from the situation, but with him in my apartment, it's going to be all Foster, all the time.

Also, Dr Sully wrote a note to my boss and she's approved two additional weeks off to care for my new patient. She sent me a text this morning and said I was an absolute saint of a person to take this on, but considering this experience might kill me, I feel more like a martyr.

After what feels like an endless few hours waiting on discharge paperwork, we finally reach the lobby of my ancient apartment building. Foster stands beside me, his clothes rumpled and disheveled from the hospital stay. He wears a pair of blue scrub pants, and the black T-shirt and slides Matty brought him yesterday when they thought he was flying home. His tired eyes scan the lobby, taking in the marble floors and wall of locked mailboxes.

His right hand rests heavily on a cane, as he looks at the elevator with dismay. 'This thing still doesn't work?'

'Yeah, well, my landlord is more concerned about him living the good life, not his tenants. Hmm... how are we going to do this?' I ask myself, staring up the stairs.

As I look back at Foster, I can see the clear signs of pain etched on his face. I rack my brain, trying to come up with a plan to get him to the third floor quickly. Easily.

'While I think, you walk, it'll get the blood flowing.'

'Walk where?' he asks.

'Um, to the mailboxes and back, five times.'

'Five times?' he moans, but does it, slowly.

Suddenly, an idea strikes me – I pull my phone out of my pocket and navigate to Phil's contact. I press the speaker button, hoping he's home.

'What's up, sugar?'

'I'm in the lobby, and I need your help.'

'Lawd, honey, don't tell me you bought another new mattress. It's too soon! That thing almost killed us last time. Pivoting wasn't enough. I thought you'd end up squashed against a wall before you even slept on it.'

That was a complete fiasco. I regret not ordering one of those mattresses that come in a compact, rectangular box. Instead, I bought it locally, refused to pay extra for delivery, and got it home myself, just barely.

'It's not a mattress this time; it's a man.'

'A man?' he asks quizzically. 'For me?'

'No.'

'For you?' He perks up. 'Oh, honey, finally! I was beginning to wonder if the Sahara Desert had taken root in your undergarments.'

Foster's deep, rumbling chuckle fills the air, causing his broad shoulders to shake with amusement as he walks. He tilts his head down coyly and hastily wipes the smirk off his lips as soon as my gaze meets his.

'I'm sorry,' he says, another laugh escaping his lips.

'No one here needs to know a thing about my undergarments,' I say, my tone firm and unwavering as if scolding two misbehaving children. 'Our arrangement is clinical, and what goes on in my panties is private.' My words hang in the air, thick with tension and unspoken emotions. The weight of our past interactions lingers between us, threatening to break through the facade of professionalism I am trying to maintain. But I can't let that happen – this is strictly business.

'Oh, this sounds interesting! I'll be right down, sweets!' Phil says enthusiastically before the phone goes silent.

Foster clears his throat, the sound echoing through the lobby. A hint of amusement dances in his voice as he speaks. 'Clearly it's a touchy subject, but I can't resist asking. Has the Sahara Desert taken up in your pants?' His eyes sparkle with mirth, and a sly grin tugs at the corners of his mouth.

I glare, shoving my phone into my back pocket. 'I can confirm, it has not.'

'Also, I thought you hated pet names, Jellybean?' he asks, while still on lap number three.

'I do hate pet names, Mr Wonka. However, much like you, Phil doesn't care about that because that's just how he speaks. Everyone is honey to him, even you – just wait.'

'Will I also be sugar? 'Cause I sort of like that one.'

'Careful, he likes the masculine type.'

'Are you saying Phil isn't your boyfriend?'

I laugh. 'In the same way Kait and Jess are my girlfriends, yes. To speak your language, we're bros, brah.'

A low rumble of laughter fills the hall, but the lines on his face betray a tinge of annoyance. 'I can assure you, I have never once uttered the term "brah",' he retorts.

I look him over, wishing he weren't so frickin' handsome right now. There's not much to pick on. Not that I want to roast the guy – he's been through enough recently – but it's going to be hard to set rules for our game of house considering we've done just about everything two people in love could ever do, and now we're supposed to dance around it and be patient and nurse.

I spent last night painfully overthinking how to handle this situation. I've decided I need to set some boundaries here – no more flirting. I suspect flirting will lead to places we'll never return from, and I can't take the heartache.

'You've never said "brah"?'

'Nope.'

'Well, the flat-bill hat on your head says otherwise.'

It's puzzling to me how that particular item made its way into his personal belongings bag, while his clothes were left out. Sure, it's part of the off-duty FMX boy uniform, but I thought for sure he'd have grown out of it by now.

He rolls his eyes. He's always had the FMX rider look. He could pass for twenty-five instead of thirty-five, and not just with his looks. He's got a young heart, mouth – and probably brain, if I had to guess by his condition right now.

The sound of someone jogging down the stairs relieves me a bit. Finally, a piece of my world that is familiar to me after weeks of chaos.

'On my way, hon!' Phil's voice echoes through the hallway, announcing his arrival before we even catch a glimpse of him.

I quickly whisper to Foster as he meanders back to me from the mailboxes after his fifth lap, 'Don't react when you see him.'

'Why?' Foster asks. 'Does he have two heads?'

'No, he's just... colorful.'

He grins. 'I don't judge, sugar. He could come down here wearing diamond-studded glasses and a rainbow suit, and I wouldn't bat an eye.'

'He's not Elton John. But he's also not many steps away from that.'

'I like Elton,' Foster murmurs.

'Let's see this ma—' Phil stops mid-sentence as he begins to descend the last set of stairs, his eyes on Foster. I can't blame him there.

While he's not wearing the exact outfit Foster alluded to, he wasn't far off. Instead, Phil's clad head to toe in a bright neon orange sweatsuit, zipped halfway open to reveal a lush garden of chest hair. A sparkly bracelet on one wrist that matches the necklace shining around his neck completes the look. And if his outfit weren't enough to catch your attention, his choice of shoes would surely do the trick – a pair of silver joggers that seem more fit for a disco than a jog.

Phil exudes an aura of confidence and flamboyance that is both impressive and slightly intimidating. The man is built like a Greek god, and despite the fact that he's very clearly into men, women never pass up the opportunity to admire his good looks.

'Well, well, well,' he drawls, taking in Foster's appearance with a critical eye before turning to me. 'He is beautiful, darling.' Suddenly he cocks his head. 'But what's with the bandages? Did you run him over?' His words drip with sarcasm and amusement as he continues to scan Foster up and down like a piece of art.

A chuckle threatens to escape my lips, and I fight to stifle it. 'No, but if I had, he deserved it,' I tease, playfully nudging Foster's arm.

Foster rolls his eyes in response. 'It was a motorcycle accident.'

'Oooh. You're a daredevil; I like it. She needs some excitement in her life.' Phil gives me an approving thumbs up while behind Foster. 'Does he have a name, love?'

'Foster.'

'Foster...?' He awaits the rest of his name.

'Just the one name,' Foster says. 'Like Madonna.'

Phil's face lights up with a smile that conveys his interest in the conversation. We seem to have hit all the right notes, sparking his curiosity and engaging his attention. Foster, on the other hand, appears relaxed and at ease despite being the object of a gay man's unabashed admiration.

'Alright then, Foster. Let's get you upstairs,' he says.

Without hesitation, he reaches out and grabs Foster's hand, throwing his good arm over his shoulder. Together, they make their way up the stairs, Phil trying to take short breaks at each landing.

'Where are we putting him?' Phil asks.

'In my room,' I say.

Slight panic sets in as soon as the words leave my mouth. My tiny apartment is not equipped to handle a guest. I wasn't lying when I told Matty that. My bed is too small for two people and my couch is uncomfortable at best. But I can't bear to think of Foster suffering on my lumpy hand-me-down couch.

'Your room?' Foster asks, clearly confused.

Phil can't contain his excitement and lets out a swoon. 'Ohhh! He's going in your bed?' he exclaims. 'This just keeps getting better and better.'

With each step, the tap of Foster's cane echoes through the stairwell, a constant reminder of his injury. But he climbs determinedly, one step at a time, refusing to let it slow him down.

'No, I've already uprooted your entire life. I don't need your bed too,' he declares, reaching the first landing and turning to face Phil. 'I need a two-minute break,' he says, his voice strong and resolute, but laced with pain, exhaustion evident in his eyes.

I stop at the landing with them. 'Trust me when I say the couch would be a backward step in your healing. A few nights on that thing and you'll need a chiropractor too.'

But Foster shakes his head, determination set in his features. 'I can handle it.'

Phil looks at him with admiration, bordering on awe. 'You definitely are a daredevil,' he exclaims. 'Do we need a second break?' he asks between staircases.

Foster stands tall and defiant, shaking his head. 'Not taking a break *or* your bed, and that's the end of that conversation. Let's keep going.'

'We made it!' I say proudly, turning the key in my door.

I push it open, gesturing for Phil and Foster to enter first. Phil walks in confidently and Foster follows closely behind, his steps hesitant and uncertain.

'Have you ever been here before, or will this be your first time in Evie's bed?'

'I'm familiar with her bed, but put me on her couch,' Foster says, side-eyeing me with amusement.

I'd only just rented this apartment when he and I met. So he was familiar with my bed five years ago and as I mentioned earlier, this bed is brand new. A Foster-free bed – until now.

'Phil,' I say sternly. 'Put him in my bed.'

'Evie,' Foster pleads, looking at me with puppy dog eyes. 'You can't sleep on the couch in your own apartment.'

For a second, my mind races with memories of past nights spent in his arms. If he's suggesting we sleep in the same bed, that's way too risky.

'I've already decided. Plus, you're sort of at my mercy, so, don't make me be mean?' I say, like I could ever be mean.

He heaves a sigh, nodding his head like he's a sore loser. 'To her bed, I guess,' he says.

Phil turns his head swiftly, his eyes widening in amazement as he lets out a gasp. 'Why have I never heard of him before?' he asks, leading Foster the short distance from my living room to my bed, sitting his butt first and then helping get his legs up.

'It's a story I don't like to tell,' I say, watching Foster frown. 'Comfy?' I ask him, adjusting the pillows behind his head as he sits back.

'No,' he admits.

'A story you don't like to tell?' Phil asks. 'You better get over it because it's a story I want to hear all about. Spill the tea, sister. It can't be Cowardly Cayden bad.'

Foster's gaze suddenly snaps at the mention of the name Cayden. His brow furrows in confusion and he speaks up, his voice laced with surprise.

'Who's Cayden?'

'Just another ex I'd rather not remember.'

'Another ex?' Phil asks. 'Wait, is this one an ex too, or just a one-nighter?'

'Husband,' says Foster.

'Ex-husband,' I say, as Foster and I speak in unison.

Phil lifts a single eyebrow. When his gaze meanders back to Foster, he looks confused. 'Why are you wearing scrub pants?'

'He's from Florida,' I say.

'And scrubs are on trend there?'

'He has nothing with him.'

Phil rubs his chin, clearly concerned. 'What are you, six foot? A size large?'

Foster nods.

'I'll set him up.'

Foster shakes his head, his eyes fixed on Phil's bright orange sweatpants. 'No, no. No need to do that,' he says firmly. 'I can order the things I need from Target or some other store and have them delivered.'

'Nonsense,' Phil says, waving a hand. 'That's a process, darling, and it seems like you have enough on your plate. It's no problem at all. I'll be back in a jif.' He exits my bedroom, me following close behind.

'Thanks, Phil,' I say, dropping my keys and purse on the counter.

Instead of trotting off to his apartment, he turns, stopping the door from closing with one hand. 'I'm going to want to hear the details of this ex-husband I knew nothing about, so when I come back, I'll have wine – be ready.'

'It'll take at least two bottles for that story.'

'I'll bring three,' he says with a gleeful smile. Phil loves gossip. So, with that settled, he disappears down the hall and toward his apartment, two doors down.

I close my front door, walk into my room, and turn to Foster. 'Are you comfortable? Do you need adjusting or more pillows?'

'Pain meds. Bring me the pain meds,' he moans.

I glance at my Apple watch, then shake my head. 'Sorry, mister. You've got another hour before those are due. I've got a schedule.' I grab the discharge paperwork from my dresser and flash it before him.

'When's my sponge bath?' he asks coyly.

I scan the paperwork. 'Oh, they seem to have forgotten that order. Too bad.'

He frowns.

'Also, I've got one rule while you're here.'

'Hit me with it,' he says.

'No flirting in my apartment.'

He cocks his head, giving me a 'you can't be serious' stare. 'I've been flirting with you since the day we met. I don't even know how to speak to you without doing it.'

'I guess it's a good thing you'll be asleep a lot then, huh?' I say with a laugh. 'Just behave, alright? And don't make it weird.'

'No promises there,' he says, leaning his head back against the pillows and closing his eyes.

'Here's the remote.' I open the bedside table drawer and set it on his chest. 'Watch whatever, but the doctor said to sleep as much as you can, so you can either go quietly or...' I grab another pillow, slowly lowering it toward his face.

'Or you'll put me to sleep? Nice.' He chuckles.

'I'll fill your water cup.' I grab the hospital-issued plastic cup.

'Can you fill it with vodka? I hear drinking with pain meds makes them work better.'

'OK, new rule – no drinking while you're here,' I laugh. 'But I could poison it with anti-freeze? Interested?'

His usually upbeat face (because he can be Mr Sunshine at times – annoying) drops, and he goes serious.

'You don't actually hate me, right?' His words carry a tinge of sadness and apprehension.

I take a deep breath, letting out a heavy sigh as I settle down near his feet, positioning myself to face him.

'You heard that, huh?' I ask, thinking back to my phone conversation with Jess recently. I'm surprised it took him this long to ask about it.

He nods.

'Truthfully, Fost, this has been such a whirlwind that I haven't had a chance to properly evaluate my feelings yet, because I never expected to see you again.'

'Everything about us has been whirlwind-style, right from jump,' he says, lifting his good shoulder in a shrug like he just can't help it.

'I know,' I say. 'Because of that, I can confirm that I *thought* I hated you. I say I hate you. You're not my favorite person on the planet any more. But then you were suddenly in my trauma room and things I thought were settled suddenly feel complicated.'

He nods, as if he understands. And maybe he does?

'I'll take that,' he murmurs in a low voice, his eyes half-closed. 'For the record, in the future, when I'm not high on morphine, and you're not feeling overly complicated, we should probably have a conversation.'

I look at him with curiosity. 'I'm OK with us not rehashing the past.'

Before I can exit the room, he grabs my hand. 'Evie... thank you – for doing this. I'll repay you somehow.'

I nod. 'I know, Fost. I'll wake you up for meds, OK?'

''Night, Jellybean.'

Why is my heart palpitating? Is it Foster? Or maybe the stress is finally going to do me in? I don't have long to think about it because within minutes, Phil is back.

'Knock, knock, love,' he says, opening my door and inviting himself in.

He's pulling a suitcase behind him, and a vase of daisies that I know was on his kitchen counter is in one hand. He gives it to me. 'Be a dear and put these in his room? Flowers help with healing, this much I know. Now, give me a sec and I'll be right back with the wine.'

'Always the hostess, aren't you?'

I sneak into my room, setting the daisies on my dresser. They remind me of the flowers I carried during Foster's and my wedding. Sigh. *Don't start thinking of those moments yet.* I glance at Foster, lying in my bed, fast asleep, soft snoring flooding the room. Yet I feel content with him here? Almost like I've missed him? Have I?

I exit my room, as Phil walks in bear-hugging three bottles of wine against his chest. I unzip the bag he packed for Foster, pulling things out one by one, and stacking them on my kitchen counter while he works on opening the wine.

'These are some very colorful choices,' I say to Phil with a giggle.

The vibrant colors of the leggings catch my eye. A bright purple pinstripe pair. A Hawaiian gift-shop-inspired design. And a lovely pink floral print. The extra underwear is also a sight to behold, featuring a range of eye-catching Technicolor tighty whities. Among the T-shirts, one stands out with the bold phrase: 'I look good. *Real* good' printed across the front. Phil even included all the necessary toiletries and hair products, though I suspect I'll be the one using those since Foster has never been interested in styling his hair beyond a quick brush-through.

'I have a feeling that boy is built like an Abercrombie underwear model under those scrubs and sling. Am I right?'

I let out a heavy exhale at that image. 'Yeah, you're right,' I say, grabbing the red wine he just opened, and taking a swig straight from the bottle. 'Are you going to be offended if I don't use a glass? These past couple of weeks have felt like an eternity.'

'Of course not,' he says, maneuvering the corkscrew in another bottle, the pop sound filling the air as he pulls the cork. Without hesitation, he tips it up, taking a long swallow, skipping the need for glasses altogether.

'Talk,' he says, tapping his bottle to mine, then sitting back in anticipation of new gossip.

'So, Foster and me...'

15

GUY 'FOSTER'

'Eve?' I call out, knowing damn well she's inches from the closed bathroom door. She's been hovering since she heard me stir earlier.

'Yes?' she chirps.

I can picture her as the nurse who answers every call-button request quickly and with a smile on her face, ready to do whatever the patient requests.

'Can you maybe step away from the door? You're giving me stage fright.'

I'm a guy who prefers a private bathroom. Rows of urinals are not my friends. A line of people listening outside a port-a-potty, it's just not happening. I have no idea why I just can't let go enough to do my business.

'Stage fright?' she laughs. 'Since when are you one to get shy?' she teases, her voice laced with amusement.

'That sounded flirty,' I say, remembering her 'only rule'.

A few silent moments provide me with the exact relief I came in here for. Finally, I readjust the purple striped leggings riding up my ass, loaned to me by the very flamboyant Phil. They wouldn't be my first choice for sleepwear, but they'll do. I push open the door with a sheepish grin.

'I wasn't flirting,' she says.

'I'm nervous, I don't want to break the rules because I don't want a cup full of antifreeze,' I admit.

Her jaw drops. 'I wasn't serious.'

'I know,' I say, moving slowly toward her bed so as not to jostle anything. 'I do prefer flirty Eve as opposed to a murder-y one. Should I be sleeping with one eye open?'

'No,' she says with a laugh.

That's when I spot the flowers on the dresser. Were those there when I got here?

'Aren't they pretty?' she asks, noticing my gaze. 'Phil brought them last night.'

'Ah,' I say with a nod, sitting on the edge of her bed like I'm a hundred and fifteen years old. 'Do they remind you of anything?' I ask, curious if she's having the same memory I am right now.

She sighs sharply, leaning against the doorframe of her room and watching me get back into her bed.

'The sight of a single daisy reminds me of all the things,' she says, her tone insinuating that she'd rather not relive the story. 'Ready for your morning meds?'

She changes the subject flawlessly as she grabs the basket she's bundled my medications in and sits on the bed at my feet. She hands me a water bottle that I didn't even notice her holding and goes to work prepping my meds into a frosted shot glass that says STAY WEIRD in neon green.

'You're seriously the best nurse,' I say. 'When we were together, I could only vaguely picture it, but now—'

'Now I get the award for Number One nurse and not hottest track girl?' She finishes my sentence with a wide smile.

I laugh out loud, groaning when the jostling hits my ribs. 'You will hold that title forever.'

'Here.' She hands me a tube full of Ritz crackers. 'Eat some of these before you take your meds. It'll help with possible nausea and will keep you from breaking my one rule.'

'I can't help it,' I say, doing as I'm told, leaning my head back against the pillow with my eyes closed, munching on crackers. My head is pounding as is most of the rest of my body since the previous meds are wearing off. 'I see your beautiful face and I just want to flirt,' I say between crackers. 'You bring it out in me, Evie.'

'Yes, I know. But right now, I need you on your best behavior.'

I look at her, feeling dumbfounded. 'I don't know how to do that with you.'

She chuckles at my expression, handing me the shot glass full of medications.

Without hesitation, I toss all the pills back in one swallow, drinking half the bottle of water in the process.

'Eat a few more crackers,' she advises, her voice soft and soothing.

I comply, munching on the crackers obediently, stealing glances at her delicate features as she tidies up the medical supplies on the bedside table.

'You're the best nurse,' I say, grateful for her care, yet struggling with conflicting emotions swirling inside me. The way she effortlessly tends to my needs brings back memories of moments we once shared, juxtaposed with the pain and heartache that followed. I've missed her, more than I thought. It's unsettling yet I want to sort it out. I watch her graceful movements, a pang of guilt washing over me – why wasn't love enough?

'Yeah,' she says. 'You said that already.'

'I did?' I think back, barely remembering it. 'Well, I meant it. Portland doesn't know what they've got, for real. I've never been more proud of you.'

Eve looks up from the basket now refilled with my bottles of medication, meeting my gaze with those warm, compassionate eyes that have always seen past my FMX boy facade. There's a flicker of something in her expression, a vulnerability that tugs at my heartstrings. Yep, I hurt her, possibly as much as she hurt me.

'Thank you.'

'You're welcome,' I say. 'Also, I'm sorry. For everything.'

She stops after standing from the bed – frozen in place.

I want to say more, but the words linger somewhere in the back of my mind, unable to be spoken yet on the tip of my tongue. I swallow them down with the last sip of water and hand her back the empty bottle.

'I know, Fost.' Her tone is gentle but pained. Without another word from either of us, she exits the room, and for the next bit, I listen to her bustle around the apartment. The sounds of her loading the dishwasher, then the gentle hum of it running, lull me to sleep.

16

EVE CASSIDY

He's sorry? For everything? Well hello, they're words I never thought I'd hear.

My mind races as I lie on the couch, his apology hanging in the air like a delicate thread waiting to be pulled. Part of me wants to grab onto it and unravel the years of uncertainty, and finally find some closure. But another part of me hesitates, afraid that this new-found honesty might just be another temporary moment of vulnerability that'll suck me back in only to spit me out worse than I was before. Would he ever have apologized had he not been hurt and ended up here?

I dunno. What I *do* know is that it's way too soon to be having these thoughts. I mean, I figured we'd end up having some conversations about our history, but so soon? That surprises me, considering this is all I ever wanted to hear five years ago, yet he did not pick up the phone or show up at my door and say it when I needed it. For that reason, I thought I didn't mean much to him. Now I'm second-guessing things.

The couch beneath me is soft, worn, and a little bit lumpy. The room is enveloped in darkness, but the moon's pale light filters through the windows, casting long shadows on the floor.

Usually, I'm the most calm, cool, and collected person you'll ever meet. It's why I'm great at my job – nothing frazzles me. Tonight though, with his recent confession of regret, my thoughts are like a spider weaving intricate webs, constantly unraveling and spinning new ideas and fears into existence.

Did he finally say the words too late? The whirlwind of emotions sweeping through me says otherwise.

There is no way I'm going to be able to sleep. So, instead, when I hear the soft snores emanating from my room and I know the pain meds have knocked him out, I grab my phone and enter his name into the browser search bar.

Guy Foster, Famous 15. Enter.

The once blank page now fills with photos, articles and videos mostly all about the person I'm looking for. One particular image catches my eye, where he's mid-air with his brightly colored bike, his arms spread out as if he's soaring through the sky as he hovers just above it. He. Is. Nuts. Tempting fate every day of his life. I'm shocked it took him this long to end up in ICU, truthfully.

I click through the pages of search results, each with images of him performing daring stunts, showing off his tattoos and athletic build. They are a combo of goofy, fun Foster, and FMX pro Foster with an intense look of concentration as he performs for stadiums full of strangers.

Then I notice a video, dated only weeks ago. I tap on the preview and my Instagram app automatically opens to the Red Bull profile page. I unfollowed them a long time ago, precisely so I didn't get caught up in this kind of stalker behavior. Keeping tabs on a boy you dumped isn't usually my style. But here I am, in a world turned upside down by that exact boy – again.

This is the video Matty mentioned – the one Foster didn't want to watch. I hit play. I need to see it. My heart races as I watch Foster riding toward the ramp with an exhilarating speed that makes my breath catch. The crowd cheers as he performs a jaw-dropping backflip, holding on only to the back fender of the bike, then landing smoothly on the dirt track. His smile is infectious, his eyes shining with pure joy and adrenaline when he rips his helmet off as he comes to a stop. That is a Foster I know, and I can't help but feel a surge of pride watching him do what he loves.

I swipe to the next sequence and this time, it's the exact one I feared – of the accident that has him sleeping in my bed.

This is why I couldn't watch him perform every day of the week when we were together. I was in awe of him but was also so in love that I feared exactly this would happen, right before my eyes, and I was certain my heart wouldn't be able to take it. Based on how rapidly it's galloping through my chest as I hit replay on the video, I'd say it's not loving seeing it second-hand either.

How was he not killed? Seeing him in the ER now makes more sense, though even just thinking of it gives me the same anxiety I feel watching the video.

He lived. The lull of his snores right this second is proof.

I scroll through the comments to distract myself from watching the video for a third time and get caught up seeing fans gushing over him.

#PleaseBeOK-I luv u Foster!! <3

The profile picture looks as if this girl is still in high school. Disturbing. I continue scrolling comments.

Give the guy the grand prize for living through this! #OUCH

Crazy wipeout! Dude's a legend! #FearlessFoster #Famous15

There's the nickname he earned long before we ever met. And a new one that perfectly encapsulates his spirit and determination that I've no doubt he'll adore – 'Fearless Foster'. Yep, that's him.

Without thinking it through, I find myself clicking on his profile, scrolling through the images and videos that document his daring feats and adventurous life. It's like getting a glimpse into a world I hardly knew. One where Foster shines brighter than ever – the exact same Foster I fell in love with.

My hand instinctively presses against my chest, feeling the rapid thumping of my heart. My fingers tremble slightly as I scroll, the tips tingling with a mix of anxiety and... something I'm unfamiliar with. Confusion? Hesitation? Regret? Old photos and videos flood my vision, transporting me back in time to moments that we shared together. My eyes well up as I repeatedly see the familiar smile on his face, the same one that used to light up my world.

Each scroll of my screen is like trying to hold onto a swarm of butterflies, each carrying a different memory, all overwhelming and bittersweet. A sudden rush of emotions, a longing for the past, and a deep ache for what could have been, nearly suffocate me. I lay my phone screen down onto my chest, close my eyes, and inhale deeply through my nose and slowly out of my mouth.

This is why you made yourself never look back, Eve. Just relax. Breathe through the incoming panic attack. In through your nose, out through your mouth.

I do the breathing taught to me by my therapist a couple of times – just for good measure. Why does the logical part of me want to push him away? That's right, because getting over him hurt. I was a mess for months. Yet now that I'm over him, the part that still remembers the way his touch felt wants to believe that maybe, just maybe, this apology is sincere – just really, really late. Does that fix the part of me that he broke? Do I want to find that out? Shouldn't I have thought of this before I offered to nurse him back to health?

In through your nose, out through your mouth.

* * *

Five Years Ago

'You nervous, Jellybean?' Foster asks, patting my ass as I pace the tent.

'How are you *not*, Candy Corn? You're about to go out there and do something incredibly stupid, all for cheers from the crowd.'

'Cheers, money, fame, women...' Jeff mumbles in the background.

'Listen to those roars,' Foster exclaims, ignoring Jeff like it's his job, with amusement in his voice. 'It's like a surge of adrenaline rushing through my veins. It's fucking awesome.'

'I think that's probably the five energy drinks you've downed since we got here. Your heart is going to explode.'

I have never been this worried about someone in my life. The first time I saw him do this, I had no emotional attachment, and I pictured a crash more like the 'hockey fights' of FMX. Now, my boyfriend, a man I have fallen head over heels for, is going to tempt fate right in front of me.

'Have you ever wrecked?' I ask, the words slipping out fast enough that he lifts an eyebrow.

'Yes,' he says, his voice lowered as he gathers my hands into his. '*Every* rider's had their share of falls. You walk it off and get back on yer horse,' he utters in a deep velvet purr, drawing me in further with its hypnotic rhythm and seductive tone. His southern accent slips in and once again my heart melts at every word.

'Was it bad?'

'I didn't die.'

This snaps me out of the lovesick spell. My eyes widen as if experiencing terror on his behalf.

'Yet,' I say.

'Are you worried about me, Evie?'

'Yes.'

He lifts both my hands, kissing my knuckles. 'Not gonna lie, it's cute, but don't stress. I've been training my whole life. No matter what happens, I'm ready.'

I start to swoon at the hand-kissing but then my mind wanders to 'no matter what happens'.

'You're ready for death?'

His smile is crooked but sincere. 'I'll be fine,' he assures me. 'Cross my heart and hope *not* to die.' He makes the motion, then kisses my forehead, throwing an arm over my shoulders and pulling me close. 'The only thing you'll witness today is me winning first place.'

Finally, he cracks me and I begrudgingly chuckle at his arrogance – he's not really. Well, maybe on the track, but all these guys are like that – it's sort of like WWE in that way, where the riders sort of spur one another on when they're on the track in front of a crowd but behind the scenes, they all seem to have one another's back.

Foster and I stand together, overlooking the racetrack. His arm is around me as if trying to convey a sense of safety and comfort or maybe just claiming me as his own, which I'm cool with. My silence must be making him nervous because after minutes of silence, he speaks again.

'You've got nothing to worry about. This isn't a sport that you can just pick up a bike and excel at. It takes years of dedication and practice, not to mention a certain degree of natural talent. Take a look at Tommy over there, he's up next. He's exceptionally skilled and one of the younger riders. Of course, he's not where I was at that age.'

'Puh-fucking-lease,' Jeff, technically a member of Matty's team along with Foster, says.

Foster laughs, flipping him off. 'Never listen to Jeff the Heff. He's all sorts of jealous,' he says with a smirk.

The dynamic between these two can best be described as a blend of competitiveness and friendship, or 'frenemies', if you will. My gaze shifts toward the track, where Tommy is stationed at the starting line, eagerly anticipating the signal to go.

'He's most likely doing his standard crowd- and judge-favorite stunts; the Superman or an upside-down Nac-Nac. Although these tricks are difficult to execute, he's only been riding about five years so that's usually why he doesn't earn high scores.'

'Supermans, Nac-Nacs, I don't care how easy or hard they are. For *me*, a girl who knows nothing about this sport, and thinks the solid ground is safer, every trick is terrifying.'

Foster gently takes hold of my arms, turning me to face him. His touch sends a shiver down my spine. As I meet his gaze, his voice drops to a low and intimate tone. 'Do you trust me?' he asks, his eyes searching mine for an answer.

I find it strange that my heart races every time I even think about this guy I have known for only a few weeks. As I gaze into his eyes, I feel like I'm tumbling through a kaleidoscope of emotions, each one more vibrant and alluring than the last. And despite my rational mind telling me that this is too soon, I *do* trust him.

'Yes, but—'

'No "buts",' he says, shaking his head. 'I'll be OK. You'll be incredibly impressed. And tonight, instead of partying with the guys, you and I will celebrate my win – romantically. Deal?'

'Deal,' I say without skipping a beat.

He doesn't have to beg me to hang out with him because it's literally all I want to do. I feel like a teenager in love as he kisses me softly. My skin is electric as his fingertips slide down the back of my arms and I like it – a lot.

'Coming up, Famous 15, Guy Foster.' An announcer's voice rumbles through the track, detailing some of Foster's achievements. I read about these things when I googled him after we met. He's never bragged about them, but I'm seriously impressed. He's placed in the X Games – many times.

'Go. Win,' I say, pushing him from me with one hand on his chest.

He steps back, smiling excitedly. 'I'll be alright, I promise. I'm always alright,' he says, grabbing a helmet and sliding it over his handlebars, then speeding off to the track, doing a quick run around the outside to flirt with his fans.

His riding gear is black, white and green and covered in sponsor logos. His bike is a bright grass green color. The duplicate riding shirt I got when we met is on and tied at my waist. My eyes are on him and despite the danger of this sport, he is incredibly sexy while he does it.

'He'll *probably* be fine,' Matty says, stepping beside me.

'Reassuring,' I say, not exactly amused. 'And if he's not?'

'He's pretty damn tough. I've never seen him not walk away from a fall. But if this is the moment he doesn't, I could set you up with Jeff. He's single and hot for pretty much anything that walks. He wouldn't even think twice.'

I glare over at him. 'I am *not* interested in Jeff the Heff.'

Matty laughs. 'You say his name like poison! Just like Foster does. He's really gotten to you. Are you in love with our boy?'

'It's been three weeks,' I remind him. Not long enough to fall in love.

'Instalove is a real thing,' he says with confidence. 'Just ask my wife...'

There is no way that's a thing. I don't think... Then again, with the way my heart is racing in my chest as I see Foster stop at the start position, this can't be normal. This is the racing heart of someone *on* the bike, and I'm standing on solid ground. Crap-ola. Am I in love with Foster after three weeks?

17

GUY 'FOSTER'

I groan as I open my eyes, my stomach growling and my body aching. After a few confusing moments, I realize I'm still injured, at Eve's instead of at the hospital, and I'm sleeping in her bed. And this is not night number one. The lingering effects of morphine make my head throb, but my mind is starting to work again after a couple of days (weeks, really) of endless sleep.

As I sit up, I take notice of Eve's room – something I didn't bother to do yet besides noticing the flowers yesterday. The curtains are a sheer navy lace, fluttering in the gentle breeze through the open window – that I don't remember opening. Each wall is adorned with a mismatched array of paintings and photographs, while string lights create a dreamy ambiance. A pile of vintage clothes sits in one corner, waiting to be sorted through. Soft, romantic touches intermingled with bold, free-spirited elements and I'd bet money just about everything is vintage, thrifted, or antique. She could never drive by a second-hand store because 'what if something that spoke to her soul was there and she missed it'? I can see now that each item has a home in her space, and it all works together and somehow equals her.

I push aside the patchwork quilt covering me. My feet sink into the softness of the shag rug beneath me as I make my way toward the bathroom, using the walls for support.

'Morning!' her sweet voice greets me before I see her.

All I can do is grumble something incoherent as I enter her bathroom, which is just as eclectic as her bedroom. The sink is an old-fashioned pedestal style, adorned with baskets of make-up, hair products, and antique bottles filled with various bath salts and oils. The shower curtain is a bold paisley print, adding contrast to the otherwise soft and romantic space.

'Thank you for not listening outside the bathroom door this morning,' I say, making my way into the kitchen and sitting down at her tiny kitchen table.

Eve chuckles a melodic sound that fills the cozy kitchen. She places a steaming cup of coffee in front of me, the aroma instantly invigorating my senses.

'You only need to tell me once,' she replies, her tone laced with playful sarcasm. Her smile is infectious, and I can't help but feel a warmth spreading through me despite the throbbing headache. 'It took me a few to remember how you like your coffee, but I think I got it? Heavy on the cream and sugar, aggressively stirred.'

I laugh at her 'recollection'. I take a sip of the strong, rich brew, feeling its comforting heat soothe my insides.

'It's perfect. Just like—'

'Don't finish that sentence,' she says, shaking a wooden spoon at me.

'Right,' I say shamefully. 'I almost forgot – no flirting,' I repeat her rule as I glance around the kitchen. This is the first morning where I've felt alive enough to leave her room. Her apartment isn't exactly as it was the last time I saw it, but some things are. Like the mismatched mugs hanging from hooks above the sink, each telling a story. The shelves are packed with cookbooks, spices, and quirky vintage kitchenware – those were all there before.

'So.' She sits at the chair across from me. 'I figured after breakfast you and I would go on a walk around the third floor to get your blood pumping.'

I groan, but nod because I know it's going to happen.

'Movement is the key to healing,' she says, frowning at my lack of enthusiasm.

'You medical folk are dedicated to your talking points. When do I get to rest?'

'When you're dead,' she says with a grin. 'Seriously, Fost, exercise will help reduce your pain, increase your range of motion, and enhance your overall mobility. If you want to get back to that bike, you better get on board.'

I scrunch my face, running my one good hand over it. 'You gotta bring my bike into this? I'm trying not to think about her.'

'Her?' She laughs, sipping from her pastel purple pottery turned coffee mug, the letter E front and center.

I sigh, slightly embarrassed to have to explain this to her for the second time. The first being when she and my bike first met. 'You know I consider her sexy as fuck, only trumped by one other girl.'

This gets a full-out laugh from her. 'If you had to rate us both...?'

'No,' I cut her off. 'I will never answer that question. At least not right this second. It's too soon.'

'Too soon for what?' she asks, her tone interested, to say the least.

I shake my head, and motion to zipping my lips and tossing the key.

'OK, OK,' she says, standing from the table as she rolls her eyes playfully. 'No more questions about your other girlfriends. Are you hungry?'

'Famished,' I admit.

'Perfect, because I've been up for two hours and figured I'd make breakfast.'

'You made breakfast?'

She nods, pulling a plate from the oven and setting it in front of me.

'I did. French toast with fresh blueberry compote, complete with butter and powdered sugar. Orange juice, low pulp. And bacon, extra crispy.' She grabs a slice of bacon from my plate and munches on it, before setting it before me and meandering to the coffee maker and filling another mug.

'Aren't you going to eat with me?'

'I ate while I cooked. It's my bad habit. But I figured we could catch up after you eat, on our walk.'

Our walk. I'd nearly forgotten after she mentioned my bike. Without waiting, I try her French toast and drop my head back in shock. 'Sweet baby Jesus. Why aren't you the head chef at that hospital?'

Eve's grin widens at my reaction to her French toast, a glint of pride in her eyes.

'If they served great food, nobody would ever want to leave,' she says.

'There are plenty of worse things about that hospital than the food,' I say, taking another bite of her delicious French toast, savoring the sweet flavors that dance on my tongue. The blueberry compote is the perfect balance of tart and sweet. I'm beginning to think perhaps Eve is good at everything she does. 'A lack of clothing for the patient, for starters. No one asks, they just look at everything. Intubation tubes. Needles. ORs. And morphine-laced thoughts.' With each thing I list she nods in agreement, until the last one where she lifts a single finger into the air as if having an epiphany of some sort.

'I am a pro at translating morphine-laced thoughts. It's part of what I get paid for.' She settles in her chair, sipping her coffee as she watches me pretty much devour the breakfast in possibly record time.

'Ready?' she asks, the moment my fork settles on my plate.

'Shouldn't we wait thirty minutes to prevent cramps?'

She laughs. 'Wives' tale...'

'Really?'

'Scientifically, it's completely unfounded, so yeah. Now come on, you don't want to lose your uh – firmness?' she asks, looking horrified that she's said it as she touches my bicep.

I stand, wiping my mouth with the napkin I had on my lap. 'If you're going to spend our walk complimenting me like that, I'm in. Please, keep a tight grip on my firmness,' I say, patting her hand wrapped around my good arm.

'If Phil gets wind of this conversation, we'll never hear the end of it...' she says, leading me out of her apartment and into the hallway.

Four apartments, two facing two, are on either side of the out-of-service elevator, creating a big square for me to do laps around. Perfect, a built-in gym I didn't expect. Not that I hate the gym, I'm there often. What I hate is how lazy this morphine makes me. *Let me sleep the pain away, please.* But no, she's right. Movement is key.

'So,' she says. 'Pretending the last ten seconds never happened, let's start over. How've you been?'

'We're doing the "hi, how are you" routine?'

'Why not,' she asks, innocently looking up at me. 'We haven't really even spoken about it yet and it's been weeks.'

She's got me there.

'All right then, well, there's not much new with me that you haven't probably already googled or witnessed.' I look at her questioningly, knowing full well she has done exactly that. She probably knows more about me than I do at this point.

Pink fills her cheeks, and her stride speeds, causing me to have to pull her back a bit.

'My bruised spine and broken ribs request a soft stroll, not a speed walk.'

She smiles through the blushing and slows her step.

'How about we start with you. How are you feeling with me in your apartment unexpectedly?'

The sigh she exhales says she's not sure.

'Confused,' she says.

'About what?'

Her head snaps my way and her look says, 'Have you lost your mind?'

'You. Me. Us. Everything. The past. The present. And the future.'

'You're confused about all that?'

'And then some.' She shakes her head, glancing around the hall as if looking for her thoughts. 'I may have even possibly fallen asleep while scrolling your Instagram last night. But it was unintentional – the Red Bull account is what led me down that hole.'

'Really? Find anything good?'

Why do I like the idea of this?

'Or should I ask, see anything you like?' I joke, winking at her flirtatiously.

Eve rolls her eyes, a playful smile dancing on her lips as she meets my teasing gaze.

'No flirting,' she quips.

'*In* your apartment – your words. Technically, we're outside of it so flirting is allowed.'

'You've made sub-rules to my one rule?'

I nod. 'Morphine thoughts.'

'Fine,' she laughs. 'Get it all out while you can. I'll probably regret this, but flirt away.'

Excitement bubbles within me, overpowering the pain I'm feeling on this walk. 'If I could rub my hands together with anticipation right now, I would. Your breakfast was to die for, thank you.'

'Flirting with manners – nice.'

'Don't get too hopeful,' I say. 'I'm just getting started. Are you aware that you've gotten prettier since I saw you last?'

'Maybe chronically tired is my look?'

'*Something* is doing it for you. You're a damn smoke show and I won't be surprised when I get caught ogling you as you clean one day.'

'You're ogling me behind my back?'

'I am,' I admit with a wide smile.

'And you're proud of it,' she says, leading me along the hall. 'OK then, well, I hope you get a good look because you'll have to stop once caught – those are the rules.'

'Fair enough,' I say, admiring her for a few steps. 'Seriously, Jellybean, I've missed you. I always knew, but being with you in person, that's really driving it home here,' I say, touching my chest. 'And also, here.' I point to my head, stopping her in her tracks.

'What do you mean?'

'Medication-laced dreams help our past echo through my subconscious while I sleep. Every moment my eyes are closed, I'm dreaming of us.'

For a moment she stares at me with hope in her eyes, and a silent conversation happening that her face can't hide. Her brows furrow and she shakes her head. 'Foster, there is no "us" any more.'

Ouch. The morphine isn't strong enough for that sort of rejection.

'I think I'm ready for bed again.'

'OK,' she says, guiding me back towards her door.

We don't speak – because I made it weird by allowing morphine to choose my words. But she deserves to hear what I'm really thinking, doesn't she? I mean the woman is voluntarily nursing me back to health. Which I will make right when this is over. But now that my head is somewhat clear, I'm realizing that what I lost five years ago was so much more than I've allowed myself to remember up to now. I can't pretend it's not.

'I'm having them too,' she says almost under her breath as she hands me the cup containing my meds.

My hand is partially around hers for the shot glass exchange when she says it, and with her words, I hold it there.

'You're having what?'

'Dreams. Flashbacks. About us.'

'Really?' I ask, taking the cup as she pushes it into my palm.

She stands from the bed, handing me a bottle of water from a little snack and drink area she's made on her dresser top. Staying with her is more like a five-star hotel than a hospital. I guess now I see why. She's dreaming of me.

'Yes. And I didn't want to mention it because I thought it would be weird.'

'Is it?' I ask at her pause.

She shrugs, suddenly twisting a ring on her thumb. 'I don't know. I really don't know.'

I lift the glass and swallow my pills, chasing them with half the bottle of water. 'Then let's not decide what it is right now. We've got time.'

'Yeah. Time we have.'

'Now give me a goodnight kiss,' I tease to lift the mood and with a soft laugh from her, it does.

'We're going on a five-minute speed walk after this nap, so mentally prepare while you dream of me.'

I hold my ribs as I laugh. I swear, just the motion of taking the pain meds and muscle relaxers activate something in my brain to make me tipsy the moment I swallow them down.

'Don't hurt me, pretty lady,' I say as she walks out, shaking her head. She likes it. I'm pretty sure she likes it. Time to let myself wander back into the depths of my heart to relive some moment, and hope it doesn't shatter as quickly as it did today with the words 'there is no us' the next time I open my eyes again.

18

EVE CASSIDY

Foster's brow is furrowed in confusion, his gaze fixed on me as I sit on the floor in front of the toilet. He just woke up from his morning nap.

'You're doing what again?' he asks, staring at me from my bed.

'I'm installing a bidet because I'd really rather not wipe your butt for you.'

He lets out what seems to be a sigh of relief, slapping his forehead with his good hand. 'My God you're smart.'

'The smartest,' I tease, working like a home repair man, pretending I know what I'm doing; but truth is, I'm relying heavily on these overly simplified, yet confusing, instructions.

A sharp, sudden knock on my front door startles me out of my concentration. I halt mid-thought, straining my ears to confirm if it was a real sound or just my mind playing tricks on me. I haven't slept much lately and when I do, it's constant memories of the 'us' I no longer want to be a part of.

The noise of urgent, persistent pounding reverberates through the door, growing louder and more frantic with each strike. It's as though the person on the other side is in a hurry, desperate for someone to respond.

'I think the fuzz is here,' Foster says.

'Then they're here for you because I am a law-abiding citizen,' I state confidently. 'I've never even been pulled over,' I add as I rise from the floor.

'Never? Not even a warning?'

'Not even a warning,' I say proudly, now making my way toward the front door.

'Wow, super-citizen!'

I laugh. 'What color should my cape be?' I ask, pulling open the door. Jess is pushing in. 'I knew you were home,' she says, like me being here is some kind of secret.

'Of course I'm here, I live here.'

'You should be at work.'

'Can a workaholic woman never take a day off?' I ask, confused why she's broken her doctor's orders for this.

'I know you, Eve. You don't take days off.'

I huff, offended she thinks she knows me better than I know myself. Did I intentionally lie to her and Kait and tell them that I helped Foster board a plane home days ago? Yes. Mostly because I wanted to avoid Jess 'nesting' and over-parenting me in anticipation of motherhood.

'I have too, taken a day off. Once. For a gynecology appointment. And at one time I'd scheduled an entire two weeks off for a post-engagement vacay. I lost money on that.'

'Aruba,' Jess says with a sigh. 'I was so jealous. It would have been the most romantic engagement holiday.'

'Yes,' I say flatly. 'Please remind me of more... You're supposed to be home on bed rest! You can't go into labor in my apartment because it will make a total mess, and I am not prepared for another medical emergency.' I step in front of her, blocking my bedroom door.

She stops, crossing her arms over her enormous belly and shooting me daggers. 'I want to see it with my own two eyes,' she says, glancing at the couch and then frowning. She takes a few steps and peers into my room, turning immediately to look at me with disappointment.

'He's in your bed?'

'Look at him,' I motion, watching him give her his best pouty face. 'How could I make a guy this injured sleep on a fifty-year-old couch?'

'By remembering how it felt when he love bombed you, married you, moved you across the country to be his housewife, then went right back to his career and left you behind?'

'I didn't love bomb her,' Foster says, defending himself. 'I loved her, it just—'

'—wasn't enough,' I finish his sentence but the way he scrunches his face says he might not agree.

Jess narrows her eyes at him. 'You are a heartbreaking asshole.'

I shoot her a warning look before turning to Foster. 'Ignore her. She's hormonal and protective because she's due any day now. It also seems that she's forgotten I'm a full-grown adult who does not need the supervision or approval of my big sister.'

Jess frowns, moving her hands to her hips. 'You don't want my approval?'

'I'd like it, but if it's not possible, it's not going to sway me from making my own decisions.'

'What kind of decisions?'

'The hypothetical kind...'

She looks between us. 'There's been no romance here? No stolen kisses? No "I miss yous" or "what ifs"?'

Foster's and my gaze meet and I immediately know what he's thinking. *Keep it to yourself.* If there's anything I know, it's that getting family 'overly involved' can be bad too. We can only protect our own hearts.

'I'd say the romance weather meter is reading in the negatives nowadays,' Foster says.

Not a word of that was a lie. No mention of the 'miss you' conversation. You can't explain what you don't understand yourself.

Jess cocks her head, her dark hair pulled into a messy bun.

'I suppose I can respect that. You've grown a lot over the last few years, Eve. I just worry, ya know?' Her tone softens and of course I forgive her – she's my sister.

'Totally understand. But fret not, dear sister, Mr Foster here is only a temporary presence until he's healed enough to get back to his first love, his motorcycle.'

'That's probably best because with me getting ready to deliver a baby, I'm not going to have time to drag you out of a heart-shattering, earth-moving personal crisis like last time.'

Without even thinking about it, Foster and I glance at each other. He looks confused, clearing his throat awkwardly. 'Heart-shattering? Earth-moving?' he repeats.

Why would she go and say that?! Never once have I muttered the words 'you broke my heart' to this man. He didn't deserve to know what he did to me, at least not in my head at the time. Now she's let them loose and even with medication clouding his head, he's heard them, and nearly choked on them.

Finally my insides settle like confetti, allowing me to speak. 'Listen, Foster and I aren't reliving the past. Are there things we probably need to talk about? Absolutely. Am I interested in doing it right now? Not even a little bit. We're going to keep that mess on the back burner and focus on becoming friends again while he allows me to nurse him back to health from a horrific injury. He's my patient, not my lover.'

'And that is not a Prince song,' he says, making me laugh.

Jess cracks a smile, shaking her head and motioning two fingers between her eyes and Foster. 'I'm watching you, pretty boy. You won't break her twice.'

'Not even a thought in my mind. Currently I'm trying to figure out how to repay her for what she's doing. How many zeros do you think it'll take?'

There is no way I'm allowing him to pay me for this, and if he knows me at all, he knows that. But he's making himself the bad guy for my sake so Jess can calm her hormonal ass down.

'At least five,' she says, nodding my way.

'Five zeros it is,' he says.

'I'm done,' I say, tossing the bidet directions onto the bathroom floor. 'Bidet installed,' I announce, standing and giving it a test – pushing the different buttons and seeing what this thing can do. 'Want to try it out?' I ask, knowing Jess will definitely have to pee, considering the baby is probably smashing her bladder.

She confirms the bidet works just as intended but it takes a snack and a small rest on my couch, watching the latest episode of *Love is Blind*, before she decides to go home and follow the doctor's orders.

'How about another walk?' I ask, approaching Foster who's now sitting on the side of my bed.

'Only if you promise to touch my firmness again,' he jokes.

I smirk. 'How could I say no?'

19

GUY 'FOSTER'

My phone rings loudly, pulling me out of my sleep. I fumble around blindly, searching for it under my pillow until I finally find it.

'Hello?' I croak, my voice rough from just waking up. The daylight streaming through the window tells me I've been out for a while. How long did I sleep? All the walking – er, healing (Eve's words) is wearing me out. I don't even remember going to bed last night.

Matty's familiar voice comes through the phone, easing my mind. 'How ya doin', bud?'

'Oh, you know, just living the life as I'm glued to my ex's bed while she waits on me hand and foot.'

'I hope you're a better actor than rider if you expect her to believe you don't secretly love every moment of being there.' He bellows a laugh into the phone.

'That is our secret,' I remind him. 'Also, one wreck doesn't make me a bad rider.'

'I suppose you're right. Well, I worried this might blow up at first but it's been five days at her place and you're still alive; that's a good sign.'

'That's because our conversations have been surface level at best. And she has a "no flirting in the apartment" rule which stifles my usual ways.'

'Probably for the best.'

'She's definitely playing it safe.'

'As should you, considering your physical condition. Do you feel like you're healing?'

'Yeah. My ribs still hurt with a lot of movement but we're getting somewhere, I think. She's got me walking miles around the building multiple times a day – I think that's doing the most.'

'Good, good, so you're in good hands with Eve. I'm glad.'

'I am in gorgeous hands and since her rule is "no flirting *in* the apartment", that's motivation for leaving it and allowing her to guide me on walks with her hand in the crook of my good arm, like old times when we'd flutter around the city together.'

'You're reliving old times via flirtatious conversations in the hall? Interesting. Have you broken out the news that y'all are still married?'

I choke on absolutely nothing.

'No,' I finally reply. 'Timing hasn't been right for that.'

He chuckles lightly. 'I bet not.'

The thought of telling Eve those words feels like gazing into an abyss, knowing that once I fall into the truth, there may be no coming back. No rescue. No salvation. I'll possibly lose this woman forever. It's a bottomless pit of anguish, the kind that breaks you from the inside out and leaves you hollow for the rest of your days. And I did it on purpose – refused to sign the divorce papers, that is. The last thing I wanted was to lose her, but after she left me so coldly, the immature side of me sort of wanted to pay her back for that, so I ran the divorce papers through my shredder. When I never received anything from her or her lawyer again, I assumed it was done. However, Matty asked about it last year, and when I admitted what I'd done, his wife did some research. They had me over for dinner one night just to announce that Eve and I were still married – for four years at that point. How that happened, I've no idea, but at some point, Eve deserves to know.

'You need anything?' Matty asks.

'I'm glad you asked,' I say, glancing down at the ridiculous neon leggings on my bottom half. 'Yes, I do. I'm currently wearing Eve's very gay neighbor Phil's wardrobe which today consists of pink leggings, and a shirt that has Ryan Gosling's face on it with the words "Hey, girl".' This gets a big hearty laugh out of him.

'Yeah, it's hilarious. Please, please tell me you can bring my shit?'

'Only if you send me a photo so I can prove to the guys you're still alive – in the leggings and Gosling shirt.'

I groan into the phone. 'Seriously?'

'What's a trip across the country worth to you?' he teases.

With that, I tap into the camera app, turn the screen and snap a selfie of myself, texting it through to him without inspecting it.

He bellows a laugh, far too amused by my appearance.

'You know, anyone else might be offended by this,' I say when the laughing has gone on way too long.

'It's funny,' he says. 'Your fans are going to love it.'

'My *what*?'

'And post,' he says, laughing to himself.

'Post where?'

'On the insta thing,' he says.

'Matty! Damn it. That wasn't a photo I wanted getting out.'

'Sorry. Anyway, we've sealed the deal and I'm booking my plane ticket now. What do you want?'

'Grab me everything out of my top two dresser drawers.'

'Top two dresser drawers.' He repeats my words. 'I'm jotting this down. What else?'

'My pillow?'

'Pillow. Anything else? Want a couple trophies to make the place feel like home?'

He's kidding, but I'm game. 'Sure, throw 'em in. It'll be fun to see Eve's reaction to that. Ohhh, you know what else she might like? Top of my closet, right by the door, is a blue shoebox, taped to the hilt like it's a Dybbuk box holding in a demon, and on the top are the words "Never Open". Bring it.'

'Is this box going to get me strip-searched at the airport, Fost?'

'No, it's just… sentimental,' I reply. 'Her sister isn't thrilled I'm here and said I love bombed Eve when we met, insinuating that I didn't actually love her, and this box will prove I did.'

'Do,' he corrects me.

'The jury is still out on that. Just grab the box, please?'

This box – despite the fact that it looks like a bomb – holds pieces of my heart by way of tokens of Eve's and my shared adventures and whispered promises. I have a feeling she too wonders if what we had was actually love, and I want – no, I need – to prove that it was.

'I'll get the box,' Matty says. 'Don't tell me you're attempting to woo this woman again?'

'Maybe I am,' I say. 'Whether I can magically sweep this woman off her feet for a second time or not, we at least deserve some closure from our time before.'

'I have a feeling if you fuck up twice, it's *over* over. You ready for that?'

'I wasn't ready the first time. But I think reminding her of who I am – who we were – might help. Don't you think?'

'I suppose so,' he says suspiciously. 'Alright, then. Ticket booked, I'll be there in a couple of days, bud.'

'Thanks, Matty.'

We exchange goodbyes, and I'm left staring at the ceiling. If dreaming about each other during this serendipitous coming together is all this is meant to be between Eve and me, then the box Matty's bringing will have no impact on us.

* * *

'Pardon me, sir,' Eve says with an accent I can't quite place – Australian, English, Irish, Pirate? Somewhere in that zone.

'Yeah?' I say without opening my eyes.

Morphine is good, y'all. Why I need it sucks, and I'll stop when I no longer do, but I can see why it's become a problem for humanity. (*Don't do drugs, kids.*)

'I'm almost ready to serve dinner,' Eve says in her terrible accent. 'Would you like it here or in the dining room?' She motions toward her tiny kitchen.

A small round wooden dining table and two chairs in different styles and colors sit across from each other against the wall. It's barely big enough for two microwave dinners.

'Um—'

In an instant, her demeanor changes, and she reverts to her usual American self.

'Also, a gentle reminder from Nurse Eve: you were doing really well at my coaching so I didn't want to ride you about it, but I haven't seen you up moving at all this afternoon.'

I chuckle softly, unable to hide my amusement. 'I did sleep away a lot of the day, didn't I?'

'You did.'

'Also, how many different personalities will I be encountering tonight, Miss Cassidy?'

Her broad smile is parenthesized by a charming dimple on the left cheek, which never fails to capture my attention. Her happiness is genuine, and she is enjoying herself immensely this evening. I bet Phil brought wine again.

'You have control of that remote,' she says.

'Yikes. That's a lot of pressure.'

'I wish you all the luck. Anyhow... do you feel like taking the adventurous route and hiking your injured butt to the kitchen, or would you rather watch your friends on TV and have a cozy dinner in bed?' British Eve is back with her witty and playful tone.

Yes, I've been watching the tour I'm supposed to be on, via the Red Bull channel. Jeff is coming in first in every single one, and each one irritates me a little more. Time to click this off.

'I'll take option one, please,' I say, matching her energy because I know I'll ruin her night if I don't. She's really trying here, and the least I can do is not be 'grumpy-in-pain' guy or 'talk-about-the-past-and-confess-my sins' guy.

She extends a hand my way to help me out of her bed. 'Slowly,' she reminds me, pulling me into the sitting position, her warm hand resting on my shoulder, providing a comforting support. This part – really every part – is getting easier but if she wants to help, I'm not going to say no. I like her.

'Whenever you feel ready to stand up, use your knees and lean on me for balance,' she advises.

'I never expected you to treat me like—'

'A friend?' She finishes my sentence as I get to my feet. Her hands are lying gently on each bicep and her gaze is on me.

I nod. I was going to say 'a boyfriend', because that's really all I know around her, but she capped that.

'I guess I expected you to be a little… rougher.' I laugh, even saying the words.

She smirks. 'If you act up, I plan on whacking you with this cane. Maybe that's what you're feeling?'

'Maybe it is.'

She keeps a hand on my shoulder as she balances me. 'You good?'

'I'm good,' I say, reaching out to take my cane from her, even though I don't really need it any more. She was right, walking even short distances a few times a day has me much steadier on my feet than I was. But I also like her fawning over me, so the help is nice. I gesture for her to proceed, and she walks to the stove.

As I follow, the aroma of something delicious fills my nostrils, and I can hear the sizzling sound coming from a pan in the oven. She cooked again?

'Have you always been this good of a cook?' I ask, not remembering more than scrambled eggs and toast in our past.

Eve gazes at me, bewildered, as if my question has taken her aback. 'I, uh—took some cooking classes with someone a couple of years ago and caught the bug.' The topic of this mysterious 'someone' has her suddenly shy.

'That's good for me, then. Given that I'm usually on the road, the most convenient option is drive-throughs,' I explain. 'I live on fast food or free food at events.'

'Yum,' she says with a grimace, setting the plates on the table. She takes the bright blue chair, leaving me with the magenta one. 'This is way better than fast food. I had to do some digging for this recipe, and you just got lucky enough to end up here on one of the two nights a month I make it.'

'What is it?'

'Escargots,' she says with a sweet smile. She eagerly pierces one with her fork. Her expression turns to pure delight as she chews.

'You're a little grosser than I remember.'

She nearly snorts laughter.

'Seriously? Snails?' I ask, poking my fork around my plate. No way she's not messing with me.

'It's a very popular food,' she says. 'You'd know that if you didn't eat at Burger King every day of your life.'

'I prefer McDonald's.'

She rolls her eyes playfully.

'Fine, fine,' she chuckles. 'Stick to your fast food, Mr Gourmet.' She dabs at the corners of her mouth with a cloth napkin, her eyes sparkling with mischief as she reaches for her nearly empty wine glass. 'But you're missing out on a whole world of flavors.' She stabs at another 'snail' delicately. 'Try it, just this once. For me?' Her expression is pleading, her lips quirked in an endearing grin.

I sigh dramatically, feigning reluctance as I pick up my fork and reluctantly poke at one of the snail shapes. As I lift it to my mouth, she watches intently, a mix of amusement and anticipation in her gaze. With a deep breath, I close my eyes and take a bite.

This little liar. The cheese-filled tortellini explodes on my tongue, surprising me with its richness and complexity. Opening my eyes, I meet hers, now gleaming with triumph.

'Well?' she asks eagerly, almost unable to hold back her laughter.

Our gazes meet and if that smile didn't melt my heart, I could probably find words to say that are more flattering than 'Wow, it's familiar and amazing. You make this twice a month?'

The night we spontaneously got married, we wandered into a tiny Italian restaurant where the server convinced us to make us a special 'wedding night' meal. This was that meal. Is that why she still makes it? I mean, she did say she had to dig for the recipe; that's something, isn't it?

'This is the first time I've made it. I had to email the guy who owns that restaurant for the recipe. I thought it might be fun to relive something while we're both awake, and food seemed safe.'

She wants to relive something while not dreaming? I set my fork on my plate and rub my chest.

'Are you alright?' she asks, suddenly concerned, reaching out to touch my shoulder.

'I'm fine, just been experiencing some unexpected stabbing pain lately,' I explain. No way can I tell her – yet – that those pains are in my heart.

Regret is painful. Like physically so. I know for a fact there is nothing wrong with my heart as it's recently been inspected – but it hurts. I took her for granted and failed to show her the appreciation she deserved, and in the five years we've been apart, I've tried absolutely nothing to get her back, yet here I sit in her kitchen, eating a meal she cooked for me willingly, that reminds us both of a memory she's probably tried to forget.

'I'm glad it's not snails. Honestly, I think you made it better than the original.'

'Really?'

'Yeah.'

She smiles sweetly. 'I guess you weren't all I fell in love with that night.'

I stare at her, stunned by her words. This is the first time she's mentioned loving me. 'Are you flirting with me, Jellybean? In the apartment?'

She laughs, shaking her head and turning her attention back to her meal. 'No. Just allowing myself to remember something I'd previously forced myself to forget, that's all.'

'Did you really forget me? Us?'

'I tried,' she says with a shrug. 'But it never really worked. Once a year Facebook would remind me, and I'd spend the next three hundred and sixty-five days attempting to block it from my mind, but truthfully' – she looks up from her plate at me – 'and I promised myself I'd never say this out loud – but my heart would never let it go.'

'"It" as in me?'

She nods, tucking her hair behind her ear nervously, a hint of vulnerability crossing her features. 'Yes, you. Us. Everything we had and everything we lost. It's funny how memories never truly fade, isn't it? They linger in the corners of our minds, waiting for a moment of weakness to resurface.'

'To be fair, you should know you're not the only one who tried to bury those memories away.'

Her eyes reflect a mix of emotions – nostalgia, regret, and a hint of longing. 'I thought time would make it easier, that distance would fade the memories, but then you were wheeled into my trauma room and I realized some connections are just too strong to sever,' she murmurs.

I reach out and cover her hand with mine, the touch familiar yet tinged with the weight of unspoken words. 'I tried but never could forget either,' I admit quietly, feeling the heaviness of our shared past hanging between us like a veil.

She squeezes my hand, a silent acknowledgment passing between us – just like when I was in the hospital.

She pulls her hand from mine gently. 'This seems like a slippery slope...'

I nod. 'A little bit.'

The mood shifts, and I can almost feel her anxiety as she pokes at her nearly empty plate. 'I'll just start the dishwasher while you finish up and then we'll go for a walk,' she says, suddenly fluttering around the kitchen. The sound of running water from the sink fills the air as she starts to rinse the dishes and fill the dishwasher.

20

EVE CASSIDY

'Tonight, we have to change that shoulder and wrist bandage, which means you get to take a shower without half of your body taped inside a garbage bag,' I inform him, tossing the dishtowel over my shoulder and leaning against my counter. 'What a time to be alive, eh?'

He laughs. 'Yeah. Hashtag, blessed.'

'Hashtag, dork,' I tease.

'Hey, since it's shower night, and since I've been doing pretty good with my walking, why don't we go outside? You live on the riverfront, which is designed for exercise. Maybe I could break a sweat? It's been weeks since I did anything physical and I'm starting to feel absolutely ick. I want that shower after a good sweat feeling. Plus, look at that...' He nods at the windows overlooking the river below us. 'I haven't seen a good sunset in ages.'

He doesn't even need to use the 'please can we go for a walk' puppy dog eyes he's currently wearing. That face alone could get me to say yes to a lot of things I'd regret right now. Walking with him outside is easy.

'I'd be a terrible nurse if I said no to this.'

'You would,' he agrees.

'And a good sunset is enticing. I'd actually forgotten that about you,' I say, thinking back to the time when he told me he breaks for sunsets. He's got charm, that's for sure.

He looks confused.

'That you love sunsets. Sure, let's walk outside tonight.'

We step into the cool, early fall evening air wrapping around us like a comforting embrace. The sky is painted in hues of pink and orange as the sun dips below the horizon in a brilliant display of nature's beauty. Foster walks beside me, coming to a stop at the riverside railing along the paved sidewalk across the street from my building entrance. I walk this street daily in my normal life, and not once did I expect to be walking it with him again.

'Isn't it incredible how something as simple as a sunset can make you forget all your worries?' Foster muses, his voice soft in the fading light.

'We are just a drop in the bucket of life, for sure.'

He continues walking beside me, without his cane, his good hand on the railing for balance and he's making pretty good time. His breathing rate is up a bit, but his skin is suddenly glowing in the fading daylight. Never in all the time we spent together did I watch this man lie around his apartment like a slug. This has got to be hard for him. Not only is he hurt but his whole world just got flipped upside down.

I steal glances at him as we walk, his profile sharp against the vibrant sky. He catches me once, flashing me a cute smile that crinkles the corners of his eyes and within them, there's a flicker of something I've seen before, a vulnerability that he usually keeps hidden beneath his confident facade.

'Are you ogling me?' he asks, nudging me gently with his slinged elbow.

'I am. I installed a bidet for you and gave up my bed. I've got to get something in return,' I joke.

'Oh!' he laughs. 'Flirting while we're off property hard. I'm game. Fancy meeting a gorgeous girl like you down by the river. Come here often?' he asks, his voice low, twinged with a southern accent and flirty.

'Truthfully, I came down here a lot after we broke up when I needed to clear my head,' I murmur. 'The way you always "stopped for sunsets" made me think maybe they could help me too.'

'I thought you'd forgotten that part of me?'

I cock my head. 'Well, eventually I'd forced myself to bury everything "you" deep on "Please Forget Island" – also known as my heart – but you know how that goes.'

He frowns but then walks around me and sneakily grasps my hand in his, holding it to his chest as we walk.

'Did they help?'

Holding hands feels like tiptoeing into the flirtatious deep end. I'm not sure we're ready or have thought it through, but having his hand wrapped around mine brings me some kind of comfort I've missed.

'They did.'

'Tell me why?' he asks, stopping and turning to face the sunset. He drops our hands to our sides, his thumb stroking the back of mine.

'Watching the sun bid farewell to another day is peaceful. Whether it was the best or worst day you've ever had, you'll never repeat it. Ever. And that made me realize that no matter what happens, life goes on.'

Foster nods thoughtfully, his gaze never leaving the sky. As the last remnants of daylight fade away, he turns to me with a small smile playing on his lips.

'Do you want to hear how smart I think you are, or something ridiculously marshmallowy and over-the-top flirtatious?'

'I'll take marshmallows, please.'

He looks shocked.

'They always made me smile.'

'I remember,' he says. 'Good. Here goes: I always thought of you as my sunset. That's part of why I fell in love with them the way I have.' He squeezes my hand gently in his.

'That was so cheesy,' I say with a laugh.

'It was.'

'Really, though?'

He nods. 'One thousand per cent, Evie. Sunsets are breathtakingly beautiful and sadly fleeting, but each one leaves a lasting impression on me – just like you.'

My heart skips a beat at his words, causing me to let out a gasp as a rush of emotions floods through me. This is why I face-planted into a dirt racetrack for this man. Because he's sweet, and goofy, and charming, and handsome, and so many adjectives that I could go on for days. Most importantly though, he is beautiful inside and out, and so many people have only ever been interested in the out.

'I think sometimes sunsets help you see someone in a new light too,' I say, noticing the colors of dusk painting Foster's background in a dreamlike haze. Why didn't I get this guy for the last five years like I was supposed to?

'Do you ever wonder if maybe we were always meant to find our way back to each other?' Foster muses. 'Like two ships passing in the night, destined to collide again and again because fate decided a long time ago they were meant to be.'

I heave a sigh at the thought of fate. It hasn't done me any favors. But what if he's right and I just haven't seen them yet?

'Maybe we needed to lose ourselves before we could truly find each other?'

Foster's smile widens, a glimmer of hope and love shining in his eyes. 'Maybe. Of course, I didn't expect losing myself nearly meant *death*.'

'Neither did I,' I chuckle. 'Look at you now though, without even realizing it, we've walked six blocks and you haven't groaned even once. That's huge progress!'

He turns, his face scrunching like he's trying to see something a mile away. 'Six blocks, huh?'

'What's wrong?'

'We've got six blocks back and I'm ready for a nap *now*.'

He's tired. And here I thought he was doing so well. 'And a nap you will get as soon as we get back, after we change those shoulder and wrist bandages, and after you get that deep cleansing shower you wanted.'

'Oooh, the shower. Race ya back?' he asks, pretending to take off in a sprint but not getting very far in the skip, hop, walk he's doing.

It takes us a bit longer to get back to my building than it did to walk six blocks and by the time we're climbing the stairs, Foster is moving much more slowly.

'What did you get?' he asks, looking at the package in my hand that I grabbed from my mailbox on our way through the lobby.

'You're going to love it,' I say as I unlock my door and push it open, allowing him through first. He beelines right for my couch and drops onto it with a moan it sounds like he's been holding in all night.

I open the box and display the two purple- and green-colored containers. 'These are pill organizers. You take meds so often that I had to buy two. In the coming days, I'm going to have to go back to work and I thought if we get started with these now, then while I'm gone you won't forget when your meds are due.'

'You need a nursing award,' he says. 'The fact that I need a pill organizer makes me feel a tad elderly.'

'Considering you're nearly scientifically middle-aged, I'm not surprised. Did you know that the average death rate in America is in your seventies?'

He bellows a laugh. 'Mid-thirties are now middle-aged?'

'Double thirty-five, and you've got seventy. You think with your career, you'll live past that?'

'Yes,' he insists. 'I'm not even the oldest in the industry, Evie. Jeff's in his forties.'

One by one I separate his bottles of pills into the organizers while we talk.

'I've watched Jeff slam energy drinks like a chain-smoker, before and after performances, so I won't be surprised when his heart explodes on the track at age forty-five,' I remind him.

'He is playing a dangerous game,' Foster remarks, shaking his head as if he doesn't do the same thing. It's hard not to, considering Red Bull and Monster are some of the biggest advertisers of the sport.

'I'm going to focus more on not dying sooner than average. No more accidents, and I definitely gotta quit the energy drink slamming.'

I laugh. 'I'll cross my fingers for you. Now let's take a look at that arm.'

Once I get the sling off, his shirt delicately peeled over his head and the bandages removed, I have to grab us both water. He's sweating, and I'm just remembering how incredibly beautiful he is shirtless. I have to force myself not to kiss his glistening chest because my mind was telling me to go there.

I force him into the shower, insisting he keep the shower chair in with him, mostly because my knees were weak at the sight of him partly unclothed and maybe his are too? That's stupid. I divert my eyes as he walks out of the bathroom, in a pair of lovely black and white checked yoga pants that really accentuate his ass, much to my demise.

'How's it look, doc?' he asks once he's back on my bed.

I down half a bottle of water while unintentionally staring at him. My eyes just won't look away!

Do not jump his bones, Eve. He's injured. What if you hurt him worse by crawling on top of him to seduce the guy?

'Evie?'

'Yeah?' I ask between sips, then remember he asked how it looks. 'Looks really, really good.'

He laughs under his breath. 'You're daydreaming about that sponge bath I asked about right now, aren't you?'

'No...' I lie. 'I'm thinking my shower will be cold later because I'm having a hot flash.'

He lifts a single eyebrow. 'Menopausal in your late twenties is rough.'

I groan, pretending it's completely plausible – which medically, it is. But there is no getting away from the fact that I'm overheating from my panties up.

'Fine, I'll admit it, there's no denial on my part that you're handsome and things. Obviously I'm attracted to you, I married you.'

'True,' he says. 'But "handsome and things"? What kind of "things"?'

I bite my lip, holding back a growing smile. *Don't answer that question.*

'No flirting, mister,' I say, grabbing the bin full of medical supplies the hospital sent home with us from the top of my dresser, and sitting at his side near his injured arm. 'Not within the apartment walls.'

'Fine,' he says, leaning his head back and closing his eyes as I clean the surgical sites and rebandage him. With him not looking, my gaze can go anywhere it wants and it pauses on his tattoos. His skin is sun-kissed, and soft enough to lick. *No, Eve. Do not lick him.*

'It's healing great,' I say, hoping words will distract my screaming libido.

'Good,' he says, glancing down at the freshly bandaged shoulder and wrist. 'You think maybe I could sleep without the straightjacket tonight? It's so uncomfortable.'

'Will you promise me you won't sleep wild like a tornado?' I ask, standing and placing the medical supplies back in their place.

'Sure, but I'm not sure my subconscious will pull through.'

'Don't worry,' I tell him. 'The morphine will. You pretty much sleep still all night, just a rustle of snoring is all I hear.'

'I snore?' he asks, as if he didn't know.

'Take these,' I say, handing him a handful of pills.

He swallows them down and relaxes into my bed. I'm sure he'd be more comfortable if I were in there next to him, but intrusive thoughts be damned.

'The sling off feels so much better. Thank you.'

'You're welcome. Goodnight, Fost,' I say, leaning down and flipping off the naughty boy lamp.

'Goodnight, Jellybean.'

I wonder what he'll relive tonight? I hope it's something good. The best part of us. And I don't even understand why the thought is crossing my mind at all.

21

EVE CASSIDY

Five Years Ago

'I can't believe we're doing this!' I exclaim.

'You can't fight love,' Foster says, his fingers interlaced with mine as he gives me a reassuring squeeze. His touch is warm and comforting, and I can feel his love coursing through his grasp. 'It's like trying to hold back an ocean with your bare hands.'

I glance up at him with a smile. 'You better write that down for your vows.'

'How can I help you two?' a mousy woman behind the court registrar counter asks. She's barely taller than the vase of white daisies sitting on the counter beside her.

'We're here for a marriage license,' Foster says.

'Congratulations!' she chirps happily, reaching into a file full of paperwork. 'Fill these out and we'll need a copy of each of your driver's licenses.'

The two of us fish our licenses out from our wallets and begin completing the documents she's given us.

'Where's the ceremony taking place?' she asks.

Foster's and my eyes meet.

'That's something we haven't thought of yet,' I say to him.

'I just proposed yesterday, on a whim.'

'Yesterday?' the woman asks.

He nods. 'We're sort of doing this spontaneously.'

'How romantic!' she says, suddenly lifting a single finger into the air. 'Give me just one second.' She turns, disappearing from the small office while we finish up our paperwork.

'How do you think your parents will feel?' I ask, signing my name on the bottom of the paper.

'That I'm nuts, but that's their usual opinion of me, so no surprise.'

I laugh, leaning into him and kissing his shoulder as he finishes his document. 'You're the best kind of nuts.'

'Save that for your vows,' he says, scribbling out his usual signature, minus the 'Famous 15' he usually adds on.

When the mousy woman reappears, she has a middle-aged man in a black robe with her. 'This is Judge Ashford. Today is his twenty-fifth wedding anniversary and he'd love to marry you two in his chambers,' she offers with a friendly smile.

'Really?' I ask, the flutter of butterflies in my chest growing with each passing second. This is real. 'When's your next availability?'

Judge Ashford glances at the clock on the wall. 'In five minutes. Last wedding of the day. How about it?'

Foster glances at me, his eyes twinkling mischievously. 'What do you say, love? This wouldn't be a whirlwind romance if we didn't do this,' he teases.

I can't help but laugh, feeling the bubble of excitement in my chest. 'Are we this nutty? Met, engaged, and married – all in thirty days?'

'I think so,' he says confidently. 'Let's do it.'

The woman claps her hands in front of her excitedly then checks through our paperwork, sliding our licenses back to us across the counter.

'Everything looks good,' she says, her pen viciously moving through part of the papers. 'I just love weddings,' she mumbles as she works. 'You two seem in love.'

'We are,' Foster agrees happily.

'OK, we're all set here, just follow me.' The receptionist gathers a few things in her hands and leads us through the large reception area and through a door at the back of the room.

As we walk, I steal glances at Foster, taking in every detail of his handsome face, the way his eyes crinkle when he smiles, and the dimples that appear in his cheeks. This feels like a dream I never want to wake up from. I want to remember every single detail of today.

'This is my wife, Evangeline, but I call her Evie.' Judge Ashford motions to the woman sitting on a small couch off to the side of his office. Evangeline looks like she has just walked off the set of an Audrey Hepburn movie. She's dressed to the nines, not a speck of make-up or hair out of place, and she's beaming.

'Congratulations!' she says, standing and approaching us. 'Aren't you two just cute! Look, honey, we were young and adorable like them once.'

'We sure were,' he agrees.

Judge Ashford's office is cozy, filled with the warm glow of afternoon sunlight streaming through the windows. I stand beside Foster, a surge of butterflies fluttering in my stomach as we face each other in front of the judge.

'It's nice to meet you, and happy anniversary,' Foster says, shaking the judge's wife's hand. 'Evie, huh?' he asks, eyeing me.

'That's what he calls me too,' I say excitedly.

'Really?' the judge's wife asks.

Foster nods. 'Could this be fate confirming our decision?'

'I like the word serendipity,' Evangeline says, as she reaches for our marriage license, setting it on her husband's desk beside her.

'Serendipity,' I repeat her word softly. It does seem more plausible than fate. The word is just prettier, like a rose-colored sunrise over a field of wild flowers.

'Chris likes to plan our anniversary dates, so I drove in for a romantic evening and now I get to witness a wedding!'

'The most romantic night of our lives,' the judge says, flashing her a less than professional flirtatious smile.

'And you met Rosie a few minutes ago,' the judge continues, motioning to the receptionist from earlier. 'She'll be our second witness.'

The mousy woman's name is Rosie. 'A couple of last-minute details,' Rosie says after disappearing then scuttling back in a hurry, now approaching me with a small veil in one hand. 'Someone left this a few months ago and I was waiting for the perfect bride-to-be to offer it. May I?' she asks.

I'm the perfect bride? That's flattering.

'I didn't expect a veil but yeah,' I say, turning my back to her so she can attach it.

'Also, these,' she says when she's done fluffing the white tulle to perfection, handing me a handful of the daisies I saw on the desk in her office. 'I tied them with a blue string so you can use them as your something blue, something borrowed, *and* something new.'

'You are a genius, Rosie.'

She smirks, lifting a single shoulder proudly.

'How do you feel?' she asks, as if we're old confidantes.

'Like I'm caught in the joyous chaos of a downpour of swirling confetti, and I want to remember every single second of it.'

'Wow,' she says with a smile. 'That was beautiful.'

It's beautiful because I left out being only the slightest bit terrified that I'm making a huge mistake. I'm 99.99 per cent sure I love this man. But marriage is forever and that is a long, *long* time to spend with a guy I've known thirty days.

Long deep breaths, Eve. This is real. You're marrying Guy Foster – the sweetest, kindest, most dedicated, most handsome man you've ever met. Remember every moment.

I take the flowers from Rosie, holding them delicately in one hand and lifting them for a sniff only once, after remembering daisies smell a little like dirt – which is fitting considering my about-to-be-husband's life.

'You look beautiful,' Foster says.

'Stunning,' Evangeline adds.

'Thank you. I feel beautiful. And you were right, your handsome self really did wear the perfect shirt,' I say to Foster, laughing at his tuxedo-print T-shirt that he insisted on wearing, even though he knew we were only coming in for a license today. He wanted to 'dress the part'.

'It's completely kismet,' he says, pretending to straighten his printed-on tie.

'Are you ready?' Judge Ashford asks, glancing at the two of us.

Foster grins widely at me, his hand reaching for mine. 'More than ready.'

The judge clears his throat before reading out of a book in his hand. 'Marriage is a shimmering vision, like a mirage in a desert. It's a path that is seen clearly only by two people and appears to glow with the light of love, leading to an unknown yet exciting lifelong destination with your best friend.'

His voice is gentle yet powerful and I can tell this isn't the first time he's made this speech.

'Over the years, my Evie and I have learned that love can be like trying to hold onto smoke, ethereal and elusive, constantly shifting and changing, yet always present and powerful. It's a dance between two souls, a language spoken without words, a feeling that consumes every fiber of your being. I can see exactly that when I watch the way you two look at each other.'

We glance at each other nervously. He can see all that?

Foster squeezes my hand reassuringly as the judge continues.

'Marriage is not just a legal union, but a promise to stand together through all the storms and sunshine life may bring. It's a commitment to love, respect, and support each other, no matter what challenges may arise – love should be enough.'

'It will be,' Foster says, his gaze so intent I feel it.

'For sure,' I agree.

'Do you, Guy,' he reads Foster's name off our paperwork, 'take the lovely Eve to be your lawfully wedded wife, to have and to hold from this day forward, for better or for worse, for richer or for poorer, in sickness and in health, to love and to cherish until death do you part?'

Foster's eyes never leave mine as he answers confidently, 'I absolutely do.'

'And Eve, do you take your handsome Guy here to be your lawfully wedded husband, to have and to hold from this day forward, for better or for worse, for richer or for poorer, in sickness and in health, to love and to cherish until death do you part?'

Our witnesses giggle at his name pun as I take a deep breath, feeling the weight of his words. This is it, the moment that seals our fates together, forever intertwined – until death do us part.

'I do,' I say, looking into Foster's warm gaze, feeling a sense of calm wash over me like the gentle waves on a serene beach.

'By the power vested in me by the state of Oregon, I now pronounce you husband and wife. You may kiss your bride.'

Foster doesn't waste a second, pulling me into his embrace and capturing my lips in a kiss that speaks of promises, passion, and a love that knows no bounds. The room fills with applause from our witnesses Rosie and Evie and we break apart, breathless and giddy with the weight of our new-found commitment.

The judge shakes Foster's hand and then mine, congratulating us once again as we exchange smiles with our witnesses.

'Let's just get this paperwork signed,' the judge says, handing us the pen one by one.

Once we've signed, Foster turns me toward him, his hands on my waist. 'Well hello there, my beautiful wife,' he whispers, his voice full of wonder and happiness.

'Hi, my gorgeous husband,' I reply softly, a smile breaking through my tears.

Judge Ashford clears his throat gently, bringing us back from our little bubble of love. He hands us our marriage certificate, five signatures and an official seal marking the beginning of our forever.

'Before you leave,' Evangeline says, 'should we take a photo of the two of you to commemorate?'

'Yes,' I say, excitedly handing her my phone from my pocket.

Foster stands tall and proud, his arm wrapped around me in a protective embrace. In his hand, our marriage certificate glints with the official seal, a symbol of our commitment. We gaze at the photo on my phone, our smiles wide and our eyes sparkling with love and joy.

'It's perfect,' Foster says.

'Just like you,' I agree.

We take a couple more, one with Judge Ashford, and another with the five of us, that I text to Evangeline as she requests so they can share what they did on their anniversary on Facebook.

'Congratulations, again!' the trio says when we step out of the judge's cozy office.

I feel like I'm floating on air as we walk away from the building – married. I turn to Foster, feeling overwhelmed by a rush of emotions.

'I can't believe we did it,' I say, my voice barely above a whisper.

Foster squeezes my hand. 'It's real, Jellybean. You are officially my wife.'

I take a deep breath, inhaling the scent of a new chapter in life and Foster's cologne, committing this moment to memory.

'Wow. I'm your wife and you're my husband. Crazy.'

'We might just be,' he jokes.

This is the beginning of our happily ever after. As we reach the car, Foster opens the door for me with a flourish. I catch his eye and smile, knowing that this was just the first step of many we would take together. I settle into the seat beside him, lean over and kiss Foster's cheek, whispering, 'I love you.'

'And I love you,' he replies, his words carrying the weight of a lifetime of devotion.

And as we drive away, our hearts full of love, I know that even though we haven't been together long, and the journey ahead may be uncertain, as long as we have each other, we can weather any storm that comes our way. Maybe we didn't iron out the details, but the heart wants what the heart wants. Plus, we have a lifetime to iron out the details.

* * *

Now

Blinking my eyes open, I take in the familiar sight of my apartment, feeling a hint of disappointment at the realization that the perfect wedding that I romanticized for far too long was all just a dream – both then and now. The heaviness of that settles in my chest like a stone, a slightly resentful rock.

The light seeps through the curtains, the shadows dancing on the walls, and my alarm beeps incessantly like it's mocking me for my brief escape from reality. This is not exactly how I pictured I'd feel waking up on my first day back to work after this crazy situation.

Nor did I expect to be going back to work so soon. I got the call from my boss late last night; they're short-handed. Foster doesn't even know yet, but I've set some alarms in his phone and left him a note.

I drag myself out of bed, the weight of exhaustion clinging to my limbs like a stubborn child refusing to let go. I shuffle into the kitchen, the smell of brewing coffee offering a faint promise of caffeine-induced salvation. As I sip my morning elixir, I can't help but replay the dream in my mind – it felt so real, so vivid. I get what he's talking about now – it's like I was there. Again. How can the memory of his lips linger on mine like a ghostly caress, after a dream? That's just his supernatural charm, I suppose.

Before I leave I check in on him, peacefully sleeping in my bed. He is gorgeous awake and stunningly beautiful when asleep. The perfect man that every girl talks about but only the rare actually acquire. And he's not just a pretty face, he's sweet, and funny, and I have a lot more good memories of him than bad. Looking back, maybe I was just being impatient and homesick when I left. Spoken words probably would have done more good than written ones.

He's probably dreaming of our worst day, and will wake up hating me, having no idea I just relived the one day I've tried the hardest to forget. Quite possibly the happiest day of my life – still.

I sigh, turning away and grabbing my bag to head out the door. Maybe it was just a dream, but the confusion it's stirred up is real and I'm not sure what to do with that yet.

22

EVE CASSIDY

The aroma of freshly brewed coffee drifts through the halls, mixing with the antiseptic and sterile scents of the hospital.

'My darling sweet Eve, there you are!' Adam says, already scribbling my name on a clear cup. 'I have bad news.'

'Oh?'

He nods, his lips pressed into a straight regretful line. 'I have bitten the forbidden fruit, and it has bitten back.'

I chuckle awkwardly. He's laying it on thick this morning.

'While I do appreciate you staying in character for this... what on earth are you talking about?'

Suddenly, Adam is twenty-four again. 'Heard you were taking care of your injured husband.' He glances at Genevieve who is standing at my side.

When I look at her, she looks away.

'*Ex*-husband,' I correct him, glaring at Gen when she finally makes eye contact.

'OK,' she heaves. 'So I missed one word.'

'You and I are not meant to be if you're married. It's one of the Ten Commandments,' Adam says, his voice disappointed.

Was he serious all this time? Oops.

'Or because one of us was never feeling it?' I suggest, making him frown.

The silence is heavy as we wait for our drinks to be ready.

'Warn me now. How many people did you miss one word to?' I ask Gen as we exit the coffee shop with our drinks in hand.

Before she can answer, Dr Sully is walking toward us, a blue Superman surgeon's cap on his head.

'Nurse Eve! How's Foster?'

'Still alive, thanks to you!' I chirp, waving a hand back at him like all is OK.

Him asking about Foster, I get. He did the surgery and has been his primary doctor since. Everyone else, that's gossip, probably spurred on by my bestie. Dang it.

'I dunno,' Gen answers my question, sipping her Frappuccino. 'You know how boring slow moments here can get. I may have mentioned it a time or two, but only because people were asking. It's not a big deal.'

'Eve!' Dale says, spotting me many feet away. 'Glad to have you back. How's your husband?'

'*Ex*-husband, and he's doing fine.'

'Hey,' Pam, a nurse I'm friends with only at work, stops Gen and me, resting a hand on my shoulder. 'I've been thinking of you. How is he? What's his name? I didn't even know you were married!'

'Ha ha, me neither...' I shoot Gen another glare. 'Foster and I are past tense. That said, he's doing fine.'

Pam frowns, glancing at Gen, the likely source of her misinformation. Genevieve only shrugs, but the coy smile on her face says she's not sorry at all – she's enjoying this.

We walk a few more feet only to be stopped again. This time, it's the ER Hispanic beauty, Catalina.

'Evie,' she says with a slight accent. 'Darling, I'm so sorry. How you holding up? Taking care of yourself, yes?' she asks, wrapping me in a big hug. 'Remind me later, I've got a gift certificate for a romantic restaurant Harry and me discovered a few years back. You two will need a date night after this chaos.' When she finally releases me, she does her two-handed duck-beak wave and backs down the hall, turning just in time to make the corner.

Twenty minutes, $100 in donations, one request for an autographed poster (that the young X-ray tech supplied), and one slightly unhinged 'what if' daydream about going back in time, and I'm clocked in at my workstation.

'You're back,' Chris, a fellow nurse, greets me. 'How's your little stuntman of a husband? BTW – my invitation to that wedding was rescinded because it "fell through." What's up with that?'

'That wedding *did* fall through,' I say.

'Different guy,' Gen tells him.

Chris's jaw drops open, so I turn in my chair not to see it.

'Apparently, chaos is my color now?' I ask, turning to Gen and glaring with an intensity that she can hopefully feel. 'This is not the morning back I was expecting and because you are behind that, no more talking, please,' I instruct, causing her to nurse her drink again.

After a few more questions, I stand in the middle of our nurses' station, with mostly empty patient rooms all around the big rectangular desk.

'Attention, co-workers!' I say, clapping my hands. Since I seem to be the talk of the ER, I feel like I should kill this rumor now. 'Please, keep your gifts.' I toss the cash donated onto the counter before me. 'Genevieve here' – I 'accidentally' whack her on the back of her head, causing her coffee to drip from her mouth and dribble down her front – 'forgot one teeny tiny word when discussing my situation without my permission: *ex*. Foster is my *ex*-husband.'

'Your ex? Why you taking care of him then?' Catalina asks, clearly confused.

'Yeah, Eve, why not kick him to the curb?' Gen asks, getting back at me for the slight violence.

'Because at one time, I loved this man enough to marry him, and that seems important,' I huff.

'Do you still love him?' Chris asks, as if any of this is any of their business.

'I—'

Do I?

Noooo.

'She hesitated!' Catalina exclaims, pointing my way. 'You love him.'

'I don't know what I feel for him, but it's not love.'

'You sure about that?' Gen asks, looking up at me with puppy dog eyes, insinuating love is my exact emotion. 'You did just take off weeks to pamper him.'

'There has been no pampering. And yes, I'm crystal clear in how I feel about Foster. We are just friends. So, can we move on now?'

My co-workers all watch me momentarily, and then just like a flip was switched, they go about their business, pretending none of it happened. Thank God.

* * *

'Honey, I'm ho—' I stop midway through the door, smelling something far better than the tuna melt I had for lunch in the hospital cafeteria.

When I spot Foster, he's standing in my kitchen, unbagging Chinese food containers onto the counter with one hand. Phil's hot pink floral print leggings on Foster make me laugh. I bet he'll be glad to be home and wearing his own clothes.

'What's this?' I ask, confused.

'It's your first day back at work and I didn't want you to have to worry about feeding me. So I ordered in.'

'You ordered in?' I repeat his words, setting my bag near the front door and meandering into the kitchen. 'Dinner?'

He nods proudly. 'And dessert.' He points to the pink bakery box, still unopened. 'And wine.' His gaze moves to my sink that he's filled with ice currently chilling two bottles of rosé. 'That Instacart makes life too easy.'

'Wow,' I say, legitimately surprised. 'No one ever does this for me. Usually, I walk into an empty apartment.'

He nods, a frown on his face. 'I figured as much, but after what you've done for me, this is the least I can do.'

Is this what just friends do? Sure, I've had dinner at Kait's or Phil's dozens of times, but they've never shown up at my apartment while I'm at work to make my night easier. I don't really know what to say about this.

'You kept up on your meds today?' I ask.

'I did. Actually, I missed the first dose 'cause I slept through my alarm, but I realized my pain wasn't as bad even being late, so I'm dialing back the morphine because I feel pretty good. Obviously, not good as new' – he motions to his arm still strapped to his chest in the sling – 'but better.'

With my help, we get the takeout boxes, a bottle of wine (and a single glass for me), and the box of doughnuts to the coffee table where we each grab a set of chopsticks and choose an entrée of the many he ordered.

'How was your day?' he asks.

'*My* day?' I ask, like there's anyone else in the room he could be talking to. I heave a sigh. 'Long, chaotic and annoying.'

He raises a single eyebrow curiously. 'Is that normal?'

I shake my head. 'My friend Genevieve – you guys have never met – "accidentally" told everyone I've been home taking care of my injured husband.'

Foster laughs. 'And that's bad because...?'

'Imagine the gossip mill running wild with that one,' I continue, poking at my lo mein absent-mindedly. 'I had colleagues coming up to me all day offering condolences and well wishes for your "speedy recovery". Some even felt the need to remind me that they thought the wedding had been canceled.'

Foster is holding a Chinese takeout box in his injured hand, and his chopsticks drop to the floor, a potsticker falling with them.

'Shit. Because of the canceled engagement?' he asks, leaving the chopsticks and potsticker where they are and picking up the next one with his fingers.

'Yep. Honestly, I'd rather not talk about it, but today reminded me of all the drama and gossip that *that* chaos created.'

'I'm sorry I accidentally ruined your day,' he says.

'You didn't,' I say. 'That was all Genevieve.'

Foster sits back on the couch, his eyes fixed on me, contemplating my previous words. I can see the gears turning in his head, trying to process this new information about my past – a piece of me he doesn't know. After a moment of silence, he leans forward, places his takeout container on the coffee table and then reaches out to gently hold my hand.

I can't help but be taken aback by his kindness and understanding. Most people hear about a broken engagement and want all the details. Foster isn't just any friend who happened to come over for dinner. There's a warmth between us that feels different, comforting in a way I hadn't expected.

'Honestly, Fost, you're the one who has made my day better,' I point out, offering him a warm smile. 'This' – I gesture to the Chinese takeout spread out on the coffee table between us – 'is a hundred times better than anything Cayden ever did for me. And your company is an added bonus.'

Foster's face lights up at my words, a genuine grin breaking through his initial concern. 'You know me, I aim to please.' He winks playfully, grabbing a potsticker with his fingers and popping it into his mouth. 'Happy to be the better ex over Cayden, any day.'

I laugh, not realizing he'd deemed him a competitor he needed to beat. Why does he want to be better? We haven't been together for five years. Our conversation dies down a bit and one question is running through my head. The same one I thought of when Chris asked if I still loved him.

'Do you ever wonder "what if"?' I ask.

'About what?'

'Us?'

He pauses mid-chew, his eyes meeting mine with a mix of surprise and contemplation. It's as if my question has struck a chord, unlocking a flood of emotions within him. I know because I've been feeling it since I woke up this morning.

He sets down the next potsticker, his expression serious yet tender. 'I've thought about it more times than I can count,' he admits softly, his gaze never leaving mine. 'I mean, who wouldn't wonder "what if" when it comes to someone like you? We were perfect together – you can't deny that.'

My heart skips a beat at his words as I can feel the raw honesty behind them. The weight of half-spoken truths hangs heavy in the air, and there's a vulnerability in Foster's eyes that draws me in like a magnet. I'd like to deny I've done the same but the dream that awoke me this morning says otherwise.

'We wer—' I try to answer, but a sharp rap echoes through the room, cutting through my sentence mid-word and causing us to look toward the door.

I glance at Foster with confusion. 'Who is it?' I call out in a sweet and gentle voice.

'Matty.' His voice booms through the heavy wooden door. 'I brought Foster's shit.'

'Now?' Foster asks, as if the timing is just wrong.

'He brought your shit?' I ask.

'Oh, right, I meant to tell you, Matty's stopping by tonight so I can return Phil's wardrobe. I didn't realize it would be in the middle of *that* conversation, but here we are.'

'It's not ideal, but when has anything about us been? Also, I'm going to be sad to see the floral prints go,' I say, setting my Chinese container on the table and answering the door.

'Ha ha,' Foster retorts with a heavy dose of sarcasm. 'We're continuing this conversation later...'

'Maybe...' I say, pulling open the door and allowing Matty in.

'Hello, Eve.' He halts just inside, a smile growing on his face when he spots Foster. 'Whoa, those leggings are stunning, sweetie,' he exclaims with a laugh. 'You look like a combination of The Flash and a rose petal princess.'

Foster rolls his eyes. 'Now, do you see why I called him? I'm not a floral guy.'

'I dunno,' Matty says. 'I think maybe we should do a floral print on your next set of riding gear. You wear it well,' he remarks with a laugh.

'No thank you,' Foster replies.

Matty glances at the coffee table, laden with food and drinks. 'Did I interrupt something, or not get my invitation?' he teases, raising his eyebrows and glancing at us.

'You could join us, of course,' I say, moving to the chair across the coffee table.

How am I supposed to say no? He flew across the country to bring Foster his things. Obviously he's staying for dinner, and Foster and I will try to continue our lingering – yet never finished – conversation later.

'We're just eating dinner, as all humans do, and I'm not sure there's enough for three?' Foster says, shooting me a look that reads *I'm so sorry.*

'Don't mind if I do,' Matty says, heaving Foster's massive travel duffel bag off his shoulder, the weight of it causing him to stagger as he drops it to the floor with a thud. He grabs a container of chicken and a plastic fork from the pile of cutlery that came with the takeout.

'I've delivered everything that was requested,' he announces wearily. 'All the way from the other side of the country.' He fills his face with a forkful of chicken, nodding as he chews. 'This is excellent kung pao. Also, Jeff sends his regards, although they come with a less than friendly sentiment.' He flashes Foster the finger, fork still in hand.

'Tell Jeff to fuck off,' Foster says with a smirk.

I look at the giant bag, then at Foster. 'Exactly how long do you think you're staying?' I kid.

'Until he's healed enough to take care of himself because I got shit to do and competing athletes to train,' Matty responds on Foster's behalf, still munching on the chicken.

'I'll be back at comps in six months, man. In fact, Eve's got me walking blocks a day, and I started physical therapy this week, so I'll be back better than ever before you know it.'

I shake my head. 'No. You'll be able to *start* riding again in six months, but no competing.' My words echo the doctor's instructions.

Foster rolls his eyes. 'He's a surgeon, he doesn't grasp the lifestyle of professional athletes,' he rebukes. 'We heal quickly.'

Matty agrees and the conversation moves on to how good a shape athletes are in and I'd deny it, but the proof is sitting next to me and I ogled it just recently to the point of needing a cold shower.

'Well, this was amazing.' Matty sets the now empty Chinese takeout box back onto the table. He just ate an entire container of kung pao chicken and he's not even breaking a sweat. I'd be sniffling after one portion. That's Foster's favorite and he didn't get any.

'I've only got a couple of hours between flights,' Matty says. He glances my way. 'Either take good care of him or bury him deep so I don't end up with more problems,' he says to me with a hint of laughter.

'Cross my heart and hope to die,' I say with a sly smile.

Foster shakes his head. 'Thanks, Matty. I'll call you in a couple days.'

As soon as the door closes behind him, I fix my gaze on Foster's bag, dropping to the floor to unzip and unpack it for him.

'I'm sorry about that, he was supposed to text to make sure the timing was OK. Not show up and eat all my kung pao chicken?' He grabs the container from the table, disappointed as he walks it to the garbage, stomping on the pedal to open the lid and tossing it in. 'I didn't even get one piece.'

'Sorry, Fost. We can order another box, on me since you were nice enough to put all this together?'

'Alright,' he says, grabbing his phone and tapping the screen as he sits back down in front of the coffee table. 'You don't need to unpack for me,' he insists after sitting his phone down.

'I don't mind.'

One by one I pull out an array of items. Toiletries. A pillow. Clothes. Shoes. Underwear. Not one thing in a floral or neon-colored print. However, I am confused by the blue heavily taped shoebox.

'"Never Open".' I read the words on the top aloud. 'What is this?'

Foster clears his throat. 'Um... *that* is my Eve box.'

23

GUY 'FOSTER'

Eve's brows furrow, creating lines on her forehead. Her eyes dart from the box to me, searching for answers. Her lips are pressed together in a puzzled expression, and she tilts her head to one side, clearly trying to make sense of the situation.

'What's an Eve box?' she asks. 'And why does it look like a bomb?'

I take a deep breath, my heart thudding against my ribcage. How do I explain this to her? I walk over and join her on the floor. There's a reason this lives in the top of my closet, out of sight. It hurts to see it as much as sitting on the floor does right now.

I run my fingers along the edge of the box, feeling the rough texture of the tape. The memories flood back, threatening to drown me in nostalgia.

'You asked if I ever thought of our "what ifs"?'

She nods.

'This is mine,' I begin, my voice barely above a whisper. Eve's eyes widen in surprise, a mix of emotions flickering across her features. 'It's filled with mementos from our relationship that remind me of you – of us.'

'Really?' she asks.

'Yep.'

'And it's taped closed why?'

'Because honestly, seeing these things all over my house hurt. But it hurt more to throw them away, so I boxed them up and promised never to look, but also never to get rid of them.'

Eve's gaze softens as she listens, her hand reaching out to touch the box gently. I notice a hint of vulnerability in her eyes. She leans in a little closer, her shoulder brushing mine, and her voice is barely a whisper, filled with emotion.

'I thought you just forgot about me,' she admits.

Her words hang in the air between us.

'How could I ever forget the woman I consider the love of my life?' I confess. 'I know you ended things a long time ago, but a part of me always held on to the possibility of us.'

Slowly, she nods, understanding dawning on her face. 'I get it,' she murmurs, her voice barely above a whisper. 'It's like holding onto a piece of the past, even if it stings. That said, I should probably show you something.'

Eve hands the box to me, standing and disappearing into her room. When she exits, she's holding her own box. It's bigger than mine and has the words Home Depot across the side.

She sits next to me again and opens the untaped lid, revealing the helmet I gave to her the day we met, my riding shirt that she was wearing, and a variety of other things.

I laugh as she pulls the helmet from the box – my old helmet.

'You kept it,' I say.

'I was hoping if I held onto it long enough it would be worth some money,' she jokes. 'Truthfully, like you, I used to have it on the top of my bookshelf, but I couldn't bear looking at it any more and once I started dating Cayden, it became weird to have it displayed. Like a shrine to my ex.'

'Why do I like the sound of that?'

'Because you love to be worshipped by sun-kissed women fangirling you around dirt bike tracks.'

I chuckle at her comment, feeling a mix of emotions swirling inside me. Seeing Eve sitting beside me, sharing her own box of memories – that I didn't even know she had – makes my heart ache and soar at the same time. It's like a bittersweet dance of past and present intertwining before us.

As she places the helmet back into the box, I glance at her, taking in the delicate features of her face and the way her eyes sparkle with shared nostalgia. It's in these small moments that I realize how much of an impact she has had on my life, even after all this time.

'Can I look?' I ask, sitting my box in her lap and pulling this one closer.

'Yeah, if I can snoop through yours.'

The contents of Eve's box are a treasure trove of memories, carefully preserved and tucked away like secrets in a time capsule. I see ticket stubs from concerts we attended together, the first book I gave her with a note scribbled on the inside cover, my merch bracelet and jersey, and a worn-out sweater that she used to wear when it got chilly.

But what catches my eye the most is a small photo booth strip, faded and slightly crumpled. In it, we're both laughing, our faces pressed close together as we pose for each shot. The memories come flooding back like an avalanche, overwhelming yet strangely comforting.

My fingers linger on the photo, tracing the outlines of our smiling faces. There's a wistful look in her eyes, a silent acknowledgment of the happiness we once shared. It's as if we're both revisiting a chapter of our lives that had been buried under layers of time and distance.

'I used to have that on my fridge,' she says.

'I remember this day.'

'You do?'

I glance at her, confused. 'I remember all our days, Evie.'

'I'll admit, I've tried desperately to forget over the years.'

That makes me sad. I get it, love hurts. But damn. She didn't even want to remember me?

It takes her a few minutes but eventually, she gets the lid off the shoebox and we stare into it, silently.

Among the scattered items in the box are photos I printed and framed, a crumpled movie ticket stub from the first film we watched together, a quirky fridge magnet she bought that says 'Keep Portland Weird', and a dried flower from the bouquet she held at our wedding. Each piece holds a memory, a fragment of our shared past that suddenly feels more tangible.

Eve picks up the small flower, tracing its delicate petals with her fingertips.

'You kept this?' There's a wistful smile playing on her lips as she gazes at it, lost in thought.

I watch her quietly, feeling a rush of emotions welling up inside me. Our history is heavy, but there's also a glimmer of hope, the flutter of something new and uncertain.

'I dreamed about our wedding last night,' she murmurs, breaking the silence. 'It was so weird, like I was there, reliving it.'

'And you hated it?' I ask, fully expecting that to be her answer, but she shakes her head.

'No,' she admits. 'I can't quit thinking about it, actually. Everything was so perfect.'

Her confession about dreaming of our wedding catches me off guard, making my heart race with a mixture of uncertainty and excitement.

'It was perfect because it was with you,' I say, my voice soft yet filled with sincerity. 'Despite everything that happened after, that day still holds a special place in my heart.'

Eve's gaze meets mine and it's as if we're standing at the edge of a precipice, teetering between the past and the present, unsure of which way to step next.

'I miss us,' she says, her voice tinged with regret. 'I miss the way we used to be before everything got so complicated.'

Right then her phone starts ringing. Damn it. What is with the interruptions tonight? She ignores it for a minute but when the number calls back, she answers.

'What's up, Gen?' she asks, sounding less than thrilled to have our moment disrupted. She listens to the caller on the other end. 'I already forgive you,' she says. 'A club? Tomorrow night? What? You want me to bring him? I guess so.' After a few minutes of chatter, she hangs up the phone and looks my way with a smile.

'Booty call?' I ask, completely kidding, but she laughs.

'Clubbing call – which I rarely do any more. I sort of preoccupy myself with work twenty-four seven, according to my friends. But I don't doubt you're feeling stir-crazy by now and you're doing really well at moving.'

'Ten blocks recently,' I brag.

'Exactly. So, whadya think? Will you be feeling "clubby" tomorrow night?'

Excitement bubbles inside me like recently poured champagne. We went clubbing once. I've never smiled so hard. I can't believe I'm being given a second chance to rewrite the unfinished chapters of our story, to rediscover the parts of ourselves we thought were lost.

'I doubt I'll be very dancy, but I can babysit your drinks and purse. Count me in,' I reply, unable to hide the hopeful tone in my voice.

* * *

Five Years Ago

The sun beats down relentlessly on the open motorcycle track, surrounded by rows of stadium seating and tall swaying trees. The crowd is dressed in tank tops and shorts, their skin glistening with sweat under the scorching Oregon summer heat. Colorful banners and posters promoting sponsors sway in the warm breeze, adding vibrancy to the scene. Fans eagerly line the edges of the dirt course, anticipating a chance to meet and greet their favorite riders.

Once the event dies down, I make my way toward the lingering crowd as I always do, still dressed in my riding gear. My bright green flat-bill hat with my number fifteen stitched in black on the front sits firmly on my head. I have a stack of the same ones ready to be handed out to anyone who wants one. After a few minutes of chatting with some male fans, all of the hats are gone and now you can see specks of green bobbing through the crowd as people leave for their cars.

'Could you snap a picture?' A woman hands her phone to one of the volunteers and wraps her arm around my waist, leaning her head on my shoulder as if we were together. It's one of the benefits of the job that I have no objections to – fangirls. I lean in and kiss her cheek while the blonde-haired beauty in front of us takes our photo.

'If you're ever looking for a wife...' the young woman says with a flirty giggle as she backs away, flashing a wink and a smile that'll be hard to forget.

Our photographer – the volunteer track girl wearing my jersey – doesn't smile, at least not in my direction. She simply gives the phone back to its owner and moves on to the next person in line, fulfilling her duties and taking the next camera being offered to her.

'Sign here, please.' Another woman approaches me, gesturing toward her chest and tugging at her already revealing shirt.

It's not uncommon for me to sign body parts, and I'm sure it won't be the last time. With a quick stroke of my pen, I leave my signature on the woman's skin, while my photographer gives an exasperated look, stifling an adorably crooked smirk, and takes a photo.

'I'm seriously getting this tattooed,' the fan says. 'I'll Insta you a photo.'

'Awesome,' I say with a grin. 'Not sure anyone has ever tattooed my name on them before, that I know of. I'm honored.'

'Next!' my volunteer yells, waving over the next fan. She's rolling her eyes playfully when I glance her way.

'How about you be next?' I ask.

A slight, inviting smile grows on her face, and her gaze sort of takes me aback, like there's an instant spark that we somehow both feel. Neither of us breaks eye contact for seconds, which allows me to notice her dark blue eyes, sparkling in the sun like the rolling waves of the Pacific Ocean.

'No way are you autographing *my* boobs.' She laughs, almost nervously, to herself.

She is beautiful. Her hair is in two French braids like the brand requests of female volunteers, and my riding shirt is tied at her waist and has not looked better on anyone – ever. A tiny sparkle of a diamond is in her left nostril, and you'd think it'd be the Daisy Duke shorts that catch my attention most, but I can't peel my eyes off her bright smile and that red lipstick.

'I wasn't asking to grope you. I was talking about taking a picture.'

'You've got a line of fans waiting; why waste a moment on a woman who didn't even know you existed an hour ago? These girls probably have posters of you in their dorm rooms – above their beds. They've earned a photo.'

'I can get you a poster if you want…' I tease.

Her laugh is bubbly. 'Do I have to put it on my ceiling?'

'It's not a requirement but I mean, if you need to you need to.'

'Ha!' she spurts. 'Google was right, you are a flirt, Guy Foster.'

'You googled me?' I ask, readjusting the hat on my head nervously.

'I had to,' she defends herself. 'Anytime a job requires booty shorts and "sexiness", I'm looking up the man of the brand. Did I nail it?' she asks, giving me a little spin.

I chuckle. 'You, uh—yeah—' I'm suddenly nervous and fighting for words as I pry my eyes off her.

'Cat got your tongue?'

'No—er, yes?' *This is so not smooth, Foster.* 'You know what, forget about Google me. You're not dazzled by my performance today at all? I mean, first place, Jellybean. I won a check with many zeros. I defied gravity.'

She shakes her head, her soft, red lips curving upward in a slight smile, a sparkle of interest glimmering in her eyes as they flicker toward me. 'I think you're nuts, Skittles. Never have I experienced as much anxiety as I did watching you riders tempt death, and I'm a nursing student.'

I laugh at her returning the nickname and keeping the topic candy. Also, wowzers, a nursing student? Beautiful, quick-witted, and smart – I've hit the track girl jackpot.

'Although I am enjoying women staring at you with lustful stars in their eyes, each one hoping they're the next to be that girl dating the sexiest FMX guy alive. Google said that too.'

Those words leaving her lips make my heart flutter. 'I didn't realize Google was so into me. Weird.'

She laughs.

'Come with me,' I say, grabbing her hand as I pass by her, headed to our track tent.

'I can't, I'm on duty.' She pulls her hand shyly from mine. 'I've got to stand near you and look hot, per the event director's words.'

'Trust me when I say you're succeeding. I don't know if I've said this yet, but you are easily the most beautiful track girl I've ever been assigned.'

'Lie.'

'Lie?!' I scoff. 'How?'

'Google knows everything, remember?'

'That robot showed you more gorgeous track girls than you?'

'Uh, yeah!'

I shake my head in disbelief. 'Well, I'm here to tell you, you're wrong. You are my top track girl.'

'After knowing me for what, fifteen minutes, you're awarding me first place?'

'That's it!' I say, realizing what I want to give this girl that isn't a poster above her bed. 'I have something for you.'

'I can imagine you do after that compliment...' she laughs.

'Not *that* – did you miss the part where Google said I'm also a gentleman?'

'I must have.'

'Well no, it's something cool, something I've never given out to any woman.'

She lifts a single eyebrow. 'I dunno,' she hesitates. 'What if I don't want it?'

'I think you're going to want this. Come on, Jellybean. Take a chance on me, would ya?'

She stands strong and confident, her hands resting firmly on her hips. Her eyes, however, are fixed on me with a playful glint.

'Why Jellybean?' she asks.

I nod. 'You're bright, beautiful, and small – it fits. Plus, jellybeans are my favorite candy.'

'Shouldn't we know each other better before handing out cutesy nicknames?'

I shrug my shoulders, the glint in her eye sparkling in a way I've never witnessed. 'I'm calling it now – you and me, there's something – I feel it.'

The roll of her eyes amuses me. I extend my hand, but she stares at it like I've lost my mind.

'I've heard the rumors, Casanova. You're the most desirable rider. Two women have proposed to you, with rings, track-side. I've seen the photos. Girls fall for your adorable dimples and flirtatious ways. I don't have time for falling – I've got to graduate soon.'

'Congratulations. But I feel like you might need the "not everything on the internet is true" reminder.'

'Are you saying photos lie?'

'No,' I confirm. 'Some of it's true.'

She cocks her head, crossing her arms over her chest. 'Exactly where do you want to take me, Guy Foster? And why?'

I start walking toward our mechanic's tent and to my surprise, she follows behind.

I grab my helmet and a Sharpie from my stuff. 'What's your name?'

Uncertainty is all over her face.

'It's only fair, considering you know everything about me, including my name,' I remind her.

She laughs. 'Fine, since Jellybean doesn't do it for me, you can know it. My name is Eve.'

'Eve,' I repeat, liking the way it feels as I say it. I scribble some words then my signature on the side of my helmet and place it in her hands.

She looks down at it suspiciously. 'Eve, #1 sexiest track girl alive, heart symbol, #15 Foster.' She reads the words I've written, her gaze darting from the helmet to me. Her laughter is like a symphony, filling the air with joy. Her voice is soft and melodic, like a lullaby that could soothe any troubled soul.

'Exactly how many first-place track girls get autographed helmets from the Famous 15 every show?'

I take the helmet from her and slide it onto her head, patting it right on top. 'Only one so far, and you look adorable,' I say. 'Absolutely photo-worthy. Where's your phone?'

She pulls it from her pocket, taps the camera button, reversing the screen to see herself. 'I look like Gazoo from *The Flintstones*,' she says. 'Why is it wet?'

'I was just wearing it.'

'Ew,' she groans, but it's mixed with a giggle.

I take her phone, slinging my arm around her shoulders, pulling her close, and taking a selfie of us. While she struggles to remove the helmet, I quickly text the photo to myself so I've got her number.

Her phone plays a short bubbly melody and she glances at the screen, helmet in one hand, phone in the other, biting back half a grin. 'Well look at that, I'm officially off-duty.'

'Already?' I ask, glancing at the Apple watch on my left wrist.

'Time flies when you're wearing booty shorts – thank God,' she giggles.

'Can I be ballsy?' I ask.

'You can, if you're cool with how I receive it.'

My smile grows. 'How can I see you again?'

She smirks, glancing at her phone. 'Well, considering you violated my privacy and texted yourself from my phone, maybe you can use that number?'

I drop my head like I'm ashamed I did that, but far from it. If I didn't already have her number, I'd be on my knees right now asking for it – in a matter of minutes this woman has commanded my attention and I don't hate it at all.

'Caught,' I say with a chuckle. 'How about this? Tell me you feel no connection between us and I'll delete the whole thing from my phone and pretend this day never happened.'

She purses her lips playfully, backing away from me. 'Don't tell me you just fell in love with me?'

Nervous laughter leaves my lips. 'Love? Hmmm... that's a biiiig word, Jellybean.'

Her cheeks actually flush as she pats her hair to make sure nothing is out of place after wearing my helmet. She tucks the stray hairs behind one ear. 'You're cute, Gummy Worm.'

'Oh, yeah? Must I remind you that you said "sexy", earlier?'

'Did I?' she asks, cocking her head like she's already forgotten. This girl is adorable with the splatter of freckles across her nose that is now scrunched as she pretends not to flirt with me.

'You did...'

She laughs to herself. 'Pretty sure those were Google's words. But on that note, I suppose you have my permission to text since you have my number. Wouldn't want it to go to waste.'

The smile spreads across my face.

'Good luck, Foster. I hope you're as good at flirting as you are at riding.' With that, she spins on a toe and heads toward the parking lot. She glances back once, flashing a smile that sends a spark of electricity through the distance between us – at least for me.

I have a feeling this girl is as beautiful on the inside as she is on the outside. This is going to be fun.

24

EVE CASSIDY

'Any telling dreams for you last night?' I ask as I drive down the freeway toward our destination. I don't know why Gen thinks a night at the club will make me like her more, but I don't want her going alone.

Foster gives me one single nod, his eyes darting in my direction. 'Relived the day we met.'

'Really?' I ask, surprised that my latest was our wedding but his is the day we met. 'Do you still consider that a good day?'

His brows furrow as he shakes his head, looking confused. 'It was the day the most beautiful woman I've ever met came into my life. Yeah – that still stands as a good day.'

I continue driving, passing when need be, taking whatever exits I know will get us to this club clear across the city.

'Is it still a good day for you?' he asks after a few long minutes of silence.

I look his way, then back at the road. 'Yeah,' I say. 'It's still a good day for me too.'

He sits back a little further into his seat, relaxing with my words. I don't hate him. Not even a little bit, it turns out. I didn't expect to be contemplating some of these things, that's for sure.

As the evening sky darkens into a deep shade of blue, I can't help but notice Foster's intense gaze fixed on me from the passenger seat. His eyes are like two pools of liquid silver, reflecting the city lights as we drive toward the club. When I pull in, the hum of the engine and the distant sounds of music blend into a symphony that seems to match the rhythm of my racing heart, and I catch Foster's eyes on me.

'Why are you staring?' I ask.

'Sorry, not sorry,' he laughs. 'You're just the prettiest thing in Portland right now, yet the outfit intrigues me.'

Pulling into a spot, I park my car, reach into the back seat, and grab my new straw boho cowboy hat to complete my 'look'. I pull down the visor to make sure I don't seem utterly ridiculous before grabbing the second one, which I bought just this morning – along with mine. I pull off Foster's ball cap and set the Western hat on his head.

'Achy Breaky Heart?' He reads the sign at the top of the building. The street light we're parked near illuminates the expression on his face, highlighting the panic in his eyes. 'This is a country bar, isn't it?'

'The cowboy boots and outfit make more sense now, don't they?' I say, exiting the car and running to his side to help him.

He's getting much better now that we're many weeks into his healing. Not only is he walking six to ten blocks multiple times regularly, he's also getting up and down all on his own with just the slightest look of discomfort. He might be right, maybe professional athletes do heal quicker?

'Western bars aren't really my thing,' he insists, following me toward the club's entrance.

'Oh, it gets better…' I tease. 'It's a line-dancing country bar. Get ready for some good ol' southern fun, y'all!' I plaster on a smile, making Foster laugh at my ridiculous southern accent. He claims he's outgrown his as he travels too much for it to stick, but I still hear it sometimes when it's just the two of us.

I lead him toward the entrance, feeling the vibrations from the speakers fill my body the closer we get.

'After you,' I say, pulling open the door for him.

He stops, shaking his head and reaching for the door handle. 'I can handle doors, Jellybean. It's ladies first, in my world.'

'Still a gentleman,' I say with a smile. 'Why thank you, sir.' I enter the club ahead of him at his insistence.

Genevieve and I have been here before because a guy she sometimes 'sees romantically' – Brady – works as a bartender.

Stepping inside, I am immediately transported to the Wild West. The air is filled with a chaotic mix of country and club music, pulsing loudly through the room. The walls are lined with rough, weathered barn wood, giving off a rustic charm. Interspersed among the wood are numerous mounted animal heads, their glassy eyes staring out eerily at the patrons. Vintage photos of legendary cowboys like Jesse James and Billy the Kid cover every inch of wall space, adding to the Western theme. Along one side of the room sits a bar made of heavy wooden beams and illuminated by neon blue lights reflected in mirrored shelves – the bottles on display glisten enticingly.

As I make my way to the bar, the Western theme continues with saddle-shaped bar-stools, a fun touch that adds to the atmosphere. The dance floor beckons, its polished surface already crowded with enthusiastic dancers moving to the beat. On the stage stands a DJ instead of a live band, but it doesn't matter as long as the music keeps playing. Across from the bar, a mechanical bull ring catches my eye and I know I have to give it a try after a few drinks. My outfit is fitting for the occasion: a short jean skirt with ruffled eyelet patterns that barely reach mid-thigh, paired with a plaid blouse tied around my waist to show just enough skin without being too revealing. With a smile on my face, I know this will be a night to remember.

I scan the place, searching for Gen. My eyes light up as I spot her sitting at the bar, her long legs crossed elegantly in a side-saddle style. Brady stands in front of her, already giving her his bedroom eyes. He wears the same thing I always see him in, the bar's standard bartender uniform of a flannel shirt with suspenders, Levi's, a gun in a holster on his hip, and a handlebar mustache to complete the look.

'Over there!' I point and grab Foster's hand, making our way through the crowd to reach her.

She looks me over and nods approvingly. 'You look perfect!' she exclaims, her gaze moving to Foster on my right – who, honestly, doesn't quite fit in with the rest of us dressed up to match the theme. 'And this must be the famous Foster?' she asks. 'You look way better than you did when we originally met.'

'We've met?' he asks, shaking her outstretched hand.

'She works the trauma room with me,' I tell him, speaking loudly over the music.

'Ah,' Foster says with a nod. 'So, you've seen me at my finest then,' he jokes.

'You clean up nicely,' Gen teases him before turning back to me. 'What are we drinking?'

I stare up at the menu; every drink has a Western flare but even though I'm weighing my options, I know I'll probably choose the same thing I always do.

Brady, whom I've met many times before, looks at Foster and me curiously. 'I thought Eve didn't date?' he asks, his gaze on me.

Foster's eyebrows shoot up in surprise and he looks at me expectantly.

'Too many broken hearts can do that to a girl,' I quip.

'This guy break it?' Brady asks, acting all protective over me.

Foster's gaze moves to me.

'Our relationship is complicated,' I reply vaguely.

Brady grins. 'You're a woman, I'd be concerned if it wasn't,' he jokes. 'Whatcha drinkin' tonight?'

'Um, can I get a Sweet Tea Moonshine?'

'You're *starting* with moonshine?' Foster asks, his tone laced with concern.

I nod. 'And you're loaded on morphine. We're even,' I joke.

He smirks, his gaze drifting toward the dance floor where people step in time to the twangy country music playing in the background.

'I'm definitely not loaded enough to line dance.'

I playfully nudge him with my elbow. 'Come on, Fost. You grew up in the South. Isn't country music y'all's theme or somethin'?'

He lets out a sigh, his eyes still fixed on the dancers. 'Florida doesn't really qualify as the South, Evie. Maybe up north in Tallahassee, but it's more diverse than that everywhere else.'

A sudden thought strikes me and I can't resist asking, 'Didn't you grow up near Tallahassee?'

Foster lets out a wry laugh, a smirk growing on his face. 'Technicality. Now I spend so little time in Florida it affects my taxes.'

That I know – considering I lived with him for a while and he was never there. I chuckle at his response, taking a sip of my drink which is served in a glass shaped like a cowboy boot – a nice touch for this country-themed bar. Gen and I chatter about nothing really, considering we can barely hear each other, bouncing to the music, and as I finish the drink quicker than expected, I feel emboldened by the alcohol and decide to push Foster a little further.

'OK, Mr Serious,' I say with a playful grin. 'Time to relax and have some fun. How about for one night, you let that accent free and be the southern boy you pretend you're not?'

Foster raises an eyebrow at me, a hint of amusement in his eyes. 'And why should I do that?'

25

GUY 'FOSTER'

Eve shrugs, her delicate shoulders rising and falling in a gesture of nonchalance. However, the pleading look in her eyes betrays her true feelings. 'Because I'd like it,' she says, her voice soft and earnest. 'Is that enough?'

Yes, the fact that she'd like it is more than enough for me. It always has been. I want to say that to her, but there is no way I am bringing up the past again. We never even finished our conversation from last night, but I feel like we got somewhere despite that. We each kept our past hidden away because we couldn't let it go. That's something, in my book.

'Alright,' I say, laying the accent on thick. 'Southern Foster reportin' fer duty – at yer request, Miss Eve.' I tip my brand-new cowboy hat, feeling my heart swell with pride as she beams at me for granting her absurd request.

'Well, howdy there, Mr Foster,' she replies playfully. 'What brings you to a place like this?'

'A beautiful girl – or fate, perhaps,' I respond with a grin.

Pink fills her cheeks. 'Thank you, handsome. Speaking of fate... I should warn you that I plan on mounting that bull over there at some point tonight.'

Mount the bull. *Christ, Evie.* I can't help but laugh.

'If I weren't already broken, I'd break whatever record this place has.'

'I once went nineteen seconds,' Gen boasts with a mischievous twinkle in her eye. 'Got free drinks for the rest of the evening.' The sound of clinking glasses and laughter fills the air around us.

'And I'm sure that had nothing to do with the fact that she's "doing" the bartender,' Eve teases her.

'Don't tell all my secrets!' Gen responds with a playful nudge to Eve's arm as the song changes. 'Oh, I love this one! Come on, we gotta get out there.'

'Coming?' Eve asks, turning to me for confirmation.

I shake my head, feeling slightly overwhelmed by the rowdy atmosphere. 'Not sure I could keep up even if I wanted to.'

Eve lets out an exasperated sigh. 'OK then, party pooper. I'll be back,' she says, handing me her now-empty glass. 'Order me another?'

'Jesus, you drank that already?' I ask in disbelief as I hold up the empty glass.

She smirks, cocking her head at me. 'We're having fun like we used to tonight, remember?'

'I mean, yes, ma'am,' I quickly correct myself, using the southern accent I grew up hearing but have since trained myself out of. The music grows louder and more infectious as people dance and mingle around us.

I make my way back to the bustling bar, weaving through the dance floor where Eve and Gen are effortlessly line dancing to an Alan Jackson song. Their boots tap in perfect sync with the lively music, their faces aglow with joy. I can't help but smile at the sight of Eve in her cowgirl get-up, a straw hat perched on her head, and the flannel showing off her midriff, hugging her petite frame.

A sweet, sugary scent wafts toward me, emanating from the drink I ordered for her. The glass is deceptively innocent, its contents hidden by a layer of frothy foam. Curiosity gets the best of me and I take a sip, only to be hit with an unexpected intensity that nearly has me choking. Startled, I catch the attention of the man sitting next to me, who looks at me with concern. I quickly wave him off, assuring him that I'll survive this potent concoction. My taste buds come alive as I realize that this drink is no ordinary cocktail. It's definitely moonshine, and judging by its strength, at least a double shot. This girl will be riding that bull after this drink, I promise.

As I gaze out at the dance floor, my eyes are immediately drawn to Eve who moves with grace and fluidity as she twirls and dips. She's the center of attention, sparkling like the diamond she is, lost in the joy of dancing with a crowd of people moving as one. Her skirt flounces and sways with each step, and her blonde hair bounces under the cowboy hat perched atop her head. Every time she turns toward me, her whole face lights up and she gestures for me to join in on the fun.

With a playful grin and a wink, I lift her drink in response to each invitation. 'Gotta keep an eye on this,' I shout over the booming music, knowing she probably can't hear me. But she's too busy twirling and laughing to care.

'Come on, Fost,' she begs, approaching me when the song is over. 'One dance probably wouldn't even exert you as much as ten blocks do.'

'A break-dance might.'

'Do you break-dance?' she asks, looking confused at this new information.

'No.'

'Then how about a slow song?'

'I'd love to, honestly, but I'm afraid if I jostle my insides too much, I might drop dead, and I can't possibly have in my obituary that I died country line dancing.'

She laughs, the sound like tinkling bells on a summer breeze. 'The physical therapist says movement is good, as long as you don't over-exert yourself – remember?'

'You remind me every day, Jellybean.'

'And every day you get a little bit better, so I must be doing something right.'

As the song changes to one she knows and likes, her body sways expertly to the beat. She stands in front of me, her drink in hand and straw between her lips. Suddenly, she reaches for my free hand and pulls me onto the dance floor.

'It's a slow one,' she says, her voice low and sultry. 'I'm sure you can keep up. Just sway with me.' Her hand moves to rest on the back of my neck, while her other hand grips the glass tightly. 'Even the bad dancers get away with swaying on the slow songs.'

I raise an eyebrow at her teasing remark. 'Are you insinuating that I'm a bad dancer?' I ask. But as I hesitantly slide my free hand around her waist and pull her closer, I can't help but feel the electricity between us and suddenly, I couldn't care less if my dance skills were the worst of the worst.

My God, this girl smells like a fresh summer day. Her perfume fills my senses and it's unlocking memories I'd buried deep after realizing she wasn't coming back. Yet here we are now, swaying to the music together and it feels right. Like no time has passed at all. As we move in sync, our bodies pressed close together yet not too close, I realize that maybe some things never truly die.

'The backflip and hip thrusts you do after winning hardly qualify as dancing,' she remarks, a teasing glint in her eye as she looks up at me.

'Hey, backflips in your thirties aren't as easy as they used to be, you know. But the fans love 'em,' I say with a hint of pride in my voice. 'So I gotta give 'em what they want.'

For a few brief years as a child, I did gymnastics because I was into it. If nothing else, it helped me understand gravity. I've still got a few gymnast party tricks up my sleeve that I break out on the track at times.

With a graceful shake of her head, Eve moves from side to side, taking charge and effortlessly carrying the dance. Her movements are like poetry in motion, fluid and mesmerizing. I can't help but savor her company as we listen to the song's lyrics about hating love. It perfectly captures her essence.

'You really relate to this one, huh?' I remark with a playful grin.

Her lips curve into a mischievous smile as she sings along to the lyrics. 'Love sucks,' she declares with conviction.

A gentle tap on my shoulder startles me, causing me to step away from her and turn toward the source of the interruption. A tall, light-haired man stands before us, his gaze fixed solely on Eve.

'May I cut in?' he asks politely, gesturing toward her with his hand. His confident presence and piercing stare make it clear that he won't take no for an answer.

Eve's eyes blaze with an intense rage as she gazes at the man before her. The air between them crackles with a charged tension, like a storm about to break. So much so, I want to step away but feel like for her sake, I shouldn't. Their faces twist in familiar contempt. It's clear they have a history together, one filled with animosity and resentment.

'I'm not sure she's up for it,' I say, but he's not paying attention to me. His eyes are on Eve.

'I've missed you,' the man says to Eve, whose brows pinch together with fury. That's the face of a woman who hasn't missed him back. I step closer, holding a hand out to keep the stranger at a distance.

'Maybe this isn't a great id—'

Before I can even finish my sentence, the man falls to his knees in front of me, his hands frantically grasping at his throat as he struggles for air. His eyes bulge with surprise and fear, his body heaving in a desperate attempt to breathe.

I turn to Eve and see her rubbing her fist, a fierce determination in her fiery gaze.

'Did you just throat-punch him?' I ask, my voice filled with shock.

'I did. Ouch, that hurt more than I expected.' She shakes her hand, attempting to alleviate the pain.

'My God, Eve!' the man bellows when he can finally speak, attempting to get to his feet. His voice is strained and desperate, like a wounded animal.

'You *miss* me?' she hollers, her seething anger seeping through every word. I've never seen this side of her. The patrons around us instinctively take a step back, sensing the intensity of their exchange. 'How about you go choke on a poisonous cock!'

Dang. I stifle a laugh at her choice of words. Thank God she's never said them to me. They for sure know each other, and not in a great way. I step forward again to help – even though with all my injuries, I may die doing so. She's worth it. But before I can reach them, a hand on my shoulder pulls me back. Genevieve stands beside me with a half-guilty grin on her face.

'Don't,' she advises, shaking her head. 'Trust me, she doesn't need us. He's earned this, so we'll wait to step in until just before she kills him.' She waves a hand at Brady, still behind the bar. He throws a towel over one shoulder and makes his way toward us.

'What?' I can't believe what I'm hearing.

My attention snaps back to Eve as she commands the dance floor, her voice ringing out with a barrage of insults and profanities directed at the man kneeling before her. The girl hardly ever swears and here she is letting every dirty word that exists loose. The object of her contempt remains frozen in place, one knee pressed to the ground as if he's about to propose, but his face is twisted in pain; it's clear he's already been hurt deeply.

Curiosity and concern tug at me as I turn to Genevieve, needing to know more about this explosive situation.

'Who is he?'

She takes a casual sip of her beer before answering, 'I don't know if she's mentioned him to you yet, but that is Cayden, her ex-fiancé. I'll let her tell you the rest because sometimes I share too much and it's not my story to share.'

My jaw literally drops open. Thank God I backed off the morphine recently because this is a lot of new information all at once. 'This is Cayden?'

Wow. I knew she was engaged to him but that's literally all she said before dropping that she didn't want to talk about it. And judging from the way Cayden's body language mirrors hers, it's clear there are still a lot of unresolved emotions between them. My heart aches for whatever pain he put her through.

'Yep,' Gen says. 'The same guy who ripped her heart from her chest and stomped it nearly to death in front of everyone she knows.'

Eve's voice quivers with a mix of anger and contempt, rising above the pulsing music that fills the room. Her eyes blaze with fury as she addresses her former lover, her words dripping with disdain. 'And to answer your question, *no*, I absolutely do not miss you at all because I am happily married to someone way better than you ever were!' With that declaration, she lifts her cowboy boot-clad foot and forcefully shoves it into his shoulder, sending him sprawling to the ground. 'I hope she cheats, you bastard!'

Now she's storming toward me, and I can't help but feel a twinge of fear. She grabs my bicep in a vice-like grip and pulls me through the crowded club like we are indeed a couple, and I am the 'someone way better' she just referred to. I'm torn between feeling proud and scared.

'What is happening right now?' I manage to ask as we exit the building and continue walking toward her car at an urgent pace.

'Nothing is happening,' she says through gritted teeth, obviously still seething with anger.

I struggle to keep up with her speed as she leads us to her parked car. 'Injured guy here,' I remind her.

'Stop lagging,' she snaps when I fall a few steps behind. 'We gotta leave before the police are called.'

'I'm not exactly in a condition to run from the fuzz right now, Evie.' Finally, I step in front of her, standing between her and her car. 'Let's slow down for a second. Take a breath, Jellybean,' I suggest gently, placing a hand on her shoulder.

Reluctantly, she closes her eyes and inhales deeply, exhaling slowly.

'Good, good,' I say. 'Now again.' This time I do it with her. 'Feeling better?'

'No,' she says, her eyes snapping open.

'OK, well, how about you give me your keys then?'

'Why?'

'Because you're not driving me anywhere.'

'And why not?' Her voice is sharp, punctuated by the anger that has yet to die down despite the breathing exercises.

'Because you've been drinking, and since I was tasked to keep an eye on your drink, I taste-tested it for poison or roofies and nearly choked to death.' I glance around at where we are. It's a mix of bars, restaurants and closed boutique shops. 'Let's go for a walk and cool down.'

For a second she only stares at me, then she slaps her keys into my still open hand and starts to blow past me in some sort of speed walk, but I grab her hand and gently pull her back. 'We're not racing, just going on a casual stroll, like we do lately, Evie. I'm injured, remember?'

As the fire in her eyes gradually dims, she nods silently, slowing her pace and walking alongside me on the cracked sidewalk, her hand firmly clasping mine. Her breathing is heavy as we walk. So, we continue silently until it seems she's settled a bit as we reach a small neighborhood park with only a weathered swing set as its play equipment. Eve heads toward the swings, and I follow, sitting on a nearby bench while she settles in the middle swing of the three.

'I can't believe he had the audacity to approach me,' she mutters between each push off the ground. 'And then had the balls to say he misses me?' Her voice rises with each word. 'How can you miss someone you destroyed?' She swings higher and higher, her skirt billowing with each movement, but she seems unconcerned – her mind is elsewhere. 'Gawd...' she groans. 'Why did I tell him I'm happily married?'

'I'm guessing because you wanted to hurt him back. Not even knowing the story, and based solely on a side of you I've never witnessed before, it seems like he deserves it. Besides, it's not that much of a lie,' I say, watching as the moon casts a soft glow on her face. How is she pretty in all lighting?

'Both happily and married were total lies.'

I laugh under my breath, so as to not piss her off. 'Well, technically. But I'm not unhappy tonight. For you I am, but being out with you was the highlight of my year. Because of that, I bet we probably did look happy on the dance floor, and we have been married.'

For five years now. That's a marriage milestone, yet she has no idea. *You have to tell her sometime, Foster.* Maybe not when she's tipsy and ready to kill a man in public, though.

Eve scoffs, her voice dripping with disdain. 'Pfft. It's all so stupid. Love is stupid.'

'I couldn't agree more,' I reply, my tone matching hers.

My heart sinks as I realize the gravity of the situation. Cayden broke her heart, and it makes me wonder if this was how hurt she was when we split. Was I just another throat-punchable boy in her life? Is that why she never talked to me about it and only left a note? Did I do the same kind of damage to her that losing her did to me? I can't even think about that right now, it's too painful.

26

EVE CASSIDY

'Do you think less of me?' I ask, looking up at Foster as the swing slowly comes to a stop.

'Less? *Haill* no,' he responds, accent front and center, with a chuckle. 'Am I scared? A little. But I'm impressed as fuck too. From the angle I witnessed it, I don't doubt you just taught him a lesson he'll never forget.'

'Good.' I let out a sigh of relief. At least someone's on my side.

'That was Cayden, huh?' Foster asks, already knowing the answer.

'Yeah.' The word tastes bitter.

Tonight was the first time I've seen Cayden since we broke up a year ago. And the sight of him brought back all the pain and anger that had been simmering inside me.

'He cheated and told me after I'd made a speech at our engagement party – which was me spewing some nonsense about him being such a great man and the love that changed everything for me.' I glance over at Foster, who's listening intently. 'Great man he was not. That one hurt pretty good, and humiliation has never stung the way it did that day. So, I knew I'd be pissed when I saw him,' I admit, 'but not to the point of physically hurting the guy.'

'He's an asshole. *I* should have hit that tool,' he says, clenching his one good fist.

'No,' I say quickly, shutting the whole thing down. There's been plenty of violence for me tonight. 'He's not worth it in your condition.'

'For the record,' Foster says, 'he did deserve what you gave him.' His tone is as serious as I've ever heard.

'A bruised voice box?' I ask, finally laughing about it.

'Don't forget the likely bruised Adam's apple.' He smiles, chuckling with me. 'You're one hell of a nurse, but I think if you ever needed a change, boxing might be your thing.'

'How flattering.'

Our laughter dies down and he sighs audibly. 'Can I ask you a serious question?' His arm is propped on top of the bench and he's still wearing the cowboy hat with stitching on the rim 'cause it's all I could find.

'Why not? You've already seen the worst of me.'

'First of all, he's at the top of my shit list for making you feel that way at all. Not a second of that was the worst of you. It was the best. You stood up for yourself, fearlessly. I've never been prouder of you than I am right this second.'

A small smile tugs at my lips. It's nice to have someone looking out for me.

'Not that I could hurt him now,' Foster continues, 'but I volunteer if it needs to happen in the future. Is that clear?'

His protectiveness and loyalty toward me are heart-warming. I remember how safe I always felt in his presence. Even now, I'm not triple-checking that I locked my doors.

'That's sweet, but not necessary,' I assure him with a small smile.

'Onto my question,' Foster says, his tone shifting from protective to nervous. 'Now that you've faced us both – post-break-up – is there one of us who hurt you more than the other?'

How do I even begin to answer that when the answer is so obviously *him*? I hurt *for* Foster in the trauma room that day – to the point of nursing him back to health willingly. Tonight, I chose violence with Cayden and hit him because I hate him. Truly.

'Are you sure you want to know the honest answer?'

He forces a smile and tilts his head, looking anything but sure. 'Yeah,' he says. 'Lay it on me, Jellybean.'

***

Five Years Ago

'Congratulations!' my aunt Diana exclaims as she hugs me warmly. 'What does he do?' she asks.

'He's an FMX rider.'

She stares at me blankly.

'What's that?' she asks after a beat of uncomfortable silence.

'He rides motorcycles, professionally. He's won best in his sport at multiple X Games, and Red Bull is one of his sponsors.'

'A real Evel Knievel, huh?'

I cock my head. 'Eh – if you overlook Evel's alcoholism and wife-beating, I guess sort of.'

'Does he make money doing that?'

'More than I'll make as a nurse.' He risks his life, and I save them, yet he'll make more in a year.

'Is that so? Interesting. So, if I wanted to google the FMX, do I type it in just like that?'

I laugh under my breath. 'Just don't add on too many Xs and you should be fine.'

She nods, visibly making a mental note by tapping her temple.

'When do you two plan on having babies? Do you want to start immediately, or are you considering enjoying a few years of honeymoon bliss first?'

I raise a quizzical eyebrow. Why is this question so commonly asked? Life isn't a predetermined path that everyone must adhere to. We are not all the same. Sure, my family has preached (and followed) the 'graduate high school, then college, find an impressive well-to-do spouse, and knock out some kids' lifestyle, but we don't all want the white picket fence in the 'burbs while we stay home as a submissive housewife cleaning, cooking, and popping kids out like a Pez dispenser. I haven't even started my dream job yet.

'We just got married last week. Any baby decisions are long down the road. *Long*. Maybe we'll choose to have none at all.'

'No children?' she exclaims in surprise. 'What do you plan to do with your life then? Who will be there to look after you as you grow older?'

'Hopefully, someone with a medical degree,' I joke. 'Truthfully, Aunt Diana, why worry about the future when I'd rather focus on where I am and enjoy this party?'

'Right. So, where is he? This Foster fella, introduce me.' She glances around the room. 'Your mom said he's handsome, like a young Mark Ruffalo.'

I heard my mom say that recently and it caught me off guard because I don't see it. I guess maybe the hair is similar. And obviously his handsome face.

'Unfortunately, his schedule got in the way of today. He's on a plane, but only just, and it's an eight-hour flight.'

Her lips pinch into disappointment. She is definitely my mother's sister. 'He's missing his own wedding reception? That's not a great start, sweetheart.'

It's not like they've booked the Plaza – or whatever the Portland equivalent to that would be. We're literally standing in my great-uncle's pizza shop. Once my mom learned I'd raced out and got married to some random dude, she wouldn't let it settle without at least throwing us a reception. She said she'd forgive me for not inviting her to my wedding if I said yes. So here we are. In the middle of a wedding reception where only one half of the blissful couple has arrived.

I lift the iPad in my hand. 'He's not completely missing it. Once he's allowed to turn on his electronics he's going to attempt joining us via video.'

'It's cute,' Jess says approaching us from the rear, a glass of champagne in her hand that she gives me, saving me from tackling Aunt Diana alone. 'Like that scene from *New Girl* when Schmidt can't make it to their wedding.'

Another 'the lights are on but nobody's home' stare, her head moving between us. 'Who?'

'He'll be here shortly,' I say, waving the iPad and allowing my sister to steer me away from the partygoers who have questions and opinions galore.

'Eve, honey.' My uncle Steve steps in front of Jess and me. 'One month? You think you know him after one month? Sweetie...' He grabs my free hand. 'I've been married to Leigha since you were a baby. She says things I never knew every single day. I bet you didn't know he was going to miss this party?'

'Well, no, I didn't. But sometimes things happen – nobody's perfect.'

Shall I remind you of your three-month stint in the clink for a 'misunderstanding that was never revealed', Uncle Steve?

He nods, repeatedly, as if I should still be talking.

'You know how I am,' I continue. 'I like to follow my heart,' I declare, fully aware of my tendencies.

'I remember,' he says. 'The basketball player. He's in our family photos. Who was that again?'

'Josh,' I say, preferring not to have him on my mind right now. It feels taboo to be discussing the man I thought I'd marry at sixteen while at my wedding reception to someone else.

'Poor Josh. Had you two discussed breaking up when he went to college?'

'Nope,' I say, downing the champagne, completely over the entire day at this point.

My mom made it clear that I needed to be on my best behavior at this event. She knows that I tend to speak before I think. And while I usually don't regret what I say, the same can't be said for how my family receives it. So, I'm working on myself and taming my tongue for the sake of my future patients.

I glance across the room and catch sight of my mother. Her expression speaks volumes as she shoots me the 'don't say whatever you're thinking' look. I'd know it anywhere, as I get it often. She knows me so well that she can read my mind from a distance, especially regarding her annoying little sister.

'Evie,' Jess says, jabbing me with her finger. 'The iPad is ringing.'

I glance down and notice the incoming FaceTime request, walking away from the crowd to greet him.

'Hey,' I chirp.

He smiles at the sight of me, grabbing his chest like he's been shot by Cupid's arrow. God, I wish he weren't so handsome. Then I could actually tell him how disappointed I am that our marriage is starting with him being constantly on the road.

'Hello, beautiful girl.'

I crack a smile, dropping my head to hide it. I'm mad at him so he can't see it.

'I'm sorry,' he says. 'You know I didn't expect to miss any of this, but we got married without warning and I already had commitments. We didn't really consider the after, you know?'

I nod. 'I know. I'm not mad.'

'Yeah, you are,' he says, a slight knowing smile on his lips. 'And I plan to apologize however I can while I'm in your presence, for the rest of our lives. But for now, all I can offer is me, and my new friend and seat-mate Dave, who has invited himself because it's been a long time since he's been to a wedding.' He shakes his head slightly, a perplexed look on his face before panning the camera to an elderly man wearing dark-rimmed glasses.

'Hello! I'm Dave. Congratulations!'

'Who the hell is that?' Kait asks, walking up behind me, my sister at her side.

'Hello there. I'm Dave. Did you know this guy's a professional cycler? Like Lance Armstrong!'

'Motorcycles, Dave. I race motorcycles.' We hear Foster's voice before seeing his face.

'Is that right?' Dave asks as the camera finally fills with Foster's gorgeous face.

I laugh. 'This is not the wedding reception I always imagined.'

Fost frowns, his eyes moving to my right. I glance over my shoulder only to jump back at how close Kait and Jess are.

'Would you two go away?' I ask. 'I promised you could carry him around to meet anyone you want later. For now can I speak privately? To my *husband*?'

The two of them back off and I look back at the screen.

'Your husband,' he repeats the words. 'I love the sound of that.'

'Me too, but it's still really weird to say!'

'Evie?'

I look at his face. 'What?'

'You should move in with me. Get a job here. What do you think?'

My jaw drops. 'I just got my Oregon nursing license and have an interview with OHSU tomorrow. You were excited for me. Now you're asking me to move across the country and start the whole process over?'

He frowns, his eyes narrowing. 'Will you at least think about it, like you asked me to think about moving there?'

Dang it. It's been a month and he knows me enough to back me into a corner. Now I see his point.

'Yes,' I say. 'I will think about it. We're a team now, right?'

'Right. I've got your back and you've got mine.'

'As long as we both shall live,' I say with a wink.

'I love you, Jellybean,' he says. 'Now pass my face around the room and let your family interrogate me. I'll call you later?'

'You better,' I say, blowing him a kiss and handing the iPad to my sister who gladly chatters as she walks away from me.

* * *

Now

'Honestly, Fost, if I had to choose who broke me more, it'd be you.' My voice trembles as I speak, nervously glancing up at Foster from the swing I'm on. I can't believe he's here, after all these years, and I'm admitting this stuff to him. Memories of the first time he let me down flood back and my heart aches. 'When our relationship spiraled out of control, it changed me forever. I was so deeply in love with you that the pain that followed caught me by surprise.'

Foster nods silently, his head still lowered.

'But I understand,' I continue, swallowing past the lump in my throat. 'You weren't ready for marriage. Neither of us were. It just took me three months to realize it, and by then, it was too late.' I pause, as regret floods my chest. 'I'm sorry for how I ended things.'

I stop swinging and walk over to where he's sitting, watching me intently like a protective parent. I sit next to him, one leg folded on the bench beneath me and the other hanging over the edge.

'You left a note,' he reminds me, his eyes never leaving mine. 'Wasn't I even worth a phone call? I came home to an empty house one day.'

'I didn't take everything,' I protest weakly.

'Empty of *you*,' he clarifies. 'The only thing that mattered.'

'I didn't want to bother you.'

He reaches out and cups my cheek with his hand, his thumb brushing against my skin softly. 'You were never a bother. You were the most important thing to me. But I had prior commitments that I couldn't break.'

'I understand that. But please be honest with me,' I plead. 'Was I just not important enough for you to take a small break and celebrate the big decision we made?'

'Evie,' he says, leaning closer to me. 'You were more than enough for me. I didn't know how to be married. But damn, I never expected to lose you so quickly. Man, if I could go back—'

The sudden loud blaring of my phone cuts him off, startling us both. I pull it from my pocket and see my mother's face flashing on the screen. She rarely calls me, so I immediately answer it.

'Mom?'

'Eve, the baby's coming!' her voice sings excitedly through the speaker.

'The baby?' I turn to look at Foster with wide eyes. 'And I'm supposed to be there for that?'

'It's your nephew, Eve,' she lectures. 'This is a family event. It's his birth day and you need to be here to welcome him into the world and celebrate. Unless you want Kait, who's already here, to be his favorite auntie.' I can almost hear her foot tapping as she speaks. 'Hurry up and get here soon.'

27

GUY 'FOSTER'

The timing of this baby is truly terrible, as most babies' grand entrances tend to be. Just as I was about to pour my heart out to Eve and tell her that I would do everything all over again, without any hesitation or regret, we were interrupted. It seems to be a recurring theme for us lately.

'You don't have to stay,' Eve says as we follow a hospital guide through the maze-like hallways on our way to Labor and Delivery. Despite Eve telling the woman that she works here and knows her way around, the guide insisted on directing us. 'You can drive my car home and I'll have my mom bring me back,' she says.

'Don't be ridiculous,' I reply with a shake of my head. 'You came here for me, now it's my turn to return the favor.'

She gives me a slight smile. 'Are you sure? My family aren't exactly your biggest fans.'

I look down at her walking at my side, still wondering how she pulls off the cowgirl get-up so freaking well. 'And why's that?'

She shrugs, guilt written all over her face. 'A girl's got to confide in someone about her problems. Plus, let's not forget that you missed every important event they planned to celebrate us after our last-minute nuptials.'

I frown, ashamed that I did indeed do that. I was so obsessed with my career that I figured the five-minute ceremony was enough for us to live happily ever after. Now I'm realizing it wasn't. Was I even trying?

'Well, considering the little I know about what Cayden did in front of them, I'd wager they hate him more than they hate me for not being around. So, I'll take my chances,' I reply, hoping that these people can eventually forgive me for hurting their daughter.

And I get that she was hurt. But I didn't come out of this relationship unphased. No. I was a mess. Matty is taking things to the grave I was so torn up. Now, with Eve in my presence again, all I want to do is make it right.

The elderly guide leads us to a stop outside of room 411, Jess's birthing suite. 'Here we are,' she says with a kind smile. 'The family waiting room is just down the hall near the fire exit if you'd rather wait there.'

'We're good for now, thank you,' I reply, pushing open the heavy door for Eve to enter. I follow closely behind her.

The Labor and Delivery suite greets us with an air of sterility – white walls, floors, and furnishings. The air is thick with the smell of bleach, mixed with the faint aroma of disinfectant and the underlying musk of baby powder – the scent of a new life. I hear the steady beeping of a monitor, but it's slightly muffled by the chatter of Eve's parents, sister, and Kait, who's decked out in a pair of light blue scrubs.

'Hi, you guys!' Eve greets everyone enthusiastically, walking straight to Jess and gently patting her swollen belly. 'He's on his way, huh?'

The room falls eerily silent as everyone turns to look when they spot me.

'Foster.' Kait's eyes widen as she acknowledges my presence. Her gaze flickers over to Eve, then back to me as she mutters under her breath, 'You brought him?'

'I'm right here,' I remind her with a smile.

'Yes, you are,' she says, crossing her arms over her chest.

Eve could be right. These people may hate my guts.

Luckily, Kait's gaze moves over to Eve, and half a smirk creeps up on her. 'Where were you guys? At a rodeo?'

'In my condition?' I ask with a laugh, shaking my head. 'No, your sister brought me to a country bar,' I say, tipping my hat playfully.

'We went with Gen,' Eve explains. 'You know that guy she pretends she's not into, Brady? He works there. And I figured Foster was getting stir-crazy in my apartment and he missed the fun we used to have together, so I brought him with.' She suddenly turns to me, still a bit glassy-eyed. 'Shoot! I never got to prove to you that I can ride that bull!'

I chuckle. Clearly, she's still a little tipsy. 'There will be other chances for bull-riding,' I say, patting her back.

Eve's mother, who has been watching our exchange with mild confusion, finally speaks up. 'You two are back together?'

Eve shoots a panicked look at her sister. 'You didn't tell her?'

'Why would I? He's not my problem.' Her words hang heavy in the air, revealing the underlying tension amongst us all.

'Did, uh—did she do this to you?' her father asks, his eyes crinkling in a hint of a proud smile as he takes in the sight of my bruised and bandaged body.

I shake my head, wincing at the pain that's now breaking through, considering I've dialed back on the morphine and didn't take any at all this evening, just to make sure we made it to and from the bar.

'Motorcycle stunt gone wrong.'

'You know Foster,' Eve says with a fond smirk. 'He's a true adrenaline junkie, always pushing the limits of gravity.'

'Not just gravity,' Jess adds in a low murmur.

'She wasn't enough for you to show up before, but you came to her while you're hurt?' Jean – Eve's mom – asks.

She's never really been a beat-around-the-bush sort of woman. If she has a question, she's asking it. The first thing she asked me when we met was how much money dirt biking could possibly make. So I pulled up my bank account and showed it to her. If that was her only worry, I had it covered.

'Mom,' Eve interjects, shaking her head in exasperation. 'It wasn't like that. I volunteered to help.' The air around us seems tense as we wait for her mom's response, the only sound coming from the fetal monitor. The baby's heart thumps steadily, a soothing rhythm amid chaos. But mine feels like it's galloping through my chest, desperately trying to escape. That family waiting room has never sounded better.

Jess groans loudly, grasping tightly onto the bed railings as she writhes in pain. 'What's with this breakthrough pain?' she cries out, her eyes pleading with Kait for relief. 'Can't you up the meds? Is there a friend and family extra dosage that you forgot?'

'This isn't an oil change,' Kait says, shaking her head. 'Now, I'm not usually this honest with patients, but because you're my best friend I feel the need to warn you – you're not having a baby and feeling nothing, even with medication,' Kait says, looking at the printout scrolling from the monitor. 'Contractions are getting closer, though. I should probably prep the room.'

'I'm here! I'm here!' Suddenly, a tall blond man bursts through the doorway, his movements frantic like he's been running. In one hand, he holds a vibrant bouquet, and over his shoulder is a bag packed to the brim. 'I can't believe we forgot the bags!' he exclaims, setting them down on a nearby chair before turning toward the room and spotting me – a stranger. He furrows his brow in confusion, before blurting out, 'Who are you?'

The attention of the entire group shifts toward me again.

'Scott,' Eve says, stepping closer and sliding her hand around my bicep. 'Meet Foster, an old friend of mine. Foster, this is Jess's baby's daddy, Scott.'

Jess lets out an exasperated sigh and interjects. 'Old friend my ass. Foster's her *ex*-husband, the one I told you about.'

A flicker of discomfort crosses Eve's face but she quickly regains composure, forcing a tight smile onto her lips.

'This is the FMX star?' Scott asks, pointing at me.

My reputation precedes me, probably in more ways than just the one, too.

The whole room nods.

Scott turns to face me, his hand extended in greeting. 'Well, howdy, partner.' His eyes shift to my head, then to Eve, confusion filling his face.

'We were at Achy Breaky Heart when we got the call,' Eve informs him, flouncing her skirt with her fingertips as she explains our 'looks'.

'I've heard so much about you,' he remarks, causing Eve's jaw to visibly clench.

'All good, I'm sure,' I tease playfully, glancing at a glaring Jess while earning a hearty laugh from Scott.

Eve grins, relief painted across her face. Maybe they don't all hate me? All this guy knows is that I showed up during an important event in Eve's life – the birth of her nephew.

A low, guttural moan escapes Jess's lips and she immediately clutches Scott's hand, pressing it tightly against her chest. The pain etched on her face is evident as she lets out another cry of agony.

'That anesthesiologist said he could hit me in the leg with a hammer and I wouldn't care. Lies!' she exclaims loudly, frustration and discomfort clear in her voice. 'Get. Him. In. Here!'

'Relax, Jessie,' her husband says. 'And maybe loosen the grip on my h— aahhaaha,' he squeals, obviously getting the opposite of his request.

Feeling helpless, and a tad unwelcome, I turn to Eve and say, 'I think that's my cue. I'll be waiting for you down the hall.' As I leave the room, the sound of Jess's cries echoes through the corridor – the sound of birth control.

The waiting room of the hospital is decently sized. A couple of tables and chairs sit mid-room. The overhead lights are off and only small table lamps emit a warm glow in each corner. The walls are painted a crisp white, and on one side, a large window overlooks the city lights below and the Willamette River. You'd pay a million dollars for a home with this view. Along the walls, there are comfortable couches arranged for seating, as well as a flat-screen television playing sports highlights on mute. The only other occupant is a slight man, his eyes transfixed on the TV screen. It's hard to tell if he's actually waiting for someone or just catching up on the sports stats.

There's a faint smell of disinfectant lingering in the air, a reminder of the seriousness of the place. Posters promoting pregnancy and infant care line the walls instead of artwork. In one corner, multiple vending machines stand ready to provide sustenance and a Keurig promises a cup of hot coffee to those in need. I choose a spot on one of the couches and sink into its cushioned embrace, removing my cowboy hat and placing it gently over my face – like they do in the movies – then close my eyes and allow myself to rest.

After weeks of being confined to a bed for most of the day, I suddenly feel like I've just run a marathon. Everything hurts and I could sleep until tomorrow night, if I wanted. Instead, as I lie here, my mind races with thoughts of all the things I should have done differently. I should have brought her on tour with me, but the guys were against it because we'd only known each other thirty days – why should they have to change their lives while we lived together because I couldn't wait? They were scared it'd change the vibe of our group, and that creates a bit of havoc when you're doing daredevil things in front of a crowd. And how the fuck have I not considered having to make amends with her family if I ever tried to fix this mess? God, I wish things could be as easy as they were at first. I'd give anything to get that back.

***

Five Years Ago

As I pull into my driveway, she's standing on the porch, waving like a psychopath. A beautiful, fun-loving psychopath. I laugh, waving back as I park my car.

'Hi, handsome husband!' she exclaims, waving her left hand, now sporting a sparkling diamond as perfect as she is. She refused to let me pick the size because she didn't want to 'stand out' – that's not her, so she 'settled' for a .75 carat emerald-cut diamond, flanked by two smaller triangular-cut sky blue topazes that she claims remind her of my eyes. Sweet as sugar – that's my girl.

'Hello, beautiful wife,' I say, planting a kiss on her as I wrap my arms around her, carrying her up the porch and through the front door. Our usual, very 'casual' greeting anytime I arrive home, whether I've been gone ten minutes or ten days.

'I missed you!' she says, running a hand down my chest.

'Missed you too,' I reply, grinning as I set her down in the cozy living room. The scent of her favorite vanilla candle fills the space, mixing with the aroma of…

'Do I smell Chinese food?'

'Yes!' she says. 'I slaved in that hot kitchen all day for you.'

I laugh, patting her ass as we walk into the kitchen. 'I'll pay you back for that lie later…'

We sit at the island across from each other, because she wants to see my handsome face when she talks to me. Her words.

'Nobody on the road is this pretty,' I say, looking at her between each potsticker I eat.

She chuckles. 'Are you declaring me the prettiest girl on the planet?'

'I am.' I hop off the bar-stool and grab the trophy I just won from my bag and set it between us. 'I'll have my name and title buffed out. Tomorrow this will say, "Prettiest Girl on Earth – Eve Foster".'

She lets out a soft giggle – it's adorable – one of the many things I love about this girl. I really mean it too. I'm feeling things I've never felt before when I'm around her. Sometimes I can't even believe she fell for me. I'm usually covered in grease, reek of gasoline and exhaust, and trek dirt into the laundry with my clothing – and she sees right through it.

As we eat, we fall into our usual easy rhythm of conversation, sharing stories of our day with laughter and affectionate teasing. Sure, it's only been two weeks since we got married, but it's only going to get better. God damn. How lucky am I to have found a woman who can make even the mundane moments feel like magic?

* * *

Now

'Here we are.' Kait's voice cuts through my thoughts and pulls me out of a deep nap that felt like hours had passed. To my surprise, I see her helping a frail and weak-looking Eve over to the couch where I am sitting.

'What happened?' I ask, concerned.

'Birth is *not* a beautiful process,' Eve says with a small smile as she sits next to me on the couch, leaning her head against my shoulder.

'She fainted,' Kait explains, a slight grin on her face. 'It's interesting how she can handle trauma situations but gets overwhelmed by childbirth.'

'I'm not usually looking up my sister's hoo-ha,' she snaps. 'I'm complicated,' she continues with a sigh, closing her eyes as if to block out the memories of what she's just experienced. 'And the two moonshine drinks are not helping.'

Kait's nose wrinkles in disapproval. 'Moonshine? Is that what I smell on your breath?' She shoots a glance at me – as if the moonshine was my idea – before returning her gaze to Eve, who is now slumped against my side.

'Maybe grab her something to eat and drink,' Kait suggests, motioning toward the vending machines. 'It'll help with her blood sugar.'

Eve shakes her head stubbornly, burying her face deeper into my one good shoulder. 'No,' she mumbles, voice muffled. 'I can't eat after that.'

A smile tugs at the corner of my lips as I wrap my arm around Eve protectively. 'Don't worry, I'll take care of her,' I assure Kait as she slowly backs out of the waiting room, concern on her face but finally leaving us in peaceful silence.

I feel Eve's tension beside me as she leans into me, seeking solace from the ordeal she just went through. An image I don't want to tempt even a little bit. As I trace my fingertips gently up and down the back of her arm, I feel her muscles slowly relax under my touch. Her forehead is pressed into my neck, and it sends a shiver down my spine. It's been so long since I've held her like this, and I can't help but wonder how I ever let her go. Damn that Famous 15 side of me. The cocky – 'I *have* to win' – Guy who put that ahead of a life with her and she didn't want to wait – to put it shortly. We're in this situation because of me.

The glow of the table lamps casts a warm light on her delicate features, accentuating the curve of her cheekbones and the flutter of her lashes. How did I ever fuck things up with this incredible woman?

'Kait insisted I look to see my nephew crowning,' she says with a shudder. Just mentioning it causes her body to tremble against mine. 'Be glad you left when you did and didn't have to witness that. I'd rather be back at the playground in a less than safe neighborhood.'

'Me too, if I'm being honest,' I reply, my voice low as I inhale deeply, taking in her familiar scent. 'At least then we could finish a conversation.'

The room is so quiet you can hear the seconds tick by on the wall clock.

'What *would* you do if you could go back?' she asks, her tone hesitant. 'That's what you were about to tell me when my mom called.'

A sharp pang of regret pierces my heart as I recall the words I probably shouldn't have said, now realizing their potential to change our relationship in ways I can't predict. Will it be for better or for worse? Looks like we're about to find out.

'I would marry you again, properly this time, without hesitation,' I declare, my voice steady because I do not doubt this. I still want it.

Silence hangs in the air for a moment before she responds, her voice barely above a whisper, 'You would?'

'In a heartbeat,' I say, meaning it so much I hope she hears it. 'Evie, you're the only girl I've ever truly loved.'

She gazes up at me with tear-filled eyes, still nestled against my shoulder. 'Even now, after I broke up with you via a handwritten note?'

I nod emphatically. I'd forgotten she gets emotional when she drinks. 'Did that note break me?' I pause, allowing the heaving sigh to say it for me. 'Yes. But till death do us part, girl. Every word I spoke that day – hell, every word I ever said – was true. I was absolutely besotted with you, Jellybean.'

Her lips are parted as she listens, now sitting on her knees and facing me, her eyes focused on me intently as if I'm telling her a bedtime story.

'But I understand if you can't forgive me,' I say softly, my voice laced with genuine remorse. 'A good husband puts his wife and their relationship above all else. I didn't even try to do that. Instead, I was caught up in a career I was already dominating. In hindsight, I should have taken the time off to start our life together right. I can't change the past. But I am in control of my present.'

Eve's eyes shimmer with unshed tears as she searches my face, as though looking for any hint of insincerity. She places her hand on my cheek like she would when I was in the hospital, her fingers warm against my skin – just like then, instant tingles under my skin.

'I wish you'd have figured this out sooner,' she whispers. 'Maybe things would have been different?'

It's as if the entire world has narrowed down to just the two of us on that couch because she is all I see. I reach for her hand, entwining our fingers gently, giving her time to process everything that's been said.

'Things could be *so* different this time around,' I reassure her. 'Trust me, I've been obsessing over it since you left.'

'But you never even texted me.'

Shameful. Jesus, Foster.

'I know. We've discovered my fatal flaw. I shut down when things don't go my way, and I've worked on that.'

Her jaw drops, but she snaps it shut quickly.

'Also, I did just sort of lay this on you so don't think I expect you to respond to any of this tonight. We've got time to talk.'

Her eyes meet mine, filled with a mixture of emotions – uncertainty, longing, and a flicker of something that resembles hope. Or maybe I'm just wanting to see that last part. *Please, let it be hope.*

'I just need to think about things,' she says. 'My heart is beyond confused and the moonshine is making me cloudy.'

'Cloudy'. How is she this cute? With that I lift her hand, feeling the softness of her skin against my lips as I press them gently to her knuckles. All those dreams of our past I've been having lately come at me all at once and there isn't anything I want more than to get that back.

'I'm not going anywhere, Jellybean,' I whisper, hoping to convey all the love and reassurance that words can't express. And there it is. I know, without a doubt, that I am completely in love with this woman – since the moment we met and not a second less.

A gentle rap on the wooden doorframe of the waiting room draws our attention. Kait's face lights up with a soft smile. 'Your nephew's here,' she says, almost whispering in excitement. 'Would you like to meet him?'

28

EVE CASSIDY

The memory of my conversation with Foster at the playground and hospital continues to linger days later. We haven't talked about it at all. I've worked a lot of hours since then and lately we've just binge-watched comedies and kept our conversation light. I think he meant it when he said I didn't need to decide anything immediately.

But his words are etched deep into my mind like a haunting presence. It's hard to determine if it's friendly or horror, but either way, it's consuming my thoughts. I don't know how to feel – so I'm letting rum give it a shot. Liquor is truth juice, that always clears things up. Right?

'Wait, he actually said you were the only girl he's ever loved?' Phil's eyes widen in disbelief as he leans in closer.

'Yep,' I confirm, sipping my 'Hippie Juice' – a concoction of watermelon vodka, rum, triple sec, and pink lemonade, garnished with fresh strawberries. The drink is not only visually appealing but also dangerously delicious. Usually, I'd regret having one too many. But tonight – my Friday – I need the distraction for my mind and heart.

Phil is keeping me company until Genevieve arrives. Kait is stuck at work and my sister just gave birth to a baby, leaving me with few friends to confide in about this situation.

'Does he still love you?' Phil asks, casually sipping his Shirley Temple through luminous white straws.

I shrug, feeling uncertain. 'He didn't say. But even if he did, can I trust him? He's said it before. So has Cayden. Maybe Foster is only feeling things because he's in my presence again. I don't know what to believe any more.'

Phil nods sympathetically. 'I can't believe you let Cayden live,' he says, shaking his head in amazement. 'You've got more inner strength than me, sister.'

We share a wickedly evil laugh — as wannabe villains do — then sip our fancy drinks as we sit in our neighborhood bar like we own the place.

The 'place' being Glow, a bar that we stumbled upon one night while walking home from another bar. The walls are adorned with vibrant graffiti art done by local professionals and under the black lights, it's almost mesmerizing. As if that weren't cool enough, they even provide free glow necklaces and bracelets to add to the ambiance. Of course, both Phil and I are sporting them — his neon pink one wrapped around his forehead like a sweatband or fallen halo, and my neon blue one hugging my neck like a choker. I also have an array of neon yellow, purple, white, and pink bracelets adorning my wrist like a true Taylor Swift fan (which — let's be real — aren't we all?).

'Johnny boy!' Phil calls out to the bartender, lifting his empty glass and wiggling it in the air. 'Can I get another, sweetums?'

Johnny flashes his signature wide grin in response to Phil's theatrics, his dark eyes twinkling mischievously. 'Coming right up, sugar!' he calls back, playing along and already expertly mixing another Shirley Temple for Phil with a flourish.

I watch the interaction between the two of them with a smile, feeling grateful for Phil's presence tonight. He has a way of turning any situation into a comedy sketch, lightening the heavy weight on my heart. But despite the laughter and glittery neon lights surrounding us, I can't shake off the lingering thoughts of Foster and his unexpected words. 'Things could be so different *this* time around.' Does this mean he wants to try again?

'You know,' Phil says, leaning in closer, his voice softening, 'maybe this is fate giving you a second chance. Foster's back in town, and he's laying it all out there. Isn't that what you've always wanted? For him to at least try?'

'Five years ago, yes. That's exactly what I wanted.'

'Oh,' he says, his eyes moving to the front door.

I look over my shoulder, catching a glimpse of movement by the entrance – what he's looking at. Genevieve is walking in, spotting us immediately and waving. Then my heart stutters in my chest when I see Foster following her. A hesitant smile plays on his lips as he scans the bar, his good hand shoved into his jean pocket. Our eyes meet, and for a moment, it feels like time stands still as everything else fades away.

'She's betrayed you and brought him. How can we talk about him now?'

I let out a nervous chuckle, trying to play off the tension in the air. 'I don't know?'

'Well, get ready, because I feel like we're about to find out,' Phil replies, his eyes flickering between me and our unexpected guests.

Genevieve and Foster breeze over to the bar, their presence filling our small corner. My heart races as I try to compose myself, taking a deep breath before forcing a smile onto my face.

'Mind if we join you?' Genevieve greets us warmly, her gaze sweeping over us as if assessing the atmosphere.

Phil pats the stool next to him, which Gen beelines to, leaving the only empty one to my right. Foster gingerly takes the seat.

'Jellybean,' he says with that charming smile that sends a familiar flutter through my chest.

He looks breathtakingly handsome as always, his dark curly hair slightly tousled in a way that makes my heart skip a beat.

'Candy Corn.' I acknowledge him with an equally ridiculous nickname, keeping my tone neutral despite the chaos of emotions swirling inside me. My phone chimes on the bar so I glance down at the illuminated screen.

> **GENEVIEVE**
>
> Sorry, I thought I was picking you up and accidentally invited him!

Dang it, Gen. Why didn't she send me a warning text beforehand? I take a long sip of my drink while the screen dims to black.

'Sorry if I'm interrupting,' Foster says in his deep southern accent, sending shivers down my spine. 'But I was bored – and you're my only friend in this city.'

I hadn't thought of it that way. 'You're more than welcome,' I say. 'We were talking about tennis.'

Phil shakes his head, a clear 'what the fuck' look on his face. 'Basketball,' he says. 'Remember that boyfriend you had who loved basketball?'

I nod. I told him the story of Josh? I don't remember that. Must've been one of our wine nights.

'Basketball and... things,' he adds, trying to help but clearly uncomfortable with Foster's presence.

'Tennis, basketball-playing boyfriends, and things, eh? You sure there were no motorcycle-riding exes in that conversation?' Foster asks, raising an eyebrow and ordering a Coke instead of a cocktail since he's on medication and shouldn't be drinking.

The way Phil shakes his head screams 'lies'.

Foster leans in closer to me, our shoulders brushing against each other, and I'm hit with his cologne. Christ almighty, I will never make it through this night. I've been keeping my distance at the apartment, but I can feel his breath on my neck and goosebumps are quickly overtaking me. 'Considering we haven't really talked much in a couple of days, I assume that "thing" is me?'

He shouldn't be able to read my mind the way he does. 'Not entirely.'

He smirks.

Genevieve shoots me a quick apologetic glance before turning her attention back to Phil, engaging him in a lively conversation about some new show they both enjoy. It's like she's trying to give me space to navigate this unexpected chat with Foster.

'Did I say too much the other night?' he asks.

I glance at him, his piercing gaze intent on mine.

'No, no. It's not that, I just—' Taking a deep breath, I decide to be honest. 'It's not about what you said,' I start, the words feeling like a confession. 'It's about everything we didn't say before. The unanswered questions, the unresolved feelings—'

His eyes flicker with regret and he reaches out tentatively, his hand hovering in the space between us before dropping back to his side. 'I know I messed up,' he says earnestly.

'You did. And then with the Cayden mess, I've lost a lot of trust in men over the years.'

'I get it.'

'Then there's the fact that you're going to leave here eventually. And that's just one more thing for me to get over.'

He cocks his head, fidgeting with the straw in his drink. '*Were* you over me?'

I meet his gaze, the glacier-blue depths of his soul searching mine for a hint of the truth. There's a vulnerability in his expression that I saw back at the hospital when we first talked after he woke up. That rawness tugs at my heartstrings despite my best efforts to remain guarded.

'I thought I was,' I admit quietly, swirling the remains of my drink in its glass. The ice clinks softly, punctuating the heavy silence between us. 'But seeing you again, hearing your voice, taking care of you... it's stirring up old feelings, Foster. Feelings I thought I'd buried deep.'

His expression softens, a hint of sadness crossing his features. 'I never stopped thinking about you after you left. Even when I was far away, doing reckless stunts and living like there was no tomorrow, part of me has always longed for you.'

My throat tightens as he speaks, a mix of emotions churning inside me like a violent storm. That's present-tense longing. Holy everything – he does still love me. I can't tear my eyes away from his handsome face, even as the alcohol dulls my senses and leaves me at a loss for words. Part of me wants to pour my heart out to him, but another part is afraid of him breaking my heart. Again.

'Tell me what you're thinking.' The words leave his lips like smooth velvet. I can't help but drop my head, feeling a bit swirly from the drink.

'I don't know what I feel,' I say with a tipsy smile. 'Getting over you once hurt. I don't think I can do it again.'

'I never in a million years meant for things to go topsy-turvy and hurt you in the process.'

'I know,' I nod, sipping my drink. 'Despite that, I was a total wreck. I cried for weeks.'

Half a shy smile creeps up on him. 'Me too.'

'You cried? Over me?'

Be. Still. My. Heart. I always assumed he just hopped on to his motorcycle and forgot about me.

'Sometimes I still do,' he says, raising a single finger to his lips as if I'm not to tell a soul.

'Me too,' I admit. 'Once a year with your stupid anniversary comment, and a lot more since you've been here.'

'I'm sorry,' he says, leaning in closer. 'I wish there were a way to easily *know* if there are any true unresolved feelings.'

'Any ideas?' I swallow hard.

I tilt my head to the side, ready to see if we are thinking the same thing. The rum says we are.

'I do have one idea.'

'Lay it on me,' I say, ready to figure this out.

'A single kiss. No tongue. Sweet. Just to test our hearts.'

'So, it's sort of like a science experiment?'

'If that helps you, yes.'

'Alright,' I say. 'We deserve to at least know, right?'

'Right,' he agrees, leaning into me.

'How should we do it? Count down? Ready, set, go? Or just do—'

As his lips meet mine mid-word, electricity courses through my veins. The slight brush of his fingers against my neck would bring me to the ground if I weren't already sitting. His lips are exactly as soft as I remember, and he tastes of the Coke he's been drinking, as well as cool mint Listerine. An overwhelming fluttering in my chest grows, nearly taking my breath away. My God – I never felt this with Cayden. Ever. I think these *are* feelings.

Gen's voice cuts through the chatter of the bar. 'Heeey,' she says in a sing-song voice, leaning over the bar and peering around Phil.

'Earth to Eve,' Phil says, jabbing my ribs hard enough that I pull away from Foster and glare back at them. 'As fun as that looks – *what* are you doing?' he asks under his breath.

Genevieve approaches my bar-stool. 'I need to use the little girls' room, wanna join me?'

It's a subtle question, but I know all too well it's code for 'follow me now'.

'Sure,' I reply with a coy smile, darting a glance at Foster who nods in understanding. 'I guess I'll be right back.'

Turning away from him, I follow Gen through the crowded bar, weaving between bodies and dodging spilled drinks. But all I can think about is how sweet he tasted and what that kiss just did to my insides – head, heart, and loins.

With a sly grin, Gen leads me into the women's restroom, shutting the door behind us and leaning against it.

'A kiss?' she asks, lifting her palms to the sky. 'What brought that on?'

I touch my lips, noticing I need to touch up my lipstick in the mirror. 'A test,' I say, pulling the tube from my purse.

'Pop quiz, huh?' she asks, shaking her head.

'He thought it might reveal if we had any feelings left between us. I dunno, it just happened.'

'And…?' she asks, tapping her toe on the floor.

'It was so *so* good.' I swoon, popping the cap back onto the lipstick tube once my lips are sufficiently painted, and sliding it into my purse.

'As good as before?'

I shake my head. 'Better.' I haven't felt like this since I was a kid on Christmas Eve. I want to run back into that bar, hop onto that man, and ride him home. But I won't, because I'm a lady.

'Wanna hear what I think?' Gen asks.

'Probably not.'

She rolls her eyes, crossing her arms over her chest. 'I like him,' she says with a wistful smile, her features softening.

'You know he's gay, right?' I ask with a raised eyebrow, catching a glimpse of myself in the mirror.

Her expression turns contemplative as she gazes at me through the reflection. 'Not Phil – *Foster*.'

Foster! Duh. *Hello, rum.* I pause, taken aback by her statement. 'But you barely know him.'

'We've been talking about the guy for five years, so I sort of feel like I do. Now witnessing you two together, while he's conscious, I can see the potential for something amazing between you.'

Her words linger in the air, causing my heart to flutter with possibility.

My mind is racing with thoughts of Foster and the chemistry that seems to crackle between us whenever we're near each other.

'Perhaps you're picking up on the intoxicating allure of attraction? We definitely have that.'

Her head shakes with certainty, dismissing the possibility. 'Nope. You probably won't be surprised to know that Phil and I have been eavesdropping on your conversation and we agree, he's completely smitten with you. It's glaringly obvious. The words pouring from his lips, the way his body leans toward yours, the intensity in his gaze.' A heavy, longing sigh escapes her lips. 'It's the same gaze I ache for from a man, Eve. I truly believe you should listen to your heart.'

I let out an exasperated groan, my hands clutching the edges of the bathroom counter for support. Somehow I knew this was where this was leading.

'What if I follow my heart, and once again he chooses himself over us? I can't go through that twice. Fool me once and all that crap.'

'What's that old saying? "It's better to have loved and lost than to never love at all"?'

'I *have* loved him. *And* I lost.'

'Maybe the timing was off?' Gen suggests, trying to offer some comfort. 'I mean, most people don't meet and get married within a month. Maybe you needed to be older so you could figure out the details.'

Our whirlwind romance flashes in my mind – the spontaneous proposal, the rush to the altar, and now the bitter aftermath. Was it all just too good to be true? And if so, why was that kiss the best one I ever remember having with him, including on our wedding day?

'Are you suggesting we forget our past like dust in the wind and pretend we don't live on opposite ends of the country? That I once again play the role of lonely housewife while he chases his dreams?'

Gen furrows her perfectly arched brows, her expression conveying a mix of pity and disbelief. It's as if she thinks I'm the most naive and foolish girl on the planet.

'You know, people make long-distance relationships work all the time,' she says in a tone that is both reassuring and patronizing. 'I have no doubt you'll figure out the logistics and eventually live happily ever after – but like anything else, it's going to take some work from *both* of you. You can't just expect him to give up his life for you, either. Can you?'

'No.'

Damn her, being all sensible. Her words hold a glimmer of hope, but my heart feels heavy with doubt and uncertainty.

'Let me ask you this,' she says, turning to face me. 'Do you still love him?'

My heart clenches at the question, the answer obvious yet complicated. In the quiet restroom, with only Gen's expectant gaze on me, I finally admit, 'Yes, a part of me will always love him. But love isn't always enough, you know? Sometimes careers, distance and life get in the way.'

Gen nods in understanding, her expression softening with empathy. She reaches out and gives my hand a reassuring squeeze. 'Love is messy, complicated and rarely simple – no matter who it is. But don't let fear keep you from taking a chance on something that could make you truly happy. I see that in you when you're with him. The day he came into the trauma room, I wondered if you'd be able to keep it together. You looked like you'd seen a ghost. And tonight, when he walked in behind me, you lit up. I've never witnessed that in you. Maybe he deserves a second chance.'

The sound of muffled laughter and chatter from outside the restroom seeps through the door, a stark contrast to the intimacy of our conversation. I meet my own gaze in the mirror, searching for clarity amidst the swirl of conflicting emotions within me. Does he?

'You're right,' I say, not thinking it through one bit, just going with my gut. A feeling of determination washes over me. What am I so afraid of? 'I can't let fear dictate my choices any more.'

Her hands clap together with a sharp, crisp sound in front of her chest. 'Now take that handsome boy home and savor every moment while he's here. Life is too short to waste on things you'll never get back,' she says with urgency. Her eyes shine with the wisdom of someone who has learned this lesson the hard way.

29

GUY 'FOSTER'

As I stand in her kitchen, I can't help but feel nervous under her intense gaze. My eyes dart to the fridge, though I'm not even hungry. I just need something to distract me from this awkward moment.

Eve paces back and forth in the tiny living room, fiddling with the ring on her finger. The silence between us is palpable, weighing heavily on my shoulders like a thick fog. Finally, Eve speaks up.

'We need to try it again,' she says, determination in her voice.

I take a few tentative steps toward her, my heart racing in anticipation of what she might say next.

'Try what?'

'The bar was too distracting and I wasn't prepared for you to kiss me,' she explains.

'You want to kiss again?' I ask, surprised by her request.

But then again, every kiss with Eve is amazing. Even that small one at the bar told me everything I needed to know – she's never left my heart.

'I need to know what I felt, Foster. You owe me at least that,' she says, almost as if she's willing to fight for what she wants.

A smile tugs at the corners of my lips as I realize Eve isn't pushing me away. She's holding onto something, just like I've been clinging to my feelings for her. It's a dance we've both known the steps to but have been too scared to fully commit to.

I close the distance between us, my hand reaching out to gently tilt her chin up so our eyes meet. 'I owe you more than just that, Eve,' I say softly, feeling the weight of all our past mistakes and regrets slowly lifting off my chest.

Without waiting for her response, I lean in and press my lips against hers. It's different this time, there's an urgency, a longing that we've both bottled up for far too long. The kiss deepens, sparking a fire within me that I thought had been extinguished after she left.

Eve's arms wrap around my neck, pulling me closer in a silent plea for more. I respond eagerly, tasting the sweetness of her lips and feeling the warmth of her body pressed against mine. Every fiber of my being sings with joy at this reunion, as if the universe itself has conspired to bring us back together.

When we finally break apart, our breaths mingling in the space between us, Eve looks up at me with a mixture of surprise and wonder in her eyes. I can see the questions swirling in her mind, the 'what ifs' and 'maybes' that have haunted us for so long.

'Shit,' she says, the word surprising me.

I bite my bottom lip. 'Is that a "holy shit!" or an "oh shit"?'

'Both?' She's standing in front of me, a hand resting on her chest. 'Wow, seriously,' she says through a laugh. 'You're the only one who's ever kissed me like that.'

'Well, that's because you're the only one who's ever made me feel like this,' I confess, my gaze locked with hers, hoping she can see the sincerity in my eyes.

Eve's lips curl into a soft smile, her eyes shimmering with unshed tears. 'I... I missed this,' she admits, her voice barely above a whisper.

'I missed *you*,' I reply.

'You felt something then?'

I laugh. 'Oh, Evie girl. Yes. I felt something from the moment I met you and as we stand now, five years later, it's only stronger than it ever was.'

She sighs in what seems like relief, dropping her shoulders and walking to her couch. I follow.

'We still have all the same life details against us, though.'

I nod, sitting on the coffee table in front of her. 'Yeah, that we do.'

'Gen says people make long-distance relationships work all the time.'

'She's probably right, I don't really know.'

'Do you think we could do it? I mean… if we decided to try it?'

I take a moment to consider her question, letting the weight of her words sink in. The idea of a long-distance relationship with Eve fills me with both excitement and trepidation. We've both been hurt before – by each other – so the thought of risking it all over again is daunting because I doubt we'd make it through another break-up. But as I gaze into her eyes, filled with hope and vulnerability, I know that I can't let this opportunity slip away.

'I think we can do anything we set our minds to,' I say, reaching out to gently take her hand in mine.

She thinks about that, staring down at our hands. 'Can we leave the door open until we see how soon you get to go home?'

'Evie girl, I'll leave the door open for you until eternity fizzles out.'

I don't expect her to kiss me, but she does, gently, almost like she's afraid to touch me – which I get, considering my condition.

'I really did miss you,' she says when she pulls away. 'I had no idea how much until I saw you again in that trauma room, though.'

'Wait,' I say, sitting up. 'You knew you felt something then?'

'Uh—' She presses her lips into a flat line, guilt flashing across her face. 'All I knew is that my reaction to seeing you wasn't one I've ever had before. Then my workaholic self took weeks off to make sure you survived. I'd say something inside me definitely knew.'

I can't help but chuckle at her admission, feeling a mix of surprise and warmth at how our paths seemed destined to cross again in the most unexpected way. The way neither of us can avoid that anniversary post. It's like the universe has been playing the ultimate matchmaker, orchestrating a series of events that led us right back into each other's arms.

'Well, looks like fate had plans for us after all,' I say, my voice tinged with amusement as I thread my fingers through hers.

'And here I tell people fate doesn't exist,' Eve replies, a soft smile gracing her lips as she squeezes my hand. 'Who knew each of us living our dreams would lead us back to each other?'

'Not me,' I say, moving to the couch next to her and throwing my good arm around her, pulling her close.

Eve rests her head on my shoulder, her presence grounding me in a way that nothing else ever has. Not even motorcycles, and that's saying a lot. Nothing is set in stone, no, but nothing is off the table, either. That is huge.

30

GUY 'FOSTER'

'Today's the day,' Eve says as she drives us to the hospital for my possible 'final' appointment with Dr Sully.

'This is it,' I say, anxiety building in my chest. I don't know what I'm more nervous about, getting a green light to go back home or starting this adventure with Eve again and leaving her behind until we figure out the details that have haunted us for years.

'Are you excited to see your bike?'

I laugh. 'I honestly don't know how it held up after this, judging by my injuries. I could be going home to a brand-new steel horse.'

'You plan on continuing riding then?' she asks, glancing my way.

'I hadn't planned on quitting, no,' I say honestly. I can't lie to her at this point. Not if I want things to work out.

She nods, the silence around us slightly thick with nerves. I know I'm not the only one feeling it.

An hour later, I've had a CAT scan and Eve and I are now sitting in a small cold doctor's office, waiting. The silence is deafening. Eve fidgets with her rings, her hair, her outfit, while I sit on the table, staring at the blue skylight covers, wondering how this is going to go. I might have to leave her soon. Shit.

'Mr Foster, how are you feeling today?' Dr Sully enters the room with a focused gaze.

Both Eve and I straighten up, our attention on the man who might change our lives sooner rather than later.

'Better than I was,' I say. 'Though I admit, most of that's been because of Eve.'

He glances at his co-worker, fist bumping her. 'She's one of the best.'

'Thanks,' she says, as if it's no big deal. She's cute.

'You think I can get this sling off today?' I ask, motioning to the straitjacket confining most of my upper half. 'It'd be nice to have two hands again.'

The doctor tilts his head sympathetically. 'I'll take a look, but after looking at your CT, you may need another surgery on your shoulder in the coming months. Though I can say your internal injuries are healing nicely. I have no doubt that your physical fitness has played a role in that progress. Now let's take a look at that shoulder and wrist.'

Doctor Sully carefully removes the sling, revealing a bruised and swollen wrist. As he begins to gently manipulate the limb, I wince in pain. It's not that bad, but it's there.

'What's your pain level – 1 to 10 – right now?' he asks, mid-motion.

'Six?'

'Still on pain meds?' he asks.

'Only at night, otherwise Eve's got me on a regular ice/heat routine and ibuprofen.'

'Good, good.'

After what feels like an eternity, the doctor brings a stethoscope to his ears and directs me to take deep breaths as he listens to my chest from both the front and back.

Finally, he finishes with the exam and carefully repositions my arm back into its sling, securing it tightly against my chest.

'Well,' he says, glancing from Eve to me. 'I'm impressed with his progress. How do you feel about going home?'

Eve's and my gazes lock, a flurry of conflicting emotions passing between us. Uncertainty, longing, curiosity and hesitation all swirl together in an intricate dance. Our eyes are the only communication needed at that moment. Neither of us are sure how we feel about all this.

'I do miss my bed,' I say, but there is a small tremor in my voice. I don't want to say the wrong thing here.

'Are you saying he's free to fly now?' Eve asks.

'I am,' he says, watching her response.

She frowns, but catches it quickly, flashing us both a smile. 'That's great,' she says. 'You can finally get back to your friends.'

When she's done speaking, the doctor hands me a list of doctors in the Tallahassee area that I can see once I'm back.

'Take it easy when you get home, Foster; you've still got some healing to do, so no extreme sports for the time being,' he says before exiting the room.

'Wow,' Eve says. 'I expected it, but I didn't.'

Now's the time. If I don't tell her now, I never will and if I put it off any longer, this ending will hurt so much more.

'Evie, I've got to tell you something,' I say, nervousness apparent in my voice.

'Sounds serious,' she says, sitting back in her chair.

'Sort of. But I'm hoping that after recent revelations, it comes as good news.'

'Uh-oh.'

'Remember when I told you I never got over you?'

She nods.

'Because of that, I never signed the divorce papers. And Matty found out not too long ago and did some research. We're not divorced – in fact, we just celebrated our five-year wedding anniversary.'

She stares at me, blank-faced, suddenly pulling her phone from her back pocket and tapping at the screen frantically.

Her going straight to her phone is never good. I thought maybe she'd be excited to know we don't have to do anything more than make our relationship work – and celebrate the anniversaries as they arrive.

She reads the screen, her shoulders dropping.

'My God, I wondered why I'd never heard anything. Here's why: "Howard Sweet, long-time local divorce lawyer, aged sixty-seven, died unexpectedly yet peacefully at home over the weekend" – two months after

I filed for divorce. Foster, do you know what this would have done to me if Cayden and I had made it down the aisle? I'd have been humiliated. Again.'

'In my defense, I wondered why it took so long to get the papers, but I had no idea you were getting married. All I knew was that I didn't want to lose you officially, so I ran the papers through my shredder thinking that would stop it. I had no idea the guy was going to die and never actually file.'

'You've known this the entire time you've been here, and you're just telling me now?'

I nod, shame likely etched across my face like a shadow.

'I wanted to tell you,' I say, my voice thick with emotion, 'to lay all my cards on the table and just get it out there. But between the pain, meds and seeing you again, then all the interruptions we were dealing with – I couldn't find the time or the courage.' A weighty silence hangs in the air between us.

'Every day I'm with you, I'm reminded of how good we were together,' I continue. 'And I knew that telling you the truth would ruin that – so I wanted to see if anything was even still there for you before I did, and I didn't know that until recently.' My shoulders slump with shame.

'Foster, you lied to me. For weeks. After I gave up so much for you. My *fucking* lord, are all men liars? I mean, what else did you lie about?' She stands up, pacing the room in front of me.

'Lie? No. Evie, I thought after our recent conversations, you'd see this as a win? We still have feelings for one another, and we're still married. Is that not a good thing?'

'A *good thing*? This makes you a liar, Fost! Do you have any idea how selfish that was? What if Cayden and I hadn't broken up? When would I have found out? While standing at the altar?'

'I want to say I would have signed them since you were engaged to someone else, but that'd be a lie too. Had I known you were engaged to someone else, I'd have been the guy objecting to your wedding.'

She purses her lips, attempting to force away the quivering chin sneaking up on her – but I see it.

'Now I'm wondering how much of what you've said since you've been here has even been true?'

'That is ridiculous,' I say, surprised she's this mad. 'Every word that's left my lips has been true and you know it. That kiss, Evie, are you telling me you're going to deny feelings we didn't even have to say out loud?'

The shake of her head says she's not buying it.

'Come on, Jellybean. Can you blame me? You left without even talking to me, using words from our wedding against me. So I was mad that the papers didn't even come with a phone call,' I continue, my voice slightly elevated unintentionally. 'For years, I wondered what the fuck was going on. I would have tried your family but come on, Evie, we'd only known each other a handful of months before we were over. I didn't know how to find you besides just showing up at your door, and considering you didn't even say goodbye, that wasn't an option for me.'

She perches her hands on her hips. 'Was, "Thanks for nursing me back to health; by the way, I think we may still be married, so you might want to look into that", not an option either? You could have said this before you left the hospital.'

'Would it seriously have changed your mind?'

She lifts her shoulders, crossing her arms over her chest. 'I should have had the opportunity to find out at least.'

Our voices are raised and this feels like a giant backward step.

'Ugh!' she stomps her foot onto the ground. 'Why does every man I fall for tell me something at the last minute that should have been said far sooner? I don't want to be someone's last thought, Foster. Getting this from *you*, after all the conversations we've had since you've been here, feels exactly like that.'

'No time seemed right, but I knew I couldn't leave without telling you.'

She huffs. 'I can't invest years of my life in men who lie to me. I've tried it, and I pass. I think we both know that if we decided to give this another shot, I'd be sitting home, waiting for you to remember I exist. Then we'd spend an amazing weekend together, and then I'd have to wait another few weeks for another glimpse at what I got married for – because you don't have time for me when you're on the road – remember saying that?'

I nod. I did say that. It was a long time ago, but the words were said. At least I spoke mine – she wrote hers.

'I want to be someone's priority,' she says. 'I need someone I know I can count on, and I'm not sure you're that guy.'

My jaw is literally hanging open as she speaks, words eluding me. Is she dumping me right now when we barely even saw what could've been?

'I think you should buy the plane ticket. We both have lives to get back to. And when you get there, file for the divorce. Irreconcilable differences.' Without me, she exits the room, storming out, slamming the door behind her, and leaving me in silence.

Fuck. Did I seriously just fuck this up again? She wants me to leave. I drop my head as my heart – or what's left of it – falls through my chest, landing like a delicate glass vase and shattering into a million pieces right here in the middle of a doctor's office. *Somebody call 911 because I'm pretty sure I'm dead.*

* * *

She left me at the sterile, white-walled doctor's office and I was forced to call an Uber to get back to her place. My limbs feel heavy and uncooperative, like they are filled with concrete as I trudge up the three flights of stairs to her apartment. I finally reach her door and knock, but there's no answer.

'Evie?' I call out, rapping on the door again.

The click of her door opening gives me hope, but it's not Eve who appears – it's Phil.

'Hi, darling.' He shakes his head. 'She doesn't want to talk about it,' he says. 'But don't worry, I've got your stuff.'

As he exits Eve's apartment, he closes the door behind him, motioning for me to follow.

Confused, I do. 'You've got my stuff? What does that mean?'

He looks at me with pity in his eyes and it only adds to the ache in my chest. As I reach his now-open doorway, I notice my suitcase behind him in his apartment.

'Shit," I run a hand through my hair. "She's that angry?' I ask, feeling a sense of dread wash over me.

Phil nods solemnly. 'Come on in,' he says, beckoning me into his vibrant and eclectic apartment. 'You can stay here until you figure out your flight arrangements.'

'I haven't even booked one yet,' I confess as I step inside his home, not sure if I'm ready to face the reality of leaving Evie behind – but I've got no choice now. She doesn't even want to see me, let alone talk.

As I sink onto Phil's couch, my phone open to a flight finder, the weight of everything crashes down on me.

'I can't believe she's giving up on us. Again.'

Phil places a warm cup of tea in front of me, the steam rising slowly, offering comfort in its simple gesture.

'You know, sometimes things fall apart so that better things can come together,' Phil says softly, his voice filled with understanding. 'You'll figure it out.'

'I wish I were as hopeful. But I'm not. This feels just like it did the first time. No closure at all, and I wouldn't be surprised if she hands you a note to give to me before I leave...'

He smiles sadly. 'Maybe I can try to talk to her?'

I shake my head. 'I can't risk pissing her off more than I already have, can I?'

As night falls outside, casting shadows that dance across the walls like memories fading into the distance, I drift off to sleep on Phil's couch, with a sense of dread settling over me. Tomorrow morning I leave – without her. If there's a way to save this, I hope it comes to me soon.

31

EVE CASSIDY

Freaking Phil. He spent most of the night convincing me via text to at least drive Foster to the airport and give him some closure.

Is that a bad idea? Probably. But here we are, strolling from my car which is parked in the airport garage. I insisted on carrying his bag even though it's almost half my size but midway through our walk, he gently takes it from me.

'I can carry my own bag,' he states. The warmth in his voice is no longer there and it stabs at my heart a bit.

I don't know what I was thinking because deep down, I knew that he couldn't stay in Portland. His life is in Florida – and on the road, with every energy drink extreme sports event available to man – and he loves it. Even I can't deny it's what he was meant to do. He's not the top FMX rider because he runs around partying and vacationing. He works his ass off, and he deserves to return to it after everything he's recently been through. Knowing Foster as well as I do, I'm certain he can't wait to reunite with his bike and hit the track again.

He flashes me a shy grin as we stop before the boarding screens to look for his flight. He casually drops his bag onto the floor, then reaches into his pocket to retrieve his phone, navigating through the screens with nimble fingers to find his electronic ticket.

'Care to share your thoughts?' he asks, casting a brief glance in my direction before shifting his gaze to the boarding screens again.

'You don't want to know,' I say, peeking at his phone to glimpse his flight number.

Then I nervously scan the departure board, half-hoping to spot the words 'CANCELED' or 'DELAYED' next to his flight number but to my dismay, it simply reads 'ON TIME'.

I can't help but feel conflicted. Part of me – a big part – wants him to stay. The other part is waving a red flag and I've ignored that before. I can't be with someone who keeps things from me. I've learned that lesson the hard way twice now.

'I don't know how I'll ever thank you,' he says, slowly strolling over to a bench just before the passenger-only zone. 'But I will pay you back,' he murmurs. 'You didn't have to step up, but you did, and for that, I'll forever owe you.'

I force a smile as if it were no big deal. Like, I'd do it for anyone. But the truth is, I wouldn't. The only person who's ever made my heart stop and caused me to take weeks off work, even after not seeing him in years, was him, and now it's time for us to say goodbye for good.

'You don't owe me anything,' I say, my voice soft, trying to convey that there are no debts or obligations between us.

'Except for one divorce,' he says, with a tinge of sadness. 'I promise I will take care of it as soon as I return.'

Why does the thought of that hurt? I insisted he take care of it, fueled by my frustration over his failure to disclose the truth earlier, so I don't doubt by next weekend, I'll be a single woman again.

'Flight 857 to Tallahassee, Florida, is now boarding at Gate 4A.' The words that I've been fearing ever since I told him to buy a ticket now reverberate through the airport corridors, enveloping us in their weighty significance.

As our gazes lock, I see a flicker of panic and perhaps a touch of regret in his eyes. Yet we remain motionless, not even making a single effort to change our positions.

He finally releases a heavy breath. 'I suppose that would be me,' he mutters, rising from the bench but hesitating to pick up his bag. Instead, he reaches his hand toward me, offering to help me up, and I accept it.

His sudden one-armed embrace envelops me, pulling me into his warmth and closeness. I respond by holding him just as tightly, feeling the strength of his uninjured arm around me, and I feel safe. I breathe him in, allowing his cologne to fill my senses, making the moment all the more intense. One I'll never forget. Is this the last time I'll have him this close? He kisses the side of my head, his lips lingering.

'I left something with Phil, for you.'

'Oh?' I say, wondering what on earth that could be.

'Yeah.'

I find myself standing there, not wanting to utter the words that will make this real. As the announcement for his flight echoes through the air for a second time, I realize that I have to let him go, even though every fiber of my being resists.

'I guess this is goodbye then, huh?' I choke the words out.

He steps back, his fingertips slowly gliding down my arm, before he grasps my hand tightly.

'I suppose so,' he says in a hushed tone.

'Text me when you land?' I request. 'Just so I know you got home safe.'

He nods, and if I'm not mistaken, I swear I see a glimmer of tears welling up in his eyes, mirroring the same emotion I feel. His eyes lock onto mine with such intensity that the overwhelming sense of his impending absence, even as he continues to stand right in front of me, nearly stops my barely beating heart. Maybe I made a mistake? I did. I made the mistake of letting him in again.

'Make sure to take your pain medication – the lower dose – once you board the flight. You don't want to be sore mid-air.' I struggle to keep my voice steady, fearing that my emotions might betray me as I anticipate returning to my apartment without him.

'I promise I'll stay on top of the weaning off the pain meds,' he assures me.

'OK.'

He lets go of my hand and stoops to pick up his bag, slinging the strap over his uninjured shoulder. He hesitates for a second, then makes his way toward the passenger-only area of the airport without saying the word goodbye.

As he walks, he looks back a few times. I manage to keep my composure each time, but I can't bring myself to leave until he's entirely out of view. Just before he disappears around a corner, he glances back once more. I raise my hand, trying to force a smile despite the turmoil inside me.

Turn back, you idiot.

He waves, but his gesture lacks enthusiasm and two seconds later he's out of my sight. Gone. I stand there, waiting, until I hear the final boarding call for his flight. That's when I know, he isn't pulling a Rachel Green. Foster is *not* getting off the plane. My heart feels like it's flatlining.

Don't die completely, heart, I say to myself, turning to leave before I lose it in public. *Please, don't die.*

* * *

'I'm sorry, honey,' Phil murmurs, perched on a bar-stool next to me, adorned with glow sticks on every limb and around his head as usual. 'If it's any consolation, he didn't walk away from you easily.'

'That's the worst kind of consolation,' I say with a heavy heart.

'He did, uh—' Phil stalls, reaching into his pants pocket, '—he left you something.'

That's right. I forgot he'd said that.

'What?'

'This.' Phil sets a folded piece of notebook paper on the bar in front of me.

For a second, I stare at it – wondering what it is but afraid to open it.

'Did you look?' I ask.

Phil nods. 'I think you should too.'

I set my drink on the bar and slowly unfold paper that feels delicate. Like it's been folded and unfolded over and over and may fall apart at any moment.

Once I've got it opened, I suck in a breath, seeing my own handwriting staring back at me.

'I can't believe he kept this,' I whisper, my heart aching as I look at the note in front of me.

'Me either. But he pulled it out of his wallet last night with tears in his eyes and said even though reading it hurt, it's the only way he knew to keep you with him after you left.'

I cry, wiping the tears away so I can read the words I'd never forgotten. 'Love *should* be enough.' Where my name was signed is now crossed out with bright pink ink and instead, his name is scribbled underneath it.

Phil side-eyes me. 'Thoughts?'

My own words being used against me doesn't feel good. I wonder if this is how he felt the first time he read them? Words straight out of Judge Ashford's mouth when he married us, used as a weapon. God, I'm a bitch.

Without realizing it, I wipe away tears that have fallen.

'It's alright, honey. Cry it out, sometimes it's all we can do,' Phil says, sliding his arm around me and pulling me close, allowing me to cry on his shoulder.

Foster kept the note I left on him at all times, for five years. Probably hoping one day love *would* be enough. And then it was, and everything fell apart again.

'He's not coming back, is he?' I say through sobs.

Phil's face contorts into a frown, and I can tell that even he wishes for a different outcome.

'It would be so romantic if he did,' he says softly.

I feel torn, like Phil is the angel on my shoulder, and my conscience is the competing demon. Thoughtfully reminding me why I shouldn't feel anything for Foster because he doesn't deserve it. But my heart is on Phil's side, unfortunately.

'I thought watching him leave would give me closure,' I admit weakly. 'But now it just feels like a sharp and painful word.'

Phil nods in understanding, knowing all too well the complexity of emotions in a situation like this.

'I'm sure you'll get over him eventually,' he says, trying to offer some comfort.

I'm not so sure about that. This feels like an overreaction to a break-up we never got to have. I wanted love to be enough last time, and I hoped it would be so much more this time.

32

GUY 'FOSTER'

Standing in my kitchen, I feel like a stranger in my own home. The familiarity of the space only amplifies the pain that lingers from my recent heartbreak. It's almost suffocating, and I wonder how I will ever survive this pain again.

The morning sun shines through the semi-closed blinds as I open cupboards, my stomach rumbling with hunger, only to find them nearly bare. I guess I haven't been home in a month, which leaves me with hardly anything edible – just a few unopened boxes of crackers and some cereal – but no milk. Great – now I need to go to the grocery store.

I purge all the expired and rotten food from the cupboards and fridge, carefully sealing them in a trash bag before hauling it out to the cans. As I step outside, the warm and humid air of Florida envelops me, a stark contrast to the cool, damp climate of Portland that I have grown accustomed to. The sensation makes me pause, unsure of which I prefer now.

On the way back in, my pocket begins to vibrate with a familiar buzz. Retrieving my phone, Eve's name flashes on the screen, catching me off guard and causing me to stumble over the threshold into my house. I barely catch myself from face-planting into the door as I read her message.

> Make it home safely?

With a heavy heart, I read the four words on my phone screen. They feel like a punch to the gut, almost knocking the wind out of me.

> Home. Thank you, for everything, Evie.

My emotions are in turmoil. I feel like a ship lost at sea without any direction or purpose. The familiar warmth in my chest that her message brought on is now gone, replaced by a hollow ache that hurts with every beat of my heart.

I stare at my phone, willing another message to appear from her, any sign that she still cares. But as the notification changes from delivered to read, reality sinks in. She's moving on without me. The 'unofficial' goodbye I never wanted.

Distraction, distraction, I need a distraction. I catch a glimpse of the Ziploc bag full of medication that I tossed onto the counter last night. I haven't taken any of my meds since I left, and I promised her I would keep up with them. I suppose I should actually do that.

With a gentle shake, I pour out the contents of the bag onto the smooth black marble of the kitchen counter. The bottles roll against each other, creating a soft symphony of sound. As I sort through the various medications, my fingers graze over a piece of paper, folded in half with my name written across one side. I pause. It's Eve's handwriting, sweet and delicate, detailing the instructions for each medication. Despite her dislike for nicknames, she signed the note, 'Love, Jellybean.'

I steady myself with my hand on the counter in front of me, the note staring back at me. It's as if time momentarily freezes, and I become intensely conscious of the rhythm of my own heartbeat. Even though she claims to hate the nickname, she chose to sign a note with it.

The familiar scent of her lingers on the paper, filling my senses and bringing back memories of our time together. With a trembling hand, I hold the note close to my chest as if it were a precious treasure. I gave one away, and I got one back. Fate.

Despite trying to fight it since we arrived at the airport yesterday, there's an overwhelming urge pulling me back to her. But deep down, I know that if she truly wanted me to stay, she would have used her words instead of remaining silent. We've come at least that far in the last month – or so I thought. I carefully attach the note to the fridge using a magnet shaped like my bike.

I spend what feels like an eternity at the kitchen island, one-handedly organizing each pill into the daily pill containers Eve so thoughtfully purchased to streamline the overwhelming process. The tiny capsules gleam in the sunlight filtering through the window; a rainbow of colors and shapes representing the multitude of medications I've been prescribed. Earbuds are nestled snugly in my ear, the haunting melody of a heartbreak playlist filling my head that speaks to my current state of mind.

As I finish my medication ritual, exhaustion washes over me like a wave crashing against the shore. In spite of this, sleep seems elusive. My bed, once a sanctuary of comfort and security, now feels foreign without Eve's reassuring presence in the next room. Instead of drifting off, I find myself staring at the ceiling for hours on end, music still playing in my head as my thoughts replay every moment since the accident and even before.

My phone disrupts the endless cycle of thoughts with its insistent ringing and with nothing better to do, I tap an earbud to accept the call.

'Ye-llow?' I try to sound upbeat, but it comes out so sad even I notice.

'Got your text,' Matty says. 'You're home? Last I knew, you two were considering driving into the sunset together again.'

'For a second I thought the same thing. But you know how I like to fuck romantic things up.'

'That, I do. What're you doin' now?'

I heave a sigh. 'Sulking in bed.'

'At three in the afternoon? Jeez, you're such a girl.'

'Thanks.'

'Well, don't sulk alone. Come on over. I had to run to the store for grilling meats so you can come and spend the evening with us. I'm barbecuing, and the guys are over. I told them you were home and you know how sappy they are.'

I chuckle. 'Yeah, I bet Jeff can't wait to see me.'

'You'd be surprised, bud. Get ready, I'll be there to pick you up in five.'

'Fine,' I say, reluctant to go. But I can't keep lying in this bed replaying where things went wrong.

I guess seeing the guys could be fun. Even though I can't ride right now, I'm excited to get back to my usual life and savor the scent of gasoline, oil, exhaust and hot metal.

Matty lives on a sprawling estate in Florida, where he's constructed an impressive FMX practice track tailored for his team of riders. The track features strategically positioned jumps and ramps, spanning a combination of hard-packed dirt and loose soil. It includes elements such as berms, rhythm sections, and tabletops to test his riders' skills. Lined with palm trees on both sides, the area is bathed in the intense glow of the Florida sun, which can be pretty relentless during the day's scorching heat. I could ride the track with my eyes closed, that's how familiar I am with it.

Heidi, Matty's wife, welcomes me with a warm smile as she opens the front door of their home.

'Foster!' she exclaims, her eyes lighting up with joy as she gives me a gentle hug. 'You look great! How are you feeling?'

It's good to be reunited with familiar faces, especially those I used to encounter daily. It's particularly nice to see Heidi, who has always been a strong source of support for me, second only to Matty.

'Not gonna lie, I've been in better shape. However, the doctors have assured me that physically, I'm on the mend.'

'Good! I was so worried, but Matty assured me you were in good hands?'

I nod, an undeniable grin at the thought of those hands. 'The absolute best by way of my ex-wife.'

'Ex?' Heidi asks with a gasp. 'I've never heard you call her that. Things didn't go the way you'd hoped?'

I shake my head. 'I lost her. Again.'

'Oh, honey, I'm so sorry.' She wraps me in another hug, this time a little tighter. 'We've missed you around here. Things weren't the same without our Famous 15. The guys are out back. I'm sure they can take your mind off things.'

Only a lobotomy could succeed in that right now. But I make my way outside and as I step onto the practice track near the back of the property, Jeff zooms toward me, skidding to a stop, his back tire practically touching my toes, kicking up a cloud of dirt that covers me.

He kills the engine of his bike and pulls off his helmet. 'You made it!' he says enthusiastically, then follows it up with a frustrated – yet not entirely serious, 'Damn it.'

'Ha ha,' I tease with a mischievous grin. 'You might be winning now, but just wait until I'm back on my bike, Jeffy boy. You won't know what hit you. Enjoy your victory while it lasts – asshat.'

He slaps on his helmet, raises his middle finger in response to my words, and then slams his right foot onto the kick-start lever. With a twist of the throttle, he sends a rooster tail of dirt flying in my direction as he speeds away. With unwavering confidence, he maneuvers through the track, cutting through the air effortlessly as he nails a double backflip, landing it without a wobble. It's a feeling I remember well and I can't wait to experience it again.

The familiar sound of roaring engines makes me feel like I'm home. This last month is the longest I've ever been away from this. I missed it.

I seat myself in a row of worn lawn chairs arranged outside the track, under the shade of a line of swaying palm trees. This spot has been witness to countless memories shared with the people who fill my days, where laughter knows no bounds, and we challenge each other with outlandish bad ideas. Here is where we push the boundaries under the open sky. It's a place where the motto is 'the bigger, the better'.

'You set up your physical therapy with Dr Dave?' Matty asks, walking up from behind me and interrupting my memories. Neither of our gazes leaves the track.

Dr Dave is the go-to doctor for taking care of Matty's riders. He specializes in sports medicine and is renowned as the best in the business. Over the years, he has helped me recover from numerous injuries sustained in crashes and accidents.

'Yep,' I reply with a nod, my gaze fixed on my friends as they take turns performing their daring stunts.

'How does it feel to be back?' he inquires.

I shrug nonchalantly. 'I dunno yet.'

'Wanna reunite with your bike? I'm sure it's missed you.'

With that, my insides light up a little. 'Yeah.'

'It's taken a while, but Jeremy has finally managed to get it in even better than its original state, just the way you like it. It looks as good as new and is all set for you, whenever you're able to get back to using it.'

As we walk into the shop not far from the track, the sight of our impressive collection of motorcycles greets me. Most of them have been generously donated by our sponsors and are worth a substantial amount of money. The walls are adorned with posters of Matty's riders – me included – performing stunts, and the floors are scattered with tools and spare parts. The center of the garage is dominated by a large workbench covered in tools and surrounded by motorcycles in various states of assembly.

Jeremy, one of our mechanics, diligently keeps our bikes in top-notch condition and race-ready. Each of us has a favorite, but we also have back-up options available for when one of them is out of commission. Unfortunately, I had the accident with my preferred bike, so I'm certain it suffered just as much as I did, and I can't wait to see it again.

'Foster!' Jeremy calls out at the sight of me, his voice echoing through the shop as he makes his way over. 'Jesus, man. I was worried. How do you feel?'

'Broken,' I chuckle, my gaze fixed on my bike. 'But look at this shit,' I exclaim with a smile as I instinctively swing my leg over the seat to climb onto it, placing one hand on the handlebar.

'Start her up!' he encourages.

As he speaks, I am already kicking her over, twisting the throttle with my uninjured hand, and reveling in the powerful roar of the engine. Ah – home. I take a deep breath, feeling a sense of calm and contentment wash over me.

'How's it feel?' Matty yells over the engine.

'It feels good,' I shout back, bouncing a little to test the shocks.

Against my better judgment, and in a move I think we all knew I'd make, Jeremy hands me a helmet. I slide it on, then engage the gear and ride out of the workshop, heading toward the track. Despite my initial apprehension, I gradually regain my confidence with each gear I shift, all the while mindful of my immobile arm. No jumps for me today. Instead, I focus on relishing the rush of riding again.

As the other bikes come to a halt, I can feel the eyes of my friends on me as I race around the track. Despite my best intentions, I'll never be able to resist the urge to pick up speed and catch some air. And it feels damn good, too. As I return to the shop, Matty and Jeremy give me a standing ovation.

'You're crazy as fuck,' Matty says as I cut the engine.

'"One-armed Bandit" should be your new name!' Jeremy teases. 'How was that?'

I steady myself by planting one foot on the ground. 'Incredible,' I say, wishing I could keep going but knowing I can't tempt fate quite yet.

'Eve woulda killed ya if she were here,' Matty says.

I drop my head, my helmet in my hand still. 'Yeah, she woulda.'

'That didn't end great, huh?'

I shake my head.

Amidst the whirlwind of emotions that arise at her mention, one memory stands out – the image of waking up in the hospital and seeing her. I remember it like it happened last night. She would be pissed if she knew what I just did yet deep down, I think she would understand. Because somehow, she gets me like no one else ever has. There's a connection between us that defies words, but despite that, I never found the courage to tell her the truth until it was too late. I never said, 'I love you' or 'I want to stay.' It's a realization that hits me like a ton of bricks – I am a fucking idiot.

* * *

'Why is it so dark in here?' Matty asks, meandering through my house the day after I visited his place, pulling open curtains and allowing the light to invade my cave of heartbreak. 'And why are you asleep at noon? And what in the fuck are you listening to?' he asks, in search of the source.

'Taylor Swift,' I answer, shoving the source of the music into my pocket so he can't take it and throw it out my front windows.

'*Taylor Swift?*' he balks, a comical look on his face. 'Why?'

I run my hand through my hair as I sit up, frustrated that I'm lying here alone and all I can think about is her.

'Because it makes me feel better, asshole,' I snap, only partially kidding.

'If I'd have known you'd come home as a Swiftie, I'd have found a way to get you here sooner.'

I shake my head. Not once have I ever listened to Taylor, and here I am stewing in it.

'I still love her, man. I can't sign the divorce papers.'

I filed as soon as I got home and got the documents in my email this morning.

Matty groans like a disappointed father.

'My God, you're a lot of work. If you love her, then why don't you act like a man and hop your ass on the next flight to PDX and tell her? It's what she wants, moron. Give her two options.'

'Two options?'

'Bring her the original wedding ring – the one she left on your nightstand. I know you still have it because you've been fighting this thing for a long time. And bring the divorce papers. Then make her an offer she can't refuse.'

'You think I should ask her to stay married to me?' I'm confused, but it might just work.

'It's been five years. So yeah, dumbass, but lace it with romance and spontaneity – the reasons she fell in love with you to begin with – and for the love of God, get on your knees and beg because you've now broken that girl's heart twice. I can't afford to have your head constantly in the fucking clouds if you're going back to competing.'

Say no more. By dark, I'm on a plane back to her. Man, I hope I'm not too late.

33

EVE CASSIDY

'I just wanna sleep!' I yell into the dark for the second night in a row. But I can't, because my mind won't shut down.

You know what, I should call him and yell. Tell him what he's done to me for the second time. Why the heck shouldn't I? I hit his contact name on my phone and put it on speaker. But it doesn't even ring, just goes straight to his voicemail.

'What's up, this is Foster. Leave me a message. Or text. I'd rather you text.'

The sound of his voice hurts physically, yet I want to call again just to hear it. I hang up, pulling up our text thread and typing one out.

> Why?

I hit 'send' but I feel like this needs more than a single word.

> Why didn't you turn back at the airport?

Send. That's better. But let's annoy him a little.

> Am I just not enough?

Send. Ouch. That one hurts to read and I sort of hope he doesn't answer it.

At some point I drift off, awaking to a relentless pounding on my door as if the person on the other side is determined to break it down. It feels like a scene from a crime movie, and at this moment – while I'm feeling particularly stabby – the thought of facing the consequences for a crime I didn't – or have yet to – commit doesn't scare me.

I let out a groan, rolling over in bed and trying to ignore the persistent knocking at the door. They've got to have the wrong apartment. But no, they don't go away and the sound continues, echoing through my skull. If I don't answer, whoever is outside will likely wake up the entire building.

'You're really brave!' I yell from the depths of my room, throwing the quilt from my body and storming toward the front door. 'You should know that I'm in the mood for murder, given the terrible few days I've had – or truthfully, the terrible few *years*. So, if you know what's good for you, you'll go aw—' I yank open the door mid-sentence and suddenly find myself frozen in place.

At my feet is Foster, down on one knee, with a stunning bouquet of daisies placed on the ground in front of him. In one hand, he holds my old wedding ring, and in the other, a set of papers.

'You *are* enough,' he says immediately.

He got my text.

'I, however, am a complete idiot. I got home and realized I only wanted to be where you are – with the only girl I've ever truly loved. My house didn't feel the same. Florida didn't feel the same. Even my bike didn't feel the same. I know you're mad that I didn't tell you about still being married sooner, but I want you to know that I have a plan.'

A weird half-cry, half-laugh exits my lips. 'You do?'

He nods. 'I've only been thinking about it for five years. I just – it took this for me to realize I'm ready. I love you, Eve, until death do us part. Still. Love *is* enough.'

Tears are streaming down my cheeks at this point. I drop to the ground on my knees in front of him. 'You love me?'

He grins sincerely, looking as emotional as I've ever seen him. 'I *really* do. Literally since the day we met, even though I don't understand how it's possible to love a stranger, but it happened the second I laid eyes on you, and I can't let you go again.' He takes a heaving breath, as if getting through that was a strain. 'But in case you don't feel the same, I also filed for the divorce, and I'll sign the papers, but only if you really, really, *really* want me to.' He looks at me with puppy dog eyes, pleading for forgiveness with a sparkle of hope that this will go the way he wants.

I cross my arms over my chest – playing hard to get even though my heart has jumped to life and is twirling in my chest. 'Are you done lying to me?'

He nods enthusiastically. 'If I *ever* lie again, I'll let you come at me Cayden-style and I'll just take it.'

I laugh through the tears. 'And what if I really, really, *really* want you to sign those papers?'

The shy, hopeful grin on his face gets a little more secure with each 'really'.

'Well, in that case, there's a question I'mma need to ask you.' He's really laying it on thick, pulling out the panty-melting southern drawl he knows I love to help convince me.

The click of a lock grabs my attention, and when I glance down the hall, I see Phil. He gasps loudly, earning Foster's gaze as well.

His eyes are wide, a baseball bat in one hand, and a muffled squeal escapes his lips as he suddenly realizes what is happening. He drops the bat on the carpeted floor.

'He's doing it! Oh my God, he came back!' he squeaks, easily waking up the rest of the floor, then quickly placing both hands over his mouth, attempting to stifle any further sound.

He came back. And here I am, in my *least* sexy pajamas, nervously biting my lip, feeling my heart race with every breath, as though it's dancing to a beat I can't hear. Could the moment so many girls dream of actually be happening to me? Again?

'Go ahead,' I say, trying to hide the excitement bubbling up inside me. If my insides burst, butterflies will flood the hallway.

Foster heaves a sigh of relief; a giddy chuckle that matches how I feel exactly slips from his lips as he theatrically tosses the divorce papers over his shoulder. They flutter to the ground like confetti as he reaches for my left hand, raising it to his lips without breaking our intense gaze.

'Evie, losing you was the worst thing that ever happened to me. I don't wanna give up. I choose you. First. Over everything else. Will you, please, *stay* married to me?'

I raise my hand to my lips, trying to conceal the silly grin spreading across my face. 'For how long this time, do you suppose?' I joke, unable to pretend I'm even considering saying no to him.

'Five, thirty, maybe fifty years?'

I laugh, nodding my head yes. 'Yes, Foster. I would love to stay married to you.'

With a swift motion, he slips the ring onto my finger, then rises to his feet, pulling me up by one hand with him, and envelops me in a tight, one-armed embrace, pressing a gentle kiss to the side of my forehead.

'I love you too,' I say into his ear, words I haven't spoken out loud in so long, but they feel so right.

Phil's emotions overflow as he starts jogging in place, his hands raised in the air, his fingers wiggling in excitement. '*Congratulations!* That was exactly what I was hoping for! Maybe not at four in the morning – I thought you were an intruder – but still, what a way to wake up! Also, for the record, this is exactly what I want, so if any of your biker friends are into Phils, please let me know,' he exclaims playfully, with only a hint of jealousy in his voice.

Foster's lopsided grin speaks volumes. He's clearly overjoyed. 'Can a Guy buy his wife some breakfast?'

I laugh at the pun but shake my head, gripping his hand and guiding him into my apartment. 'How about you, my *husband*, make me, your *wife*, some breakfast – *after* we consummate this marriage reconciliation thing, of course.'

'See ya, Phil,' he says without hesitation, closing the door behind him.

And with that, the little voice inside me while he was here healing, screaming 'he's still the one', is now singing in full chorus and I couldn't be happier. He is – and always has been – the one.

34

GUY 'FOSTER'

Five Years Later

'Uncle Foster, watch!' Ace, our nephew – Jess's little boy – comes racing past us on his child-sized dirt bike, purchased by me.

He's five years old now and a motocross prodigy. At least that's what I keep telling him. Much to Jess's disdain, he sees me as a superhero, and all he wants to be is 'like me' when he grows up. His words. I couldn't be prouder.

Eve and I are living just outside of Portland, on ten acres that we purchased a year after we got back together. Eve is now a charge nurse in the ER, barking orders and saving lives – I'm kidding, she's great at it, and as long as no relative, nor me, is brought in on her shift, she loves every second of it.

Matty spent two weeks here as he and I built my very own practice track. We've got berms, jumps, mud, and even a foam pit.

'Both hands!' Jess and Eve yell in unison when Ace rides by, one-handed.

'He's practically wrapped in bubble wrap you two, he's fine.' He's also wearing every pad and bit of safety gear available to mankind. So, I'm not worried. I've lived through worse than a one-handed fall from two feet off the ground.

Stepping closer to Eve, I can't help but chuckle at the synchronized worry in their voices. My eyes trace the lines of her face as she watches Ace with a mix of pride and concern. She's always been so attentive, and so caring. And that's one of the many things that drew me back to her.

I lean in slightly, speaking just loud enough for her to hear over the revving engines and excited shouts around us. 'You know, one of these days, he's gonna out-jump me. Then what are you gonna do?'

'Talk my sister down off the cliff?' she teases.

As Ace returns, beaming with pride, I tousle his helmet-clad head and share a knowing look with Eve. She smiles back at me, her worry melting away into amusement. It's moments like these that remind us how far we've come – from broken hearts to this family we've built together – even the ones not related like Phil, Gen, Kait, Matty, and my buddies when they visit.

'Ride with me!' Ace yells over the engine.

'You don't have to ask me twice,' I say, pecking a kiss onto Eve's lips before jogging to my bike.

'Be careful!' she hollers after me, flashing me that gorgeous smile as I slide on my helmet.

I still race. Not as much as I did, but enough to keep me happy. Mostly, though, I coach new motocross riders, like Ace and his three buddies racing around my track. He placed in his first comp recently – the trophy is front and center of Jess's fireplace mantle.

Ace takes off in a cloud of dust and I follow close behind, reveling in the roar of the engines and the wind whipping past us. He might be young, but he's got potential. I can see the determination in his eyes, just like how I used to feel when I first started out.

As we hit a series of jumps, I can't help but let out a whoop of excitement. The adrenaline rush is addictive. It's moments like these that remind me why I fell in love with motocross in the first place.

After a few exhilarating laps around the track, and one big flip that I'm sure put Eve's stomach in knots, Ace pulls up next to me, yanking off his helmet, his eyes shining with excitement. 'That was awesome, Uncle Foster!' he exclaims, his whole face lit up with joy. 'I want to jump like that!'

I kill my bike and pat him on the back, giving him a proud smile. 'You did great out there, bro. Keep practicing, and you'll be beating me in no time.'

'How about instead of beating anyone, we get this anniversary party started?' Phil says, uncorking a bottle of champagne with a loud pop.

'To ten years,' Jess says, all of our friends and family repeating her words.

We toast, clinking our glasses together.

'Ten years,' I say, looking at my gorgeous wife.

'Seems like only five,' she jokes. 'Yet I'm looking forward to eternity.' Her eyes sparkle with mischief as she taps her glass against mine in a toast to our milestone anniversary.

The sun is beginning to set, casting a warm golden glow over our little celebration. Motorcycles and music fill the air, and laughter and chatter blend into the perfect backdrop for the evening.

As we settle into the festivities, surrounded by friends and family who have become our rock over the years, I can't help but feel a surge of gratitude for everything that has led us here. From heartbreak to healing, from doubts to certainty, Eve has been my constant companion through it all.

I steal a moment with her, pulling her away from the crowd to a quiet spot overlooking the property. The engines have fallen silent now, replaced by the gentle rustle of leaves as fall starts to set in.

'Forever with you won't ever be long enough.'

'I know,' she says. 'But it's a good start.'

'That it is, Jellybean.' I kiss her lips sweetly, wishing time would slow down just a little so I never forget a moment. 'Thank you.'

'For what?' she asks.

'Being in my life. Without you, I could legit be dead. Or living without a purpose until the end of time.'

She smiles, kissing my cheek. 'I'd do it all over again in an instant.'

PLAYLIST

Now I'm in It (Bonus Track), HAIM
King of the Clouds, Panic! At the Disco
Fire!, Alan Walker, JVKE & YUQI
Heart Don't Work Like That (feat. Casey Cook), SABAI & Afinity
Linger (SiriusXM Session), Royel Otis
Ride or Die (feat. Foster the People), The Knocks
Bad Idea, Dove Cameron
Wake Up, AWOLNATION
thoughts i have while lying in bed, The Maine & Beach Weather
Feel It Still, Portugal. The Man
Hesitate, Curtis Cole & Nono
Missed You (Bonus Track), The Weeknd
I Want Candy, The Strangeloves
My Oh My, James Smith
Favorite What If, Ashley Kutcher
OH NO!, Cody Lovaas & ROZES
Trying My Best, Anson Seabra
The Best, Rachel Grae
Feeling Some Kinda Way, Kylie Cantrall
You Were Mine, Forest Blakk

Twirling, Maberry
I Guess It's Been a While, INTRN, Kayou. & Gina Livia
Something Worth Saving, Nuxe
Adore You, Miley Cyrus
Chaos, FRANKIE
love you forever (feat. Cold Illumination), Rxseboy
LOVE, X Lovers
Shake It (feat. Big & Rich), The Lacs
Chattahoochee, Alan Jackson
I Hate Love Songs, Kelsea Ballerini
Head in the Clouds, Kylie Cantrall
us. (feat. Taylor Swift), Gracie Abrams
Talk, Why Don't We
OBSESSED, Anne-Marie
Always You, Louis Tomlinson
Love Story, Taylor Swift
Love Will Keep Us Together, JACK
clue, Thomas Reid
I Guess That Was Goodbye, Lyn Lapid
Closure, Hayd
My House Is Not A Home, d4vd
Still the One, Emilee
Cupid, FIFTY FIFTY

ACKNOWLEDGEMENTS

I feel like acknowledgments get boring, always thanking the same people over and over. So, this time, I'm doing things differently and telling you where the inspiration for this story came from. No, it's not autobiographical – at all. But dreaming of this book helped take my mind off what I was going through at the time. To all my usuals (you know who you are), thank you – I couldn't write the books I do without you in my life. Oh, and I can't forget Red Bull. They have an entire channel of extreme sports and I've spent the last decades watching them, and for this book, studying the FMX trick dictionary on their website.

Onto my inspiration. There are experiences in life that change who you are. Some for better. Some for worse. This story is one of mine. On 29 July 2023, my husband of twenty-six years was critically injured in an off-road dirt bike accident. It happened a few miles from our home, which is twenty-five-ish miles from the nearest hospital. (We live in the boondocks of Montana – I mean, a town with a population of fewer than 400 with only a bar, a fire department, and a post office, miles of farms, gravel roads, in the mountains, with a windy hill of a driveway covered in ice for six months out of the year – even the post office doesn't deliver out here.)

Somehow, he was able to get back on his bike and ride the few miles home where I thought his injuries were mostly surface road rash. But because we both have medical job histories, we realized pretty quickly that he might have internal injuries. That twenty-five-plus-mile drive to the nearest hospital (which doesn't have the best reputation) through summer construction season yielding hundreds of glowing warning cones, at dusk, with terrible astigmatism and a very injured husband in the passenger seat, was the longest drive of my life.

The good news was that the only broken bones he had were many ribs. The bad news was that his internal injuries were critical. Bruised liver, bruised lungs (bruised everything), internal bleeding from a level five ruptured spleen, and extreme road rash down his left leg. He spent a day in ICU then a few days in the hospital being watched closely to see if he would need his spleen removed (they lean not to now). The surgeon decided he didn't and even though we were apprehensive to leave and go home (a thirty-minute drive away) after such a short stay in the hospital, we did what we were told.

I bought all the medical equipment he needed and set alarms on my phone every three hours to keep him fully medicated so he wasn't miserable. Because of his condition, he slept dead center of our king-size bed, while I slept on the couch. We made it through the first few days and then the 'rare' thing they'd warned us about upon discharge happened right as I gave him his night-time meds. He started bleeding out internally, from where we weren't sure. But we both knew immediately when his vision and hearing faded out and because of our medical training, I was able to monitor his blood pressure (67/45 and dropping) while on the phone with 911. Somehow we kept him alive until the ambulance got here. He made it to the ER where many mistakes were made, but ultimately, they discovered he was bleeding from the main artery leading to his spleen and needed an emergency intervention to stop it. We knew how serious this was, we've both worked in hospitals or in an ambulance. During surgery, the bleeding got worse, but after thirteen different-sized stents, they got it stopped. He was still considered critical for the next twenty-four hours but he made it through – though miserably. And after a few days of improvement, he went home, with a mountain of medication, on oxygen, and with wounds that needed care daily.

It was like bringing home a new baby. What we didn't know at the time was that he also had a possible traumatic brain injury that would cause difficulties in our future. So we went through a lot of confusing things before finally getting him healed up and back on track for now. As you can imagine, this has been a traumatic experience for our entire family, especially the night he dropped from a new medication and was in a position in a tiny bathroom where I had to maneuver him onto the ground so I could start

CPR because he'd stopped breathing. Once on his back, his airways were reopened and as I hovered above him ready to start CPR, he awoke to a 911 operator hollering instructions, our nineteen-year-old son watching, seconds before I would have broken possibly many of his ribs by starting CPR. Even the 911 operator sounded relieved. Hallelujah, he was fine and I didn't have to injure him more.

This entire situation changed our whole world. In good ways, and bad. This book was due close to when this happened and my publisher was gracious enough to extend the deadline for me. Finally, I turned in a terrible book – written while this was happening, so there wasn't a lot of 'romance'. I'm finally in a place where I could tell the story that got me through some tough times. Daydreaming about Eve and Foster kept me sane, so I hope they bring you a smile, some laughs, a little joy, and maybe you'll even fall in love. I sure did.

Thank you for reading. Without you, these characters would only live in my head, and that's no fun.

ABOUT THE AUTHOR

Aimee Brown is the bestselling romantic comedy author of several books including The Lucky Dress. She lives in Montana and sets her books in Portland. Her books with Boldwood are full of love and laughter.

Sign up to Aimee Brown's mailing list here for news, competitions and updates on future books.

Visit Aimee Brown's website: www.aimeebwrites.com

Follow Aimee on social media:

- facebook.com/authoraimeebrown
- x.com/aimeebwrites
- instagram.com/authoraimeeb
- bookbub.com/authors/aimee-brown
- goodreads.com/authoraimeebown

ALSO BY AIMEE BROWN

He Loves Me, He Loves Me Not

Love Notes

Stuck With You

Can't Take My Eyes Off You

Still The One

LOVE NOTES

LOVE IN EVERY CHAPTER

WHERE ALL YOUR ROMANCE
DREAMS COME TRUE!

THE HOME OF BESTSELLING
ROMANCE AND WOMEN'S
FICTION

 WARNING:
MAY CONTAIN SPICE

SIGN UP TO OUR
NEWSLETTER

https://bit.ly/Lovenotesnews

Boldwood

Boldwood Books is an award-winning fiction publishing company seeking out the best stories from around the world.

Find out more at www.boldwoodbooks.com

Join our reader community for brilliant books, competitions and offers!

Follow us
@BoldwoodBooks
@TheBoldBookClub

Sign up to our weekly deals newsletter

https://bit.ly/BoldwoodBNewsletter

Milton Keynes UK
Ingram Content Group UK Ltd.
UKHW021846221124
451243UK00002B/10